Sons OF Moriarty

AND MORE STORIES OF SHERLOCK HOLMES

Authorized and licensed by the
Estate of Sir Arthur Conan Doyle

Edited by
LOREN D. ESTLEMAN

TYRUS
BOOKS

F+W Media, Inc.

Published by
TYRUS BOOKS
an imprint of F+W Media, Inc.
10151 Carver Road, Suite 200
Blue Ash, OH 45242. U.S.A.
www.tyrusbooks.com

"The Infernal Machine" previously published in *The New Adventures of Sherlock Holmes* edited by Martin Harry Greenberg and Carol-Lynn Rossel Waugh, copyright © 1999 by Carroll & Graf. ISBN 10: 0-7867-0698-8 ISBN 13: 978-0-7867-0698-3.

"The Adventure of the Double-Bogey Man" previously published in *Schlock Holmes: The Complete Bagel Street Saga* by Robert L. Fish, copyright © 1990 by Gaslight Publications. ISBN 10: 0-9344-6816-8 ISBN 13: 978-0-9344-6816-9.

"The Case of the Bloodless Sock" previously published in *Murder in Baker Street* edited by Martin Harry Greenberg, Jon Lellenberg, and Daniel Stashower, copyright © 2001 by Carroll & Graf. ISBN 10: 0-7867-1074-8 ISBN 13: 978-0-7867-1074-4.

"Sherlocks" previously published in *P.I. Files* edited by Loren D. Estelman and Martin H. Greenberg, copyright © 1990 by Ballantine Books. ISBN 10: 0-8041-0555-3 ISBN 13: 978-0-8041-0555-2.

"The Field Bazaar" previously published in *The Student* by Sir Arthur Conan Doyle, copyright © 1896 by the University of Edinburgh.

"The Adventure of the Deptford Horror" previously published in *The Exploits of Sherlock Holmes* by Adrian Conan Doyle and John Dickson Carr, copyright © 1954 by Ace Books.

"Before the Adventures" previously published in *Murder, My Dear Watson* edited by Martin Harry Greenberg, Jon Lellenberg, and Daniel Stashower, copyright © 2002 by Carroll & Graf. ISBN 10: 0-7867-1081-0 ISBN 13: 978-0-7867-1081-2.

ISBN 10: 1-4405-6483-3
ISBN 13: 978-1-4405-6483-3
eISBN 10: 1-4405-6484-1
eISBN 13: 978-1-4405-6484-0

Printed in the United States of America.

10 9 8 7 6 5 4 3 2 1

Grateful acknowledgment to Conan Doyle Estate Ltd. for permission to use the Sherlock Holmes characters created by Sir Arthur Conan Doyle.

This book is available at quantity discounts for bulk purchases.
For information, please call 1-800-289-0963.

This book is dedicated, as are all my Sherlockian efforts, to the great Sir Arthur Conan Doyle, the finest entertainer since William Shakespeare. A world without Sherlock Holmes, Professor Challenger, and Brigadier Gerard is inconceivable.

I suppose every one has some little immortal spark concealed about him.

—Sherlock Holmes, *The Sign of Four*

SHERLOCK HOLMES:
AN ENDURING LEGACY

I can't think of a more wildly successful success story. Bill Gates and Steve Jobs could only dream of it.

Name someone who rose to prominence in 1887 and still permeates world culture on the covers of magazines, at the motion-picture box office, on TV, in computer games, on eBooks, in downloads. Still stumped?

While it's been said that *I Love Lucy*, a sitcom phenomenon that's been with us a mere sixty years, is playing somewhere every minute of every day, I hereby state boldly that right now, someone is reading a Sherlock Holmes story. I'm not even including the hundreds of thousands—millions—who at this moment are exposed to Holmes in some form.

His creator never saw it coming.

Sir Arthur Conan Doyle grew to hate Sherlock Holmes; he banned the name from family conversation. The skyrocketing popularity of the World's First Consulting Detective must fizzle out eventually, he thought. Holmes would soon be forgotten, and Doyle with him. He wanted to be remembered for his history of the Boer War.

Ask anyone what that war was all about. Now ask anyone about Sherlock Holmes.

Writers are often unreliable on the subject of their work.

A generation later, his daughter, Dame Jean Conan Doyle, expressed the same kind of fear, turned inside-out. Inundated with requests for permission to publish Holmes pastiches and parodies by other writers, she declared a moratorium on the grounds that the sheer volume of imitations—many, many times the weighty fifty-six stories and four novels of the original Canon—would extinguish her father's memory.

She, too, felt that the creation had devoured its creator; but this time, Holmes's endurance was the culprit, rather than his fragility.

She needn't have worried. While it's true that many people don't immediately think of Conan Doyle when Holmes's name is mentioned, those same people will instantly connect his name with his detective's.

It's a sideways kind of immortality, but hardly unique in literature. Robert Louis Stevenson is less well-known than either Long John Silver or Dr. Jekyll, and while Anna Karenina may pass muster with the bouncer at the door of an exclusive literary nightclub, Leo Tolstoy might need a reference. Daniel Defoe? Let me think. Robinson Crusoe? Oh, of course. A writer is best known for the most vivid shadows thrown by the light of his imagination.

Holmes and Watson are ubiquitous—as always. At least one film based on their adventures appeared every decade of the twentieth century, a tradition that's continued into the twenty-first. On steroids.

The old explanation, that modern audiences yearn for the order and gentility of the Victorian era, doesn't hold up. How do we account for the popularity of two new TV shows placing Holmes in our own time? What's so sexy about DNA, anyway? It can't hold a candle to footprints and tobacco-ash.

Ironically, the answer lies in the past.

When Universal Pictures took over the film series starring Basil Rathbone, the producers jettisoned the gaslight and horse-drawn cabs and replaced them with air-raid sirens and all the other trappings of World War II. Londoners enduring the Blitz needed the morale boost: Hitler had the Luftwaffe, but Britain had Sherlock Holmes.

Clearly, the age of watch-chains and bustles still has its points. It hasn't hurt the box-office success of two recent Holmes movies starring Robert Downey Jr., with Jude Law as a dynamic and sexy (as originally intended) Dr. Watson. But in our time of terrorists, serial killers, and drug gangs, the magic of television has given us Sherlock Holmes once again.

Not that Conan Doyle didn't try to take him away from us.

Divorce was out of the question. He loathed the thought of writing more adventures, but knew that simply to stop would be to invite his readers to pester him without mercy. Nothing would do but murder.

Wisely, having established his detective as without parallel, he couldn't let him be taken out by any of the petty swindlers, would-be bank robbers, and sundry trash he'd already shown he could outwit on deadline. Enter Professor Moriarty, the Napoleon of Crime; and the super villain was born. (His adapters have spent countless hours working this afterthought into Holmes's backstory.) I can't think of a suspense writer who hasn't commandeered the concept to his own ends. This pair of opposite equals would end their lives in a bloody draw.

He paid for this sin. "You brute!" wrote one outraged fan; in our modern hyper-violent world, there would be death threats.

Personally, I don't buy that Sir Arthur was committed to his plan. If he truly wanted to eradicate Holmes, he'd have done the deed in full view of the faithful Dr. Watson, and remove all doubt. Leaving a convenient note on the cusp of the grim Reichenbach Falls was the nineteenth-century equivalent of that infamous episode of the TV series *Dallas* in which hero Bobby Ewing's death was revealed to have been only a dream. No writer with the vision to invent both the world's first consulting detective and literature's first arch-fiend would fail to leave himself an out. (He was pestered anyway; even the Grim Reaper was no match for a public determined not to quit cold turkey.) At the end of "The Final Problem," he might as well have paraphrased a delicious line at the end of every James Bond film: "Sherlock Holmes Will Return in 'The Adventure of the Empty House.'"

Had he done so, however, we'd never have had that poignant *Out Our Way* panel by cartoonist J. R. Williams, showing a little boy reading in bed with a stricken look on his face and the caption: "The death of Sherlock Holmes."

With the exception of two stories—both, significantly, excluding Watson as narrator—I can't help thinking that the writer was having enormous fun with his creations, despite his grumping *en familie*. The witty banter, the circumlocutive reasoning in regard to arcane clues, and the wild races through hew hedges, Medieval thoroughfares, and down the racing Thames, fairly drip with endorphins. A writer is most enjoyable when he's enjoying himself. This much I know.

Was Conan Doyle an innovator?

On the face of it, the evidence against him is damaging. One page into Edgar Allan Poe's "The Murders in the Rue Morgue," and anyone remotely familiar with Holmes's methods and living arrangements must see that coincidence doesn't apply. Granted, characterization wasn't Poe's long suit; apart from his feats of ratiocination, the Chevalier Auguste Dupin is notable only for his insistence on keeping his curtains drawn and his candles burning to simulate eternal night, and the narrator has neither name nor apparent existence outside the association. Poe's imitator would give us the endearing, infuriating idiosyncrasies unique to his detective, Watson's private life, medical practice, and above all the caring and patience required to wean his friend from his destructive addictions to cocaine and morphine.

Well, I'm okay with that; and I've been a victim of plagiarism myself. In my case, the perpetrator merely copied a story I'd published word-for-word, changing only some character names and geographical references, and revealing no talent beyond a rudimentary knowledge of cut-and-paste. Conan Doyle at least brought skill to the enterprise. Some purists sniff and say, "That's like complimenting a thief for investing the money more wisely than his victim." Possibly so, but I can't help noting similarities in the relationship between Dickens' convict and young Pip in *Great Expectations* and that of Robert Louis Stevenson's Long John Silver and Jack Hawkins in *Treasure Island*, and Jane Smiley's *A Thousand Acres* was hardly the first attempt to recast Shakespeare in a contemporary setting, or even to select *King Lear* as the vehicle. The Bard himself borrowed freely from Plutarch and Christopher Marlowe; the Elizabethan Age was a cesspool of intellectual theft. So I'm going to look the other way, consoling myself that Poe hasn't suffered. In fact, his stories have remained in print for more than 150 years.

The pilferage, if that's what it was, didn't stop with Conan Doyle. Sax Rohmer's sharp-profiled, pipe-smoking Sir Denis Nayland-Smith and his physician biographer, Dr. Petrie, are *doppelgängers* for

Holmes and Watson, and the titular devil doctor in *The Insidious Fu-Manchu* would face legal action by Professor Moriarty were that party not smashed to bits at the base of the falls. For that matter, all the Blofelds, Drs. Mabuse and No, Svengalis, Zecks, Wo Fats, Lex Luthors, Sumurus, Jokers, (and, yes, even yours truly's Madame Sing) owe their inspirations to the fertile mind of the retired practitioner from Scotland.

Dame Agatha Christie—may her tribe increase—based the eccentric Hercule Poirot and his docile companion Captain Hastings solidly on her inspiration; the Belgian detective's boredom with commonplace crime and keen interest in the *outré* bear close comparison. I would go so far as to say that when Hollywood discovered Holmes and Watson, the "buddy film" was born.

Why Sherlock Holmes? The world has had its share or Herculeses, Robin Hoods, and Supermen. Why make room for another mythic hero?

Because the room is vacant.

There will always be a world in which the fog hovers thick around black vs. white; where the difference between goodness and dark deeds hangs on the tick of a clock, the hammer of a well-worn service revolver gripped in a steady hand; where "it is always 1895," to quote the great Sherlockian Vincent Starrett. A solitary image stands in the No Man's Land in between: a hawklike profile in a fore-and-aft cap, drawing on a curved-stem pipe, with a staunch presence at his side, poised to pounce. John Wayne's Ringo Kid, Clint Eastwood's Man With No Name, Gary Cooper's Marshal Will Caine, framed in their bright doorways, Bruce Willis in *Die Hard*, are but an extension of this Malloryan myth. It may not have begun with Conan Doyle; we must confer with Homer on that. But he will remain forever in those ranks.

"Come, Watson, come! The game's afoot!"

So it's become a cliché. What truth hasn't?

The contributors chosen for this anthology have had the candor to acknowledge their debt (and to receive the imprimature of the Sir Arthur Conan Doyle estate). They have managed to capture the spirit and cadence of the originals, and to expand the creator's vision to embrace problems that never came Holmes's way—or perhaps they did, and for Watson's own reasons were consigned to the fabled tin dispatch-box where he kept his notes on adventures he didn't publish, to be rescued and trotted out by his literary descendants. They are all well-established authors, creators of their own characters, and represent every genre including that catch-all, mainstream. With me, they share an admiration for their inspiration, as well as vivid memories of youthful evenings sitting up in bed, reading of the death of Sherlock Holmes, registering horror, then skepticism. He was never born, and so he can never die.

 —Loren D. Estleman

CONTENTS

THE INFERNAL MACHINE

BY JOHN LUTZ

Since his career began in 1975, John Lutz has published many novels of suspense, including SWF Seeks Same, *which was filmed as* Single White Female, *and hundreds of short stories of suspense. "The Infernal Machine" centers around a murder involving Richard Gatling's fearsome precursor to the modern machine gun.*

Not that, at times, my dear friend and associate Sherlock Holmes can't play the violin quite beautifully, but at the moment the melancholy, wavering tunelessness produced by the shrill instrument was getting on my nerves.

I put down my copy of the *Times.* "Holmes, must you be so repetitious in your choice of notes?"

"It's in the very repetitiveness that I hope to find some semblance of order and meaning," he said. He held his hawkish profile high, tucked the violin tighter beneath his lean chin, and the screeching continued—certainly more piercing than before.

"Holmes!"

"Very well, Watson." He smiled and placed the violin back in its case. Then he slumped into the wing chair opposite me, tamped tobacco into his clay pipe, and assumed the attitude of a spoiled child whose mince pie has been withheld for disciplinary purposes. I knew where he'd turn next, after finding no solace in the violin, and I must confess I felt guilty at having been harsh with him.

When he's acting the hunter in his capacity of consulting detective, no man is more vibrant with interest than Holmes. But when he's had no case for some weeks, and there's no prospect of one on the horizon, he becomes zombie-like in his withdrawal into boredom. And it had been nearly a month since the successful conclusion of the case of the twice-licked stamp.

Holmes suddenly cocked his head to the side, almost in the manner of a bird stalking a worm, at the clatter of footsteps on the stairs outside our door. From below, the cheerful voice of Mrs. Hudson wafted up, along with her measured, lighter footfalls. A man's voice answered her pleasantries. Neither voice was loud enough to be understood by us.

"Visitor, Watson." Even as Holmes spoke there was a firm knock on the door.

I rose, crossed the cluttered room, and opened it.

"A Mr. Edgewick to see Mr. Holmes," Mrs. Hudson said, and withdrew.

I ushered Edgewick in and bade him sit in the chair where I'd been perusing the *Times*. He was a large, handsome man in his mid-thirties, wearing a well-cut checked suit and polished boots that had reddish mud on their soles. He had straight blond hair and an even blonder brush-trimmed moustache. He looked up at me with a troubled expression and said, "Mr. Holmes?"

I smiled. "You've recently come from Northwood," I said. "You're unmarried and are concerned about the well-being of a woman."

Holmes, too, was smiling. "Amazing, Watson. Pray tell us how you did it."

"Certainly. The red clay on Mr. Edgewick's boots is found mainly in Northwood. He's not wearing a wedding ring, so he isn't married. And since he's a handsome chap and obviously in some personal distress, the odds are good there's a young woman involved."

Holmes's amused eyes darted to Edgewick, who seemed flustered by my incisiveness.

"Actually," he said, "I am married—my ring is at the jeweler's being resized. The matter I came here about only indirectly concerns a woman. And I haven't been to Northwood in years."

"The hansom cab you arrived in apparently carried a recent passenger from Northwood," Holmes said. "The mud should dry on this warm day as the hansom sits downstairs awaiting your return."

I must admit my mouth fell open, as did Edgewick's. "How on earth did you know he'd instructed a hansom to wait, Holmes? You were nowhere near the window."

Holmes gave a backhand wave, trailing his long fingers. "If Mr. Edgewick hasn't been to Northwood, Watson, the most logical place for him to have picked up the red mud is from the floor of the hansom cab."

Edgewick was sitting forward, intrigued. "But how did you know I'd arrived in a hansom to begin with, and instructed the driver to wait downstairs?"

"Your walking stick."

I felt my eyebrows raise as I looked again where Edgewick sat. "What walking stick, Holmes?"

"The one whose tip left the circular indentation on the toe of Mr. Edgewick's right boot as he sat absently leaning on it in the cab, as is the habit of many men who carry a stick. The soft leather still maintains the impression. And since he hasn't the walking stick with him, and his footfalls on the stairs preclude him from having brought it up with him to leave it outside in the hall, we can deduce that he left it in the hansom. Since he hardly seems a careless man, or the possessor of a limitless number of walking sticks, this would suggest that he ordered the cab to wait for him."

Edgewick looked delighted. "Why, that's superb! So much from a mere pair of boots!"

"A parlour game," Holmes snapped, "when not constructively applied." Again his slow smile as he made a tent with his lean fingers and peered over it. His eyes were unwavering and sharply focused now. "And I suspect you bring some serious matter that will allow proper application of my skills."

"Oh, I do indeed. Uh, my name is Wilson Edgewick, Mr. Holmes."

Holmes made a sweeping gesture with his arm in my direction. "My associate Dr. Watson."

Edgewick nodded to me. "Yes, I've read his accounts of some of your adventures. Which is why I think you might be able to help me—rather help my brother Landen, actually."

Holmes settled back in his chair, his eyes half closed. I knew he wasn't drowsy when he took on such an appearance, but was in fact a receptacle for every bit of information that might flow his way, accepting this as pertinent, rejecting that as irrelevant, acutely alert.

"Do tell us about it, Mr. Edgewick," he said.

Edgewick glanced at me. I nodded encouragement.

"My brother Landen is engaged to Millicent Oldsbolt."

"Oldsbolt Munitions?" Holmes asked.

Edgewick nodded, not surprised that Holmes would recognize the Oldsbolt name. Oldsbolt Limited was a major supplier of small arms for the military. I had, in fact, fired Oldsbolt rounds through my army revolver while in the service of the Queen.

"The wedding was to be next spring," Edgewick went on. "When Landen, and myself, would be financially well off."

"Well off as a result of what?" Holmes asked.

"We're the English representatives of one Richard Gatling, the inventor of the Gatling Gun."

I couldn't help but ask, "What on earth is that?"

"It's an infernal machine that employs many barrels and one firing chamber," Holmes said. "The cartridges are fed to the chamber by means of a long belt, while the barrels revolve and fire one after the other in rapid succession. The shooter need only aim generally and turn a crank with one hand while the other depresses the trigger. It's said the Gatling Gun can fire almost a hundred rounds per minute. It was used in the Indian Wars in America on the plains with great effectiveness."

"Very good, Mr. Holmes!" Edgewick said. "I see you're well versed in military ordnance."

"It sounds a fiendish device," I said, imagining those revolving barrels spewing death to man and beast.

"As war itself is fiendish," Holmes said. "Not at all a game. But do continue, Mr. Edgewick."

"Landen and I were staying at the King's Knave Inn in the town of Alverston, north of London. To be near the Oldsbolt estate. You see, we were trying to sell the idea of the Gatling Gun to Sir Clive Oldsbolt for manufacture for the British forces. The gun had passed all tests, and Sir Clive had offered a price I'm sure the American manufacturer would have accepted."

Holmes pursed his thin lips thoughtfully, then said, "You speak often in the past tense, Mr. Edgewick. As if your brother's wedding has been cancelled. As if now Oldsbolt Limited is no longer interested in your deadly gun."

"Both those plans have been dealt the severest blow, Mr. Holmes. You see, last night Sir Clive was murdered."

I drew in my breath with shock. Holmes, however, leaned forward in his chair, keenly interested, almost pleased. "Ah! Murdered how?"

"He was returning home late from the King's Knave Inn alone in his carriage, when he was shot. A villager found him this morning, after hearing the noise last night."

Holmes's nostrils actually quivered. "Noise?"

"Rapid gunfire, Mr. Holmes, shots fired in quick, rhythmic succession."

"The Gatling Gun."

"No, no. That's what the chief constable at Alverston says. But the gun we used for demonstration purposes had been cleaned and not fired again. I swear it! Of course, the local constabulary and villagers all say that Landen cleaned it after killing Sir Clive."

"Your brother has been arrested for his future father-in-law's murder?" I asked in astonishment.

"Indeed!" Edgewick said in great agitation. "That's why I rushed here after he was taken into custody. I thought only Mr. Holmes could make right of such a mistake."

"Does your brother Landen have any motive for murdering his fiancée's father?"

"No! Quite the opposite! Sir Clive's death means the purchase of the Gatling Gun manufacturing rights has been cancelled. As well, of course, as Landen and Millicent's wedding. And yet . . ."

Holmes waited, his body perfectly still.

"Yet, Mr. Holmes, the sound the villagers in the inn described could be none other than the rattling, measured firing of the Gatling Gun."

"But you said you examined it and it hadn't been recently fired."

"Oh, I'll swear to that, Mr. Holmes—for all the good it will do poor Landen."

"Perhaps a different Gatling Gun."

"There is no other in England, Mr. Holmes. Of that you can be sure. We crossed the Atlantic just last week with this one, and Mr. Gatling knows the whereabouts of all his machines. Understand, sir, this is a formidable weapon that threatens the very existence of nations if in the wrong hands. It will change the nature of warfare and isn't to be taken lightly."

"How many times was Sir Clive shot?" Holmes asked.

"Seven. All through the chest with large-caliber bullets, like those fired by the Gatling Gun. The village doctor removed the two bullets that didn't pass through Sir Clive, but they became misshapen when striking bone, so their precise caliber can't be determined."

"I see. It's all very interesting."

"Will you come at once to Alverston, Mr. Holmes, and determine what can be done for my brother?"

"You did say Sir Clive had been shot seven times, Mr. Edgewick?"

"I did."

Holmes stood up from the wing chair as abruptly as if he'd been stuck by a cushion spring. "Then Watson and I shall take the afternoon train to Alverston and meet you at the King's Knave Inn. Now I suggest you return to your brother and his fiancée, where you're no doubt sorely needed."

Edgewick smiled broadly with relief and stood. "I intend to pay you well, Mr. Holmes. Landen and I are not without means."

"We'll discuss all that later," Holmes said, placing a hand on Edgewick's shoulder and guiding him to the door. "In the meantime, tell your brother that if he's innocent he need have no concern and might well outlive the hangman."

"I'll tell him that, Mr. Holmes. It will comfort him, I'm sure. Good day to both of you." He went out the door, burst back in momentarily, and added, "Thank you, Mr. Holmes! For me and for Landen!"

Holmes and I stood listening to his descending tread on the stairs. Holmes parted the curtain and looked after our visitor as he emerged onto Baker Street. The shouts of vendors and the clattering of horses' hooves drifted into the room, along with the pungent smell of London.

"An extremely distressed young man, Watson."

"Indeed, Holmes."

He rubbed his hands together with a glee and animation that would have been impossible to him fifteen minutes ago. "We must pack, Watson, if we're to catch the afternoon train to Alverston." His gaunt face grew momentarily grave. "And I suggest you bring along your service revolver."

I had fully intended to do that. Where a member of nobility is shot seven times on his way from inn to home, any act of the direst nature might be possible.

The King's Knave Inn was but a short distance from the Alverston train depot, just outside the town proper. It was a large, Tudor structure, bracketed by huge stone chimneys, one at each end of its steeply pitched slate roof.

Wilson Edgewick wasn't among the half dozen local patrons seated at small wooden tables. A beefy, red-faced man with a thinning crop of ginger hair slicked back on a wide head was dispensing drinks, while a fragile blond woman with a limp was carrying them to the tables. I made arrangements for satisfactory rooms while Holmes surveyed the place. There was a young man seated at a nearby table, looking disconsolate, as if he were too far into his cups. Two old-timers—one with a bulbous red nose, the other with a sharp grey face like a hatchet—sat at another table engrossed in a game of draughts. Three middle-aged men of the sort who work the land sat slumped about a third table, their conversation suspended as they mildly observed us.

"Now, you'd be Mr. Holmes the famous detective," the red-faced pub owner, whose name was Beech, said to Holmes with a tinge of respect as he studied the guest register I'd signed, "or my guess'd be far wrong." Alcohol fumes wafted on his breath.

Holmes nodded. "I've enjoyed my share of successes."

"Look just like your pictures drawed in the *Daily Telegraph*, you do."

"I find them distinctly unflattering."

One of Beech's rheumy eyes was running, and he swiped at it with the back of his hand as he said, "Don't take a detective to know why you're here, though."

"Quite so," Holmes said. "A tragic affair."

"Weren't it so!" Beech's complexion got even ruddier and a blue vein in his temple began a wild pulsation. A conspiratorial light entered his eyes. He sniffed and wiped again at the watery one. "We heard it all here, Mr. Holmes. Witnesses to murder, we was here at the inn."

"How is that?" asked Holmes, much interested.

"We was standing here as we are now, sir, late last night, when we heard the infernal machine spitting its death."

"The Gatling Gun?"

"That's what it was." He leaned forward, wiping his strong, square hands on his stained apron. "A sort of 'rat-a-tat-tat-tat,' it was." Spittle flew as he described the sound of the repeating-fire gun. "Well, we'd heard the gun fired before and knew the noise right off, sir. But not from that direction." He waved a hand towards the north. "In the morning, Ingraham Codder was on the north road to go and see Lord Clive at the house. Instead he sees one of the lord's grey geldings and the fine two-hitch carriage the lord comes to town in. The other gelding somehow got unhitched and was standing nearby. Lord Clive himself was slumped down in the carriage dead. Shot full of holes, Mr. Holmes. Seven of 'em, there was."

"So I've heard. Did anyone else here this 'rat-a-tat-tat' sound?" Holmes managed to describe the gunfire without expectorating. "All three of us did," spoke up one of the farmers at the table. "It was just as Mr. Beech described."

"And what time was it?" Holmes asked.

"Half past eleven on the mark," Beech said. "Just about ten minutes after poor Sir Clive left here after downing his customary bit of stout." The patrons all agreed.

The young man alone at his table gazed up at us, and I was surprised to see that he wasn't as affected by drink as I'd assumed by his attitude. His grey eyes were quite clear in a well-set-up face; he had a firm jawline and a strong nose and cheekbones. "They've got Sir Clive's murderer under lock," he said. "Or so they say."

"And you are, sir?" Holmes asked.

"He's Robby Smythe," Beech cut in. "It's horseless carriages what's his folly. If you can imagine that."

"Really?" Holmes said.

"Yes, sir. I have two of them that I'm improving on and will soon manufacture and sell in great numbers, Mr. Holmes. In ten years everyone in England shall drive one."

I couldn't contain myself. "Everyone? Come now!"

Holmes laughed. "Not you, Watson, not you, I'd wager."

"Young Robby here's got a special interest in seeing justice done," Beech said. "He's engaged to Sir Clive's youngest daughter, Phoebe."

"Is he now?" Holmes said. "Then you know the Edgewick brothers, no doubt."

Smythe nodded. "I've met them both, sir."

"And would you say Landen Edgewick is capable of this act?"

Smythe seemed to look deep into himself for the answer. "I suppose, truth be told, under certain circumstances we're all capable of killing a man we hate. But no one had reason to hate Sir Clive. He was a kind and amiable man even if stern."

"Point is," Beech said, "only the Edgewick brothers had knowledge and access to the Gatling Gun. I say with the law that Landen Edgewick is the killer."

"It would seem so," Holmes acknowledged. "But why Landen Edgewick? Where was Wilson?" Beech grinned and swiped again at the watery eye. "Up in his room at the top of them stairs, Mr. Holmes. He couldn't have had a fig to do with Sir Clive's murder. Had neither the time nor opportunity. I came out from behind the serving counter and seen him step out of his room just after the shots was fired. He came down then and had himself a glass of stout. We told him we'd heard the gun, but he laughed and said that was impossible, it was locked away in the carriage house him and his brother had borrowed out near Sir Clive's estate." He snorted and propped his ruddy fists on his hips. "Locked up, my eye, Mr. Holmes!"

"Very good, Mr. Beech," Holmes said. "You remind me of my friend Inspector Lestrade of Scotland Yard."

Looking quite pleased, Beech instructed the waitress and maid, Annie, to show us to his best rooms.

Wilson Edgewick arrived shortly thereafter, seeming overjoyed to see us. He was, if anything, even more distraught over the plight of his brother. He had been to see Landen's fiancée Millicent Oldsbolt, the daughter of the man his brother had allegedly murdered, and the meeting had obviously upset him. A wedding was hardly in order under the circumstances.

Wilson explained to us that Landen had arrived here from London two days before he and taken up lodgings at the inn. The brothers had declined an invitation to stay at the Oldsbolt's home, as they had final adjustments and technical decisions to make preparatory to demonstrating the Gatling Gun to Sir Clive.

The night of the murder, from Wilson's point of view, was much as had been described by Beech and the inn's patrons, though Wilson himself had been in his room at the precise time of the shooting and didn't hear the gun.

"The next morning, after Sir Clive's body was found," he said, "I hurried directly to the carriage house. The Gatling Gun was there, mounted on its wagon, and it hadn't been fired since the last test and cleaning."

"And did you point this out to the local constable?" Holmes asked.

"I did, after Landen was taken in for the crime. Chief Constable Roberts told me there'd been plenty of time for him to have cleaned the Gatling Gun after Sir Clive had been shot, then return on the sly to his room. No one saw Landen until the morning after the murder, during which he claimed to have been asleep." Holmes paced slowly back and forth, cupping his chin in his hand.

"What, pray God, are we going to do?" Wilson blurted out, unable to stand the silence. Holmes stood still and faced him.

"Watson and I will unpack," he said, "then you can take us to examine the scene of Sir Clive's murder, and to talk to the victim's family." The rest of that afternoon was filled with the gathering of large as well as minute pieces of information that might mean little to anyone other than Sherlock Holmes, but which I'd seen him time and again use to draw the noose snug around those who'd done evil. It was a laborious but unerringly effective process. We were driven out the road towards Sir Clive's estate, but our first stop was where he'd been killed. "See this, Watson," Holmes said, hopping down out of the carriage. "The road dips and bends here, so the horses would have to slow. And there is cover in that thick copse of trees. A perfect spot for an ambush." He was right, of course, in general. The rest of the land around the murder scene was almost flat, however, and any hidden gunman would have had to run the risk that someone in the vicinity might see him fleeing after the deed was done.

I got down and stood in the road while Holmes wandered over and examined the trees. He returned walking slowly, his eyes fixed to the ground, pausing once to stoop and drag his fingers along the earth.

"What's he looking for?" Wilson Edgewick whispered.

"If we knew," I told him, "it wouldn't mean much to us."

"Were any spent cartridges found?" Holmes asked Edgewick, when he'd reached us. He was wiping a dark smudge from his fingers with his handkerchief.

"No, Mr. Holmes."

"And the spent shells stay in the ammunition belt of the Gatling Gun rather than being ejected onto the ground after firing?"

"Exactly. The belts are later refitted with fresh ammunition."

"I see." Holmes bent down suddenly. "Hello. What have we here, Watson?" He'd withdrawn something small and white almost from beneath my boot. I leaned close for a better look.

"A feather, Holmes. Only a white feather."

He nodded, absently folding the feather in his handkerchief and slipping it into his waistcoat pocket. "And here is where the body was found?" He pointed to the sharp bend in the road.

"Actually down there about a hundred feet," Edgewick said. "The theory is that the horses trotted on a ways after Sir Clive was shot and the reins were dropped."

"And what of the horse that was found standing off to the side?"

Edgewick shrugged. "It had been improperly hitched, I suppose, and worked its way loose. It happens sometimes."

"Yes, I know," Holmes said. He walked around a while longer, peering at the ground. Edgewick glanced at me, eager to get on to the house. I raised a cautioning hand so he wouldn't interrupt Holmes's musings. In the distance a flock of wrens rose from the treetops, twisting as one dark form with the wind.

After examining the murder scene, we drove to the carriage house and saw the Gatling Gun itself. It was manufactured of blued steel and smelled of oil and was beautiful in a horrible way.

"This shouldn't be allowed in warfare," I heard myself say in an awed voice.

"It is so terrible," Edgewick said, "that perhaps eventually it will eliminate warfare as an alternative and become the great instrument of peace. That's our fervent hope."

"An interesting concept," Holmes said. He sniffed at the clustered barrels and firing chambers of the infernal machine. Then he wiped from his fingers some gun oil he'd gotten on his hand, smiled, and said, "I think we've seen quite enough here. Shall we go on to the house?"

"Let's," Edgewick said. He seemed upset as well as impatient. "It appears that progress will be slow and not so certain."

"Not at all," Holmes said, following him out the door and waiting while he set the lock. "Already I've established that your brother is innocent."

I heard my own intake of breath. "But Holmes—"

"No revelations yet," Holmes said, waving a languid hand. "I merely wanted to lessen our young friend's anguish for his brother. The explanation is still unfolding."

When we reached the house we were greeted by Eames the butler, a towering but cadaverously thin man, who ushered us into the drawing room. The room took up most of the east wing of the rambling, ivy-covered house, and was oak-paneled and well furnished, with comfortable chairs, a game table, a Persian carpet, and a blazing fire in a ponderous stone fireplace. French doors opened out to a wide lawn.

Wilson Edgewick introduced us around. The delicately beautiful but sad-eyed woman in the leather chair was Millicent, Landen's fiancée. Standing by the window was a small, dark-haired girl of pleasant demeanor: Phoebe Oldsbolt, Millicent's younger sister and Robby Smythe's romantic interest. Robby Smythe himself lounged near the stone fireplace. Standing erectly near a sideboard and sipping a glass of red wine was a sturdily built man in tweeds who was introduced as Major Ardmont of the Queen's Cavalry.

"Sir Clive was a retired officer of cavalry, was he not?" Holmes asked, after offering his condolences to the grieving daughters of the deceased.

"Indeed he was," Ardmont said. "I met Sir Clive in the service at Aldershot some years ago, and we served together in Afghanistan. Of course, that was when we were both much younger men. But when I cashiered out and returned from India, I heard the news that Sir Clive had been killed; I saw it as my duty to come and offer what support I could."

"Decent of you," I said. "I understand you were a military man, Dr. Watson," Ardmont said. He had a tan skin and pure blue, marksman's eyes that were zeroed in on me. That look gave me a cold feeling, as if I were a quarry.

"Yes," I said. "Saw some rough and tumble. Did my bit as a surgeon."

"Well," Ardmont said, turning away, "we all do what we can."

"You and Doctor Watson must move from the inn and stay here until this awful thing is settled!" Millicent said to Holmes.

"Please do!" her sister Phoebe chimed in. Their voices were similar, high and melodious.

"I'd feel better if you were here," Robby Smythe said. "You'd afford the girls some protection. I'd stay here myself, but it would hardly be proper."

"You live at the inn, do you not?" Holmes asked.

"Yes, but I don't know what it is those fools heard. I was in my shop working on my autocar when the shooting occurred."

Holmes stared at Major Ardmont, who looked back at him with those unrattled blue eyes. "Major, you hardly seem old enough to have just retired from service."

"It isn't age, Mr. Holmes. I've been undone by an old wound, I'm afraid, and can no longer sit a horse."

"Pity," I said.

"I understand," Holmes said, looking at Millicent, "that Eames overheard your father and Landen Edgewick arguing the evening of the murder."

"That's what Eames said, Mr. Holmes, and I'm sure he's telling the truth. At the same time, I know that no matter what their differences, Landen wouldn't kill my father—nor anyone else!" Her eyes danced with anger as she spoke. A spirited girl. "You haven't answered us, Mr. Holmes," Phoebe Oldsbolt said. "Will you and Dr. Watson accept our hospitality?"

"Kind of you to offer," Holmes said, "but I assure you it won't be necessary." He smiled thinly and seemed lost for a moment in thought. Then he nodded, as if he'd made up his mind about something. "I'd like to talk with Eames the butler, and then spend a few hours in town."

Millicent appeared puzzled. "Certainly, Mr. Holmes. But you and Dr. Watson shall at least dine here tonight, I insist."

Holmes nodded with a slight bow. "It's a meal I anticipate with pleasure, Miss Oldsbolt."

"As do I," I added, and followed Holmes towards the door.

Outside, while waiting for the buggy to be brought around, Holmes drew me aside. "I suggest you stay here, Watson. And see that no one leaves."

"But no one seems to have any intention of leaving, Holmes."

He gazed skyward for a moment. "Have you noticed any wild geese since we've been here, Watson?"

"Uh, of course not, Holmes. There are no wild geese in this part of England in October. I know; I've hunted in this region."

"Precisely, Watson."

"Holmes—" But the coachman had brought round the buggy, and Holmes had cracked the whip and was gone. I watched the black, receding image of the buggy and the thin, erect figure on the seat. As they faded into the haze on the flat landscape, I thought I saw Holmes lean forward, urging the mare to go faster.

When Holmes returned later that evening and we were upstairs dressing for dinner, I asked him why he'd gone into town.

"To talk to Annie," he told me, craning his lean neck and fastening his collar button.

"Annie?"

"The maid at the King's Knave Inn, Watson."

"But what on earth for, Holmes?"

"It concerned her duties, Watson."

There was a knock on the door, and Eames summoned us for dinner. I knew any further explanation would have to wait for the moment when Holmes chose to divulge the facts of the case.

Everyone who had been in the drawing room when we'd first arrived was at the table in the long dining hall. The room was high-ceilinged and somewhat gloomy, with wide windows that looked out on a well-tended garden. Paintings of various past Oldsbolts hung on one wall. None of them looked particularly happy, perhaps because of the grim commerce the family had long engaged in.

The roast mutton and boiled vegetables were superb, though the polite dinner conversation was commonplace and understandably strained.

It was in the oak-paneled drawing room afterward, when we were enjoying our port, that Millicent Oldsbolt said, "Did you make any progress in your trip to town, Mr. Holmes?"

"Ah, yes," Major Ardmont said, "did you discover any clues as to the killer's identity? That's what you were looking for, was it not?"

"Not exactly," Holmes said. "I've known for a while who really killed Sir Clive; my trip into town was in the nature of a search for confirmation."

"Good Lord!" Ardmont said. "You've actually known?"

"And did you find such confirmation?" Robby Smythe asked, tilting forward in his chair.

"Indeed," Holmes said. "One might say I reconstructed the crime. The murderer lay in wait for Sir Clive in a nearby copse of trees, saw the carriage approach, and moved out to be in sight so Sir Clive would stop. With very little warning, he shot Sir Clive, emptying his gun to be sure his prey was dead."

"Gatling Gun, you mean," Major Ardmont said.

"Not at all. A German Army sidearm, actually, of the type that holds seven rounds in its cylinder."

"But the rapid-fire shots heard at the inn!" Robby Smythe exclaimed.

"I'll soon get to that," Holmes said. "The murderer then made his escape, but found he couldn't get far. He had to return almost a kilometre on foot, take one of Sir Clive's horses from the carriage hitch, and use it to pull him away from the scene of the crime."

Robby Smythe tilted his head curiously. "But why would Landen—"

"Not Landen," Holmes cut him off. "Someone else. The man Eames only assumed was Landen when he heard a man arguing with Sir Clive earlier that evening. Landen was where he claimed he was during the time of the murder, asleep in his room at the inn. He did not later return unseen through his window as the chief constable so obstinately states."

"The constable's theory fits the facts," Major Ardmont said.

"But I'm telling you the facts," Holmes replied archly. "Then what shooting did the folks at the inn hear?" Millicent asked.

"They heard no shooting," Holmes said. "They heard the rapid-fire explosions of an internal combustion engine whose muffling device had blown off. The driver of the horseless carriage had to stop it immediately lest he awaken everyone in the area. He then returned to the scene of the murder and got the horse to pull the vehicle to where it could be hidden. Then he turned the animal loose, knowing it would go back to the carriage on the road, or all the way here to the house."

"But who—"

Phoebe Oldsbolt didn't get to finish her query. Robby Smythe was out of his chair like a tiger. He flung his half-filled glass of port at Holmes, who nimbly stepped aside. Smythe burst through the French doors and ran towards where he'd left his horseless carriage alongside the west wing of the house.

"Quick, Holmes!" I shouted, drawing my revolver. "He'll get away!"

"No need for haste, Watson. It seems that Mr. Smythe's tyres are of the advanced pneumatic kind. I took the precaution of letting the air out of them before dinner."

"Pneumatic?" Major Ardmont said.

"Filled with atmosphere under pressure so they support the vehicle on a cushion of air," Holmes said. "As you well know, Major."

I hefted the revolver and ran for the French windows. I could hear footsteps behind me, but not in front. I prayed that Smythe hadn't made his escape.

But he was frantically wrestling with a crank on the front of a strange-looking vehicle. Its motor was coughing and wheezing but wouldn't supply power. When he saw me, he gave up on the horseless carriage and ran. I gave chase, realised I'd never be able to overtake a younger man in good condition, and fired a shot into the air.

"Halt, Smythe!"

He turned and glared at me.

"I'll show you the mercy you gave Sir Clive!" I shouted.

He hesitated, shrugged, and trudged back towards the house.

"Luckily the contraption wouldn't start," I said, as we waited in the drawing room for Wilson Edgewick to return with the chief constable.

"I was given to understand the horseless carriage can be driven slowly on deflated tires," Holmes said, "but not at all with this missing." He held up what looked like a length of stiff black cord. "It's called a spark wire, I believe. I call removing it an added precaution."

Everyone seemed in better spirits except for Robby Smythe and Phoebe. Smythe appealed with his eyes to the daughter of the man he'd killed and received not so much as a glance of charity.

"How could you possibly have known?" Millicent asked. She was staring in wonder at Holmes, her fine features aglow now that her world had been put back partly right.

Holmes crossed his long arms and rocked back on his heels while I held my revolver on Smythe.

"This afternoon, when Watson and I examined the scene of the murder, I found a feather on the ground near where the body was discovered. I also found a black sticky substance on the road."

"Oil!" I said.

"And thicker than that used to lubricate the Gatling Gun, as I later ascertained. I was reasonably sure then that a horseless carriage had been used for the murder, as the oil was quite fresh and little had been absorbed into the ground. The machine had to have been there recently. When Smythe here tried to make his escape after shooting Sir Clive, the muffling device that quiets the machine's motor came off or was blown from the pressure, and the hammering exhaust of the internal combustion made a noise much like the rapid-fire clatter of the Gatling Gun. Which led inn patrons to suppose the gun was what they'd heard near the time of the murder. Smythe couldn't drive his machine back to its stall in such a state, and couldn't silence it, so he had one of Sir Clive's horses pull him back. If only the earth hadn't been so hard this would all have been quite obvious, perhaps even to Chief Constable Roberts."

"Not at all likely," Millicent said.

"It was Smythe whom Eames overheard arguing with Sir Clive," Holmes continued. "And Major Ardmont, who is a member of the German military, knows why."

Ardmont nodded curtly. "When did you realise I wasn't one of your Cavalry?" he asked. "I knew you were telling the truth about being in the cavalry, and serving in a sunny clime," Holmes said, "but the faint line of your helmet and chinstrap on your sunburned forehead and face don't conform to that of the Queen's Cavalry helmet. They do suggest shading of the helmet worn by the German horse soldier. I take it you received your sun-darkening not in India but in Africa in the service of your country."

"Excellent, Mr. Holmes!" Ardmont said, with genuine admiration. "Mr. Smythe," he said, "had been trying to convince Sir Clive to get the British military interested in his horseless machine as a means to transport troops or artillery. A hopeless task, as it turned out, with an old horseman like Sir Clive. Smythe contacted us, and introduced me to Sir Clive. He told Sir Clive that if the British didn't show interest in his machines, he'd negotiate with us. And we were quite willing to negotiate, Mr. Holmes. We Germans do feel there's a future for the internal combustion engine in warfare."

I snorted. Much like a horse. I didn't care. The image of a thousand sabre-waving troops advancing on hordes of sputtering little machines seemed absurd.

"Sir Clive," Ardmont went on, "showed his temper, I'm afraid. He not only gave his final refusal to look into the idea of Smythe's machine; he absolutely refused to have as his son-in-law anyone who would negotiate terms with us. Possibly that's what the butler overheard in part, thinking Sir Clive was referring to Landen Edgewick and Millicent rather than to Mr. Smythe and Phoebe."

"Then you were with Sir Clive and Smythe when they clashed," I said, "yet you continued to let the police believe it was Landen Edgewick who'd had the argument."

"Exactly," Major Ardmont said. "To see Mr. Smythe off to the hangman wouldn't have given Germany first crack at a war machine, would it?"

"Contemptible!" I spat.

"But wouldn't you do the same for your country?" Ardmont asked, grinning a death's head grin. I chose not to answer. "The feather?" I said. "Of what significance was the feather, Holmes?"

"It was a goose feather," Holmes said, "of the sort used to stuff pillows. I suspected when I found it that a pillow had been used to muffle the sound of the shots when Sir Clive was killed. Which explains why the actual shots weren't heard at the inn."

"Ah! And you went into town to talk to Annie then."

"To find out if she'd missed a pillow from the inn lately. And indeed one had turned up missing—from Robby Smythe's room."

"An impressive bit of work, Mr. Holmes," Ardmont said. "I'll be leaving now." He tossed down the rest of his port and moved towards the door.

"He shouldn't be allowed to leave, Holmes!"

"The good major has committed no crime, Watson. English law doesn't compel him to reveal such facts unless questioned directly, and what he knew about the argument had no exact bearing on the crime, I'm afraid."

"Very good, Mr. Holmes," Ardmont said. "You should have been a barrister."

"Lucky for you I'm not," Holmes said, "or be sure I'd find some way to see you swing alongside Mr. Smythe. Good evening, Major."

Two days later, Wilson and Landen Edgewick appeared at our lodgings on Baker Street and expressed appreciation with a sizable cheque, a wedding invitation, and bone-breaking handshakes all around. They were off to Reading, they said, to demonstrate the Gatling Gun to the staff of British Army Ordnance Procurement. We wished them luck, I with a chill of foreboding, and sent them on their way.

"I hope somehow that no one buys the rights to their weapon," I said.

"You hope in vain," Holmes told me, slouching deep in the wing chair and thoughtfully tamping his pipe. "I'm afraid, Watson, that we're poised on the edge of an era of science and mechanization that will profoundly change wartime as well as peacetime. It mightn't be long before we're experimenting with the very basis of matter itself and turning it to our own selfish means. We mustn't sit back and let it happen in the rest of the world, Watson. England must remain in the forefront of weaponry, to discourage attack and retain peace through strength. Enough weapons like the Gatling Gun, and perhaps war will become untenable and a subject of history only. Believe me, old friend, this can be a force for tranquillity among nations."

Perhaps Holmes is right, as he almost invariably is. Yet as I lay in bed that night about to sleep, never had the soft glow of gaslight, and the clatter of horses' hooves on the cobblestones below in Baker Street, been so comforting.

THE ADVENTURE OF THE DOUBLE-BOGEY MAN

BY ROBERT L. FISH

The name Robert L. Fish brings smiles to many, and his first publication at age 47 is heartening to many a struggling writer. The Schlock Homes stories are rollicking send-ups of the Canon, with a kosher twist. "The Adventure of the Double-Bogey Man" is a pun-ishing exemplar of the series.

A perusal of my notes for the year '42, made in September of that year and accounting the many cases in which I had engaged with my friend Mr. Schlock Homes, gave me as rude a shock as ever I have suffered. It was in February of '42 that I had begun the study of a new method of speedwriting, feeling that a facility in this science might well aid me in both quickly and accurately annotating our adventures. Unfortunately, a sharp increase in my medical practice, possibly caused by a section of slippery pavement near our rooms at 221B Bagel Street, left me little time for my studies, and I came back to my casebook to find I was unable to translate my own hieroglyphics. In desperation I took my Pitman notebook to a famous expert, but when he announced that it was all Gregg to him, I found myself without recourse.

Even Homes, with his vast background of cipherology and cryptology, was able to be of small help. He did manage to decipher one title as *The Sound of the Basketballs*, but since we could recall no case involving sports that year, we were unable to go further. These many adventures are therefore lost to posterity, and I bitterly hold myself to blame for their loss.

October, however, brought a case of such national importance that it dwarfed all work Homes had previously done that year, for beyond furnishing him with an opportunity to once again demonstrate his remarkable ability to analyse distortions in their proper perspective, it also gave him a chance to serve his country as few men have been able to serve her. In my notes, now meticulously kept in neat English, I find the case listed as *The Adventure of the Double-Bogey Man.*

I had returned from carefully sprinkling powdered wax on the offending section of pavement, in the hopes that this might resolve its slippery condition, to find that in my absence Homes's brother Criscroft had arrived and was ensconced together with my friend on the sofa before the blazing fireplace. As I entered, they were engaged in a favourite game of theirs, and as always I stood back in reverent silence as they matched their remarkable wits in analytical reasoning. Their subject appeared to be an old-fashioned tintype of a moustached gentleman dressed in the clothing of yesteryear, stiffly seated in a bower of artificial flowers, his bowler held woodenly before him, and his frozen face reflecting the ordeal of the portraiture.

"An ex-student of the Icelandic languages, dedicated to the growing of rubber plants," Criscroft suggested, eyeing the discoloured photograph closely.

"Colourblind and left-handed," returned Homes languidly, as I held my breath in admiration.

"A one-time trampoline acrobat, adept at playing the twelve-toned gas-organ," observed Criscroft.

"A victim of the hashish habit," Homes said, smiling. "Went before the mast at an early age, and has travelled widely in Kew."

"The son of a Northumbrian bell ringer," offered Criscroft. Then, turning and noting my presence, he held up his hand. "But enough of this, Schlock. Watney has arrived and we can get down to the real reason for my visit. Put Father's picture away now, and let me tell you why I left the Home Office in such troubled times, and hurried here as quickly as possible. We are in serious need of your help!"

Once I had placed drinks in their hands and Homes had lit a cubeb, Criscroft proceeded to lay his problem before us.

"As you are probably aware," he said, "we have recently allowed some of our former colonies to join us in confronting the present unpleasantness emanating from Berlin. The representative of the former American colonies is a certain General Issac Kennebunk, Esquire, and in confidence I may tell you that it appears this gentleman will be selected to assume the duties of Chief of Staff of our combined Allied forces." He cleared his throat and leaned forward impressively. "With this fact in mind, you can readily understand our perturbation when I inform you that, as of yesterday, General Kennebunk is missing!"

"Missing?" I cried in alarm, springing to my feet. "Missing what?"

"General Kennebunk *himself* is missing," said Criscroft heavily. "Since yesterday morning when he left a War Council meeting to return to his rooms, he has neither been seen nor heard of. Suffice to say that the General is knowledgeable of all our secret strategy. Should he have fallen in the hands of our enemies or their sympathizers, it could prove to be quite embarrassing for us."

"And you wish me to locate him," stated Homes positively, rubbing his hands together in that gesture that I well knew indicated both extreme interest and poor circulation.

"Precisely. Needless to say, as quickly as possible."

"Then permit me a few questions. First, where was the General in digs?"

"The War Department arranged a suite for him at an old inn, The Bedposts, in Bolling Alley."

"He stayed there alone?"

"Except for his military aide, a certain Major Anguish McAnguish, who temporarily was sharing his quarters."

"And the Major?"

"He has also not been seen since the disappearance, but as you can well imagine our principal interest is in General Kennebunk."

"Naturally. And what steps have been taken so far?" Criscroft rose and stood with his back to the fire, his hands clenched behind him, his face ashen with the strain of his great problem and overwhelming responsibility. "The War Department brought in the military police at once, in the person of a former police agent named Flaherty, whom I believe you know. As soon as the Home Office was notified, we insisted on taking the assignment out of his hands and contacting you. The War Department was most enthusiastic in this regard; however, they still wish to also retain Flaherty, although they admit you are the possessor of the sharpest analytical brain in England today."

"Flaherty will get them nowhere," replied Homes seriously, although it was plain to see that the compliment had pleased him. "I assume, then, that I have a free hand. The rooms are under guard?"

"I have seen to it that they were immediately sealed, and that guards were posted. Orders have been issued to allow only you and Watney permission to enter."

"Fine!" said Homes, rising and removing his dressing gown. "In that case let us proceed there at once. One moment while I don suitable raiment and we shall be on our way!"

Criscroft's hansom deposited us at the mouth of Bolling Alley, and the Home Office specialist leaned over from his seat to grasp his brother's hand gratefully. Then with a wave, he drove off and we turned down the narrow lane in the direction of the famous old inn.

Our credentials gave us immediate access to the floor that had housed the missing officer, and after ascertaining from the rigid soldier on duty that there had been no visitors, we unlocked the door and passed within. At first view there was certainly nothing to indicate the forceful removal of the General. The beds were neatly made up, the furniture properly placed and but recently dusted, and the late autumn sun passing the white starched curtains gave the apartment a cheerful air. Homes paused in the doorway a moment, his piercing eyes sweeping the scene closely; then, closing the door firmly behind us, he began his search.

The dresser drawers gave no clue of anything untoward. The articles of clothing therein were neatly arranged and concealed nothing. Homes dropped to his knees to search beneath the bed, but other than some regulation Army boots, and a pair of what appeared to be spiked mountain-climbing shoes, the space was bare. Stepping closer to the closet, Homes stared at the rows of uniforms neatly arranged upon the rack; then, with a sudden resolve he pushed them to one side and probed beyond. I heard a low cry of triumph from my friend, and knew he had discovered his first clue. With gleaming eyes he withdrew oddly shaped sticks, several oversized white pellets, and some tiny wooden pins. Handling these objects with extreme care, he laid his find upon the bedspread with great delicacy and then stepped back to contemplate them, showing inordinate interest.

"Homes!" I cried in amazement, reaching for these odd objects, "what can these be?"

"Take care!" he advised, grasping my arm and drawing me back. "It's more than possible that these are strange weapons, and it would not do to destroy ourselves before our investigation has fairly begun! Let us leave them for a moment and continue our search!"

The very cleanliness of the room seemed to mitigate against finding more; the wastebasket was empty, the desk top cleared of all but essentials. Opening the desk drawer, Homes withdrew a blank white writing pad and was about to replace it when his keen eyes noted faint markings on its surface. Carrying it swiftly to the window, he held it horizontally at eye level against the light.

"Quickly, Watney!" he exclaimed in great excitement. "We have something! My bag!"

Dusting charcoal over the empty sheet, he blew it gently until it settled in the crevices left by the pressure of the quill upon the previous page, and a message appeared as if by magic. Homes placed his find carefully upon the desk, and I bent over his shoulder to read the missive with him.

"*Mammy,*" it said (or Manny; the inscription was not too clear): "*Only time for nine today; back up to fifty-six! Started off four, but I won't talk about the rest. The trouble is still my right hand, and the result is the hold hook! Talk about the bogey-man; the double-bogey man has me!*"

This perplexing message was simply signed with the initials of the missing colonial officer: I.K., E. I raised my eyes from this strange paper to find Homes with such a fierce look of concentration upon his lean face that I forbade speaking. At long last he looked at me frowningly, his mind returning from the far places of his thoughts.

"We must return to Bagel Street at once, Watney!" he said, his voice taut with urgency. "I believe I begin to see a pattern in this business, and if I should prove to be correct, we must waste no time if we are to save this General Kennebunk!"

"But, Homes," I cried, "do you mean that the answer lies in decoding this cryptic message?"

"This is no code, Watney, although there is no doubt that it contains a hidden message. Come, we have much to do!" Folding the paper with great care, he thrust it into his weskit and turned to the door.

"But these objects," I said. "Shall I take them with us?"

"No," he replied, staring at them with great loathing. "They will always be here should we require them, but I believe I already know their foul purpose. Come!"

We locked the door behind us and, passing the key to the guard, hurried to the street. A passing cab picked us up at once, and throughout our journey Homes leaned forward anxiously as if in this manner he could hasten our passage. While the cab was slowing down before our quarters, Homes thrust the fare into the cabbie's hand and sprang to the pavement even before the horses had fairly stopped. I hurried up the stairs behind him, anxious to be of immediate assistance.

"First, Watney," he said, turning up the lamp and hurriedly pulling his chair closer to the table, "if you would be so kind as to hand me the Debrett's, we can get started!"

I placed the tome in his hand and he slid his strong finger down the alphabetical list rapidly. "McAnguish, McAnguish, 224 Edgeware Mews, Hyde Park, 6-2-4 . . . No, no, Watney! This is the telephone list! The Debrett's, please!"

I replaced the volume, blushing slightly, and he fell to studying it while I watched his face for some clue as to his thoughts. He scribbled some data on a pad and handed the book back. "And now the World's Atlas, Watney, if you please." He looked up as he spoke, and noting the look of befuddlement on my face, smiled and spoke in a kindly tone.

"No, Watney, this time I am not attempting to mystify. In time you shall know all. It is simply that every minute may count, and there is no time at present for explanations. So if you will excuse me, I shall get on with my work!"

I waited as he flung the Atlas open, and then, seeing that he had already forgotten my presence in his interest in the maps before him, I quietly left and went to my room.

I awoke to find the first faint strands of dawn feathering the window-pane, and even as I wondered what had aroused me so early, I felt again the urgent pressure of Homes's hand upon my arm.

"Come, Watney," he said in a low voice, "our train leaves in thirty minutes. I have a cab waiting and you must hurry if we are not to miss our connexion. Get dressed quickly and I shall meet you below."

His footsteps diminished as he left the room and I groped for my Oxford bags with mind awhirl, sleep fighting to once again assume control. I entered our sitting room to find that Homes had already descended, and even as I picked up my overcoat I noted that the table was still covered with many volumes from Homes's vast reference library, and that the lamp was still lighted. It was evident that my friend had passed the night at work. I was turning down the lamp when a faint cry from below caused me to instantly slip into my coat and hurry down the steps.

Homes was already seated in the cab, and even as I came running up he gave the driver instructions to start, his strong hand pulling me into the moving vehicle. "Forgive me, Watney," he chuckled as we rattled off toward Euston Station. "The complete answer came to me but a short while ago, and I still had to telegraph Flaherty to meet us with some of his agents at the train. I also had to arrange our passage on the Ayr Express and see that a cab was waiting to take us to the station. I'm afraid that I left the problem of awakening you until the last."

"And the answer lies in Scotland?" I asked.

"It does indeed," replied my friend, smiling. Then, leaning forward, he cried, "Tuppence extra, driver, if we do not miss our train!"

We came clattering into Euston Station at a terrific clip and Homes had me by the hand, dragging me from the swaying vehicle while it was still moving smartly. We ran down the deserted platform, peering into the compartments of the steaming train, and then, as the cars began to move, Homes flung open a door and sprang aboard, pulling me behind him. I had scarcely time to catch my breath when we passed beneath the first tunnel, and Homes then seated himself comfortably in the first smoking compartment we passed.

"Flaherty and his men are aboard," he said, reaching into his pocket for his briar. "I noticed him in the car behind as we came along the platform. With any luck at all, we should have this case finished by nightfall!"

"But I do not understand any of this, Homes!" I cried perplexedly. "I have seen all that you have seen, and none of it makes any sense to me at all! Do you mean that you have deduced the General's whereabouts, and the plot behind his disappearance, simply from the little data of which I am cognizant?"

"Little data?" he replied in honest surprise. "Little data? Actually, Watney, I have never had a case before so replete with data! Allow me to demonstrate!"

He drew the folded paper containing the cryptic message from his weskit pocket and placed it upon the small table beneath the train window. I moved to the other side of the compartment in order to face him, and he began his explanation.

"First, Watney," he said, smoothing the sheet so that I could once again read the scrawled words, "listen carefully to what the General says. He begins by saying, 'only time for nine,' a common colloquialism meaning quite clearly that he has only time for a few words. He follows this up with 'up to fifty-six' and the words 'off four.' What can these words possibly indicate? Only one thing—they are directions! The most positive directions that exist, Watney—*latitude and longitude*! Up fifty-six. Off four. Obviously fifty-six degrees north latitude, and four degrees west longitude!

"Do we have anything to support this supposition? What else does he say? He says, 'the trouble is my right hand.' And who is his right hand? *Major Anguish McAnguish!* And Debrett's gives me the home seat of the McAnguish family as Carnoustie in Scotland, *at exactly this latitude and longitude*!"

Homes leaned back, puffing furiously upon his briar. "Let us go a bit further," he said, as I sat wide-eyed at this brilliant exposition. "The General next states, 'the result is the old hook.' I do not know if you are familiar with the slang speech of America, Watney, but the 'old hook' means that he is being pressured into something which is, to say the very least, extremely distasteful to him. And he finished by saying, 'the double-bogey man has me!' We all know what the bogey man is; it relates to demonology and the superstitions of our childhoods. And the double-bogey man can only be twice as terrifying in the imagination of this poor chap!

"On this basis, let us restate the message the General might have written if he had been permitted freedom and had not been forced to conceal his meaning from his enemies. He would have said: 'Just time for a brief note. I must go back to Carnoustie, because McAnguish is blackmailing me. There I shall be forced to undergo an experience which is too terrible to contemplate!'"

My friend stared at me broodingly. "And I am sure that I know just what this terrible experience will be, Watney! Pagan rites!"

I sat up in alarm. "Pagan rites, Homes?"

"There can be no doubt. Remember the bogey man, Watney! I do not know if you are familiar with Voodoo or any of the other pagan religions based upon sorcery, but human sacrifice often plays a part in the ceremonies, and very often human sacrifice using the most primitive of weapons! You recall, I am sure, the war clubs and wooden darts which we discovered in the rooms of our Major Anguish McAnguish!"

Homes leaned back once again and eyed me grimly. "Remember, Watney, our Aryan enemy has made Paganism its official religion. And Scotland has many Nationalists who are not out of sympathy with these enemies. There can be no doubt that somewhere on the heaths of Carnoustie this rite is either in progress or being prepared! I can only hope that we are in time to rescue this General from these fiends before it is too late, for it is quite evident who the victim of this sacrifice is to be!"

"How horrible, Homes! And it is for this reason that you brought along Flaherty and his men?"

"Precisely. There may well be fisticuffs or other violence, and besides, we have no official position in this, particularly across the border in Scotland. However, grim as the situation may be, it is certain that we shall be of small use if we do not rest before our arrival. I would suggest twenty winks while we can, for we are certain to be quite busy before the day is over!"

I awoke to find Homes in whispered conference with a heavy-set gentleman whose pocket sagged under the weight of a truncheon, and who could be none other than the police agent Flaherty.

"I understand, Mr. Homes," this person was saying respectfully. "It shall be as you say."

"You have a photograph of this colonial officer?"

"I do, Mr. Homes. He is a balding gentleman much given to wearing colourful knickerbockers and rather dashing shirts when off duty, and I am sure I shall have no trouble recognizing him."

"Good. Then we are ready. I have studied a one-centimetre map of the area, and I am convinced that there is but one heath sufficiently large and isolated as to be suitable for their nefarious purpose. The officials of the train have agreed to stop close by this heath to allow us to descend and deploy. Come, Watney, on your feet! I feel the brakes being applied at this very moment!"

Seconds later we found ourselves beside the railway track while the Ayr Express slowly gathered speed again. In addition to Homes and myself, Flaherty was accompanied by three large men, all similarly attired, and all weighted down by their truncheons. At a cautious signal from Homes, we crossed the tracks and advanced, spreading out in a widening curve, fanning across the heath.

The section of heath we fronted was well landscaped, with numbered flags, probably marking watering holes, spaced about. We were advancing slowly when, of a sudden, there was a sharp whistle in our ears and a white stone flew past to disappear in the distance. "It's a trap, Homes!" I cried, flinging him into a nearby sand-filled depression and desperately covering him with my body.

"I believe in Scotland they call these ditches 'bunkers,'" he replied, rising and dusting himself off carefully. "Come, men, we must be close!"

He leaned over the edge of the depression, studying the landscape with Flaherty beside him. Suddenly the police agent stiffened, and peering into the distance pointed his finger excitedly. "It's him, Mr. Homes!" he cried. "I don't know how you ever deduced it, but as always you were right! And he is surrounded by three others, all of whom are armed with heavy clubs! But wait!" The police agent turned to Homes with a bewildered air. "He, too, is armed!"

"It is as I feared," said Homes, watching the four men approach. "Either hypnotism or drugs, both quite common in this type of affair! In his present condition the poor man may even struggle, but at least we have discovered him before they could put their odious plan into practice! Come, men, let us spread out and surround them!"

"I'm sorry, Mr. Homes," said Flaherty, placing his hand on Homes's arm. "My instructions are very clear. You have found him, and a very fine piece of work it was, but it is my duty to effect the rescue. You must go back to London and take no part in this."

"Nonsense!" Homes cried, incensed. "Come, men!"

"No, Mr. Homes," Flaherty replied quite firmly. "The instructions come from the Home Office itself. You are far too valuable to risk in an operation such as this. But fear not; I promise you I shall get him safely away from these culprits, and this whether he struggle or not!"

"Do not fail, then," Homes replied sternly. "England depends upon you! Come, Watney, we have but forty minutes if we are to catch the next train south!"

I had opened the morning journal and was engrossed in attempting to open my eggs and turn the pages simultaneously, when Homes entered the breakfast room and seated himself opposite me.

"I believe you are wasting your time, Watney," he remarked genially. "I have already been informed by Criscroft that the General is back in London, and I seriously doubt that the censors would allow an account of yesterday's proceedings to reach the public columns."

"I am not so sure, Homes," I replied, noting a small article buried in one corner. "It is true that no great details of the affair appear, but it does say that because of a nerve-wracking experience that he underwent yesterday, General Issac Kennebunk, Esquire, is under doctor's orders to take a few days' rest."

"I can well imagine how nerve-wracking it must have been," said Homes, his eyes warm with sympathy. "However, I would judge that several days engaged in one of our pleasant English sports could well erase this terrible memory. I believe I shall suggest this to the Home Office. A letter to my brother Criscroft if you please, Watney!"

THE CASE OF THE BLOODLESS SOCK

BY ANNE PERRY

Native Londoner Anne Perry is one of the world's best-selling writers, and among the foremost practitioners of Victorian suspense. In "The Case of the Bloodless Sock," she pursues a theme familiar to her readers, the dreaded kidnapping of a child.

It was a sunny March morning in Seattle, and at 221A Baker Street, Jane Watson was preparing for a trip to visit her uncle, Robert Hunt, in Wyoming.

"Jane!" called her mother from downstairs. "We're leaving in five minutes to drive you to the airport. Finish packing and come down."

"Okay, Mom," she called back. She had been thrilled when her uncle had called and asked her to come visit. There hadn't been an interesting case for weeks, and Sherlock was becoming unbearable. He was in such a foul mood that even his parents and brother were avoiding him.

Finally, she was packed and went out to say goodbye before she left.

"By all means go, Watson," said Sherlock, who sat on the front porch of his house, reading the newspaper. "At this time of the year you will be in your town, wherever it is, before dark. Goodbye."

Jane threw her duffle bag into the trunk and got in the car. As her dad drove her away, she couldn't help but be saddened that Sherlock hadn't given her a more sanguine farewell.

Hours later, Jane got off the plane at the airport in Gillette, Wyoming, and boarded a bus to the small town where her uncle lived. As

47

a major stockholder in much of the mining activity throughout the Powder River Basin, he lived quite well.

However, to Jane's surprise, when she got off at the bus station, no one was there to greet her. So she started walking towards her uncle's house. After about four miles, when she came up to the place, a man ran up to her and said, "Have you found her?!"

Jane's look of bewilderment told him that she hadn't, and it pushed the man almost to despair.

"Who's lost?" asked Jane. "I can help you look."

"Jenny!" the man cried. "Jenny Hunt, my neighbor's daughter! She's only five years old! God knows where she is! She's been gone since four this afternoon, and it's almost ten. Please, help me look!"

Jane's guts turned to water at the news. Jenny was her cousin! It was getting dark fast, and even if she was okay, it was cold and she would be terrified!

"Absolutely!" said Jane, throwing her bag onto the front porch, "Where do we start?"

The next three hours seemed to drag on. Her uncle acknowledged her presence, but he was too overcome with fear to do anything but thank her for helping. All of his neighbors were helping, and the town was soon lit up by all of the flashlights.

Finally, Jane poked her head into a small alley and saw Jenny. Calling to the others, Robert came and picked Jenny up. She was pale and frightened, but she didn't seem to be hurt.

The next morning, when Jane came down to breakfast, she saw her uncle sitting at the kitchen table, looking over a number of business papers.

"I don't know what to do, Jane," he said when she sat down. "Jenny is devoted to Josephine, her *au pair*, but how can I keep in my employ a girl who lets a five-year-old child just wander off? But if I fire her, Jenny will be heartbroken. She's been all but a mother to that girl, since your Aunt Sophie died . . ."

"Well," said Jane, "at this point, it would probably hurt Jenny even more if she lost Josephine. I'd say give her a second chance. She'll be much more careful, now that Jenny's run off."

Suddenly, there was a clanking sound from the front door. Both Jane and Robert looked to discover that an envelope had been pushed through the mail-slot. They looked out the window, but couldn't see who had left it.

Hunt opened the letter and paled. "What's wrong?" asked Jane. Hunt passed her the letter.

Dear Mr. Hunt:

Yesterday you lost your daughter, and last night at exactly twelve of the clock, you received her back again. You may take any precautions you care to, but they will not prevent me from taking her again, any time I choose, and returning her when, and if, I choose. And if it is my mind not to, then you will never see her again.

M.

Jane's hands were shaking as she laid the paper down. Hunt snapped out of his trance and said, "I'll warn the neighbors. Anyone who isn't known in town will be watched carefully, and we'll set up a guard around the house. Excuse me, Jane, but this requires my immediate attention."

Jane nodded, but said nothing. *What would Sherlock do if he were here?* she thought, *He would do more than just defend, he'd attack. But I don't know who this "M" is.*

Jane decided to talk to Jenny first, to see how much she knew. It took a few minutes to persuade Josephine, who was deeply reluctant to let anyone disturb the girl, to let her in, but finally she was admitted.

Jane sat across from Jenny on her bed while she finished her breakfast. She knew that Jenny would not remember her, as they hadn't met since Jenny was born, so she had to approach the girl carefully.

"Good morning, Jane," said Jenny when she was done with her eggs.

"Are you feeling okay?" asked Jane softly.

"Yes," replied Jenny. "I don't need any medicine."

"That's good," said Jane. "Did you sleep well? No bad dreams?"

Jenny shook her head.

"Can you tell me what happened?" asked Jane.

"I was in the garden," said Jenny, whose voice lowered to a whisper. "I was picking flowers," Jane gathered that she wasn't supposed to do that, "and someone came up to me."

"A stranger?" asked Jane.

Jenny nodded and said, "He was old, but old like you, not like Daddy; He was big, but thin; and he talked a funny way."

"What did he say his name was?" asked Jane.

"Fessa," said Jenny.

"'Fessa?' That's a weird name," said Jane, more to herself.

"No," said Jenny. "P'fessa!"

"Oh," said Jane. "You mean 'Professor?'" Jenny nodded again.

A terrible thought began to form in Jane's mind. "He was tall, thin, and spoke with an accent," reiterated Jane. "Did he have strange eyes?"

Jenny nodded and shivered, as if with fear. Josephine gave Jane a look to suggest that she not upset the girl. By now, Jane was convinced: the man who had taken Jenny was Professor Moriarty, Holmes's nemesis!

"Where did he take you?" asked Jane.

"A house," said Jenny, "with a big room."

"How did he take you there?" asked Jane. "In a car?"

Jenny shook her head, "It was like a bike, but it was fast, like a car."

Jane deduced that she meant a motorcycle. "Okay," she said to Jenny, "was it warm there?"

"Not really," said Jenny.

"Did he give you anything to eat?"

"Yes," said Jenny, "he gave me cupcakes with lots of frosting." She smiled as though the memory was a pleasant one.

"Was there a window you could see out of?" asked Jane, a little too hopefully.

"Yes," said Jenny, "I could see the whole town!"

Jenny spent the next several minutes describing the scenery to Jane, who, by the end of it, had a fairly clear idea about where this place could be. She went back downstairs to see her uncle, who was still ashen.

"What does he want?" he asked. "I can't even comply! He didn't ask for anything!"

"Uncle Rob, can I use your computer for a sec?" asked Jane. "My friend, Sherlock Holmes, is a detective, and he'll help any way he can if I send him an e-mail."

"There hasn't really been a crime, Jane," said Hunt. "My child has been taken and returned with no ransom demand."

"It's weird enough to get him interested," said Jane.

Hunt nodded and left. Jane's e-mail contained only one word, the word guaranteed to bring Holmes to Gillette: Moriarty.

Sure enough, when Jane met Sherlock at the airport in the evening, he was very different from the miserable teenager he'd been when she'd left Baker Street.

"Moriarty!" said Holmes to Jane, as if it were some sort of charm.

"I think so," replied Jane.

Sherlock gave her a quick glance and said, "You are uncertain. What makes you doubt, Watson? What has happened since you sent for me?"

"Nothing," said Jane. "We don't know if it was Moriarty who took Jenny."

Holmes rubbed his chin thoughtfully and said, "Has any demand been received yet?" He made no attempt to disguise the disappointment in his voice.

"Not yet," replied Jane. They both got into the car that Hunt had lent her and they proceeded back to the house. On the way, Holmes was scowling slightly, as though he were brooding on something.

"I'm not going to apologize, Holmes, if that's what you're waiting for," said Jane, a bit more petulantly than she intended.

"What gave you the idea that I expected an apology?" said Holmes in a toneless voice.

"The kidnapping of my cousin is just as important as any one of your cases, Holmes," she said. "There's no reason for you to sulk just because your archenemy may not have anything to do with this."

Holmes was about to reply when suddenly John, Hunt's gardener, ran up to the car, waving his arms. Jane stopped and got out.

"What's wrong? What happened?" asked Jane fearfully.

"She's gone again!" shouted the gardener, choking back a sob. "Jenny's gone!"

Instantly, Holmes was all attention. He leapt out of the car and strode over to the man. "I am Sherlock Holmes," he said. "Tell me precisely what has occurred. Omit no detail but tell me only what you have observed for yourself, or if someone has told you, give me their words as exactly as you can recall them."

"Her maid, Josephine," said John, regaining his composure. "She was with Jenny, upstairs in the nursery. Jenny had been running around and stubbed her toe badly. It was bleeding, so Josephine went to get her a Band-Aid, and when she got back, Jenny wasn't there. At first, it didn't seem worth worrying over because the ice-cream man was outside and Jenny loves ice cream. So she went down, but Jenny wasn't there, and Mr. Hunt hadn't seen her either. We looked everywhere in the house . . ."

"But you did not find the child," Holmes finished for him, his own face grim.

The man nodded vigorously and said, "Please, help us look for her!"

"Where's the ice-cream man, now?" asked Jane.

"Percy?" asked the gardener. "He's helping Mr. Hunt search the woods."

"Is he local?" asked Holmes.

"Yes," said John. "I've known him almost all my life. He would *never* hurt Jenny, and he couldn't've because he's been with us the whole time."

"Then the answer lies elsewhere." Holmes got into the car again and said, "Watson may know where she was taken the first time and we shall go there immediately. Tell your employer what we have done, and continue your search in all other places. If it is indeed who we think, he will not be so obvious as to show us the place again, but we must look."

Jane drove with all speed to the place Jenny described, a rundown old house at the very edge of the town. They searched the house and found it empty. They didn't have time to inspect it closely, and only had flashlights to search as they could.

"She has not been here tonight," said Holmes bitterly. "We shall return in the morning to learn what we may."

They went back to the house, where Holmes questioned Hunt's entire staff and every neighbor present. Jane, having tried and failed to console her uncle, found him again out back, examining the soil for footprints.

Holmes knew it was Jane by her step and said, "This is a miserable business, Watson. There is something peculiarly vile about using a child to accomplish one's purposes. If it is in fact Moriarty, he has sunk very low indeed."

Jane had never known Holmes to have a special fondness towards children, but the look of harsh anger on his face made her proud to call him her best friend.

"I despise a coward even more than I do a fool," said Holmes. "Foolishness is more often than not an affliction of nature. Cowardice is a vice sprung from placing one's own safety before the love of truth, known as the safety and welfare of others. It is the essential selfishness, Watson, and as such it lies at the core of so much other sin."

He stood from his crouch and started pacing. "But he must want something," he said as much to himself as to Jane. "Moriarty never does anything simply because he has the power to do it. You say the child was returned last night, and this morning a note was delivered? There will be another note. He may choose to torture his victim by lengthening the process, until the poor man is so weak with the exhaustion of swinging from hope to despair and back, but sooner or later he will name his price. And you may be sure, the longer he waits, the higher the stakes he is playing for!"

The two of them then took up their flashlights and started searching again, walking what seemed like miles through fields and woodland, calling Jenny's name.

After another half-hour, everyone gathered in Hunt's kitchen to take a break when the door suddenly opened. Jenny stepped in, pale as a ghost, with one shoe off and her foot smeared with blood.

"Papa . . ." she called out, on the verge of tears. Hunt ran over to her and scooped her up in his arms, crying with relief. Many of the women did the same, and not a few of the men found the need to blow their noses and turn to regain their composure.

Jane woke up at half past seven the next morning. When she came down for breakfast, she found Sherlock pacing back and forth in the hall.

"Ah, at last," he said when he saw Jane. "Go and question the child again. Learn anything you can, and pay particular attention to who took her and who brought her back."

"You don't think one of the neighbors is involved, do you?" she asked quietly.

"I don't know, Watson," said Sherlock, clearly frustrated. "There is something about this that eludes me, something beyond the ordinary. It is Moriarty at his most fiendish, because it is at heart very simple."

"Simple!" Jane burst out. "Jenny's been kidnapped twice, even though we did everything we could to protect her. The only explanation is that he got one of these people to betray my uncle."

But Holmes just shook his head and said, "If so then it is coincidental. It is very much his own work he is about. While you were asleep, I buried myself learning something of Hunt's affairs. As you know, he is one of the main stockholders in many of Wyoming's uranium mines, as well as the owner of a large amount of land in the area, but he has no political aspirations or any apparent enemies. I cannot yet see why he interests Moriarty."

"Money," said Jane simply. "Anyone who has people that he loves can have money extorted from him by a man like Moriarty."

"It is clumsy, Watson," said Sherlock. "Money in any form can be traced, if the plans are carefully laid, and there would finally be enough of a case to place him under indictment. No, such a kidnap has not the stamp of Moriarty upon it. It gives no satisfaction."

Jane waited until nine to question Jenny again, and practically had to fight Josephine to talk to Jenny alone.

"Hello, Jane," said Jenny. "I haven't had breakfast yet. Have you?"

"No," said Jane. "I thought it would be better to see if you were doing okay, first. How do you feel?"

"I don't like it," she said. "I don't wanna go there again."

Jane's heart ached to see Jenny so upset, and she said tenderly, "I need to know everything. Was it the same man again? The Professor?"

Jenny nodded.

"Did he take you to the same place?"

"No," said Jenny. "It was a barn, I think. There was a lot of straw. It prickled, and there was nothing to do."

Jane almost smiled at this, but held back. "How did he get you out of the nursery?"

Jenny's face scrunched up as though she were thinking hard. Finally she said, "I don't 'member."

"Did he carry you, or did you walk?" suggested Jane, trying to jog her memory.

"Don't 'member. I think I walked."

"Down the back stairs, maybe?"

"Don't 'member."

Damn, thought Jane, *She was probably drugged*. Jane went back downstairs to tell Holmes what she knew. She found him reading a letter that, apparently, had just been delivered.

"This is the reason, Watson!" he said. "And in true Moriarty style. You were correct in your deduction." He handed her the note.

My Dear Hunt,

I see that you have called in Sherlock Holmes. How predictable Watson is! But it will avail you nothing. I can still take the child any time I choose, and you will be helpless to do anything about it. However, if you should choose to sell 90 percent or more of your shares in the Black Thunder Coal

Mine, at whatever the current market price is, then I shall trouble you no further.

Moriarty.

"Why would he want Uncle Rob to sell his stock?" asked Jane. "What good would it do him?"

"It would start a panic and plunge the value of the entire mine," replied Holmes. "Very probably of the other mines in the Powder River Basin, in the fear that Hunt knew something damaging about them. Any denial he might make would only fuel speculation."

"And then Moriarty could buy all of that stock dirt cheap."

"Exactly," agreed Holmes, "and not only that, but appear as a local hero as well, saving the livelihood of all the workers. This is the true Moriarty, Watson. This has his stamp upon it. Now, what have you learnt from the child of how she left here?"

"Almost nothing," admitted Jane. "I think she was drugged."

Holmes listened to what Jane knew, and then said, "We shall go back to the house. There may be something to learn from a fuller examination, and then seek the barn, although I have no doubt Moriarty has long left it now. But first I shall speak to Hunt, and persuade him to do nothing regarding the shares—"

"You can't ask him to do that!" shouted Jane. "We can't protect Jenny! Twice he's gotten her, and we're helpless to stop it from happening again."

"It is not yet time to despair," said Holmes calmly. "I believe we have some hours. It is only six minutes past ten. Let us give ourselves until two of the clock. That will still allow Hunt sufficient time to inform his stockbroker before close of business today, if that should be necessary, and Moriarty may be given proof of it, if the worst should befall."

"Do you see an end to it?" asked Jane, starting to lose hope. "Uncle Rob would give up anything to save Jenny."

"Except his honor, Watson," said Holmes rather quickly. "It may tear at his very soul, but he will not plunge a hundred families into destitution, with their own children to feed and to care for, in order to save one, even though it is his own. But we have no time to stand here debating. Have the car ready for us, and as soon as I have spoken with Hunt, I shall join you at the front door."

"What's the point if Moriarty's gone by now?" asked Jane.

"Men leave traces of their acts, Watson," replied Holmes. With that, he went to Hunt's office.

Less than half an hour later, they arrived.

"Well?" asked Jane.

"I persuaded Hunt to delay action only until two," said Holmes, tight-lipped.

"I asked around the neighborhood," said Jane. "Either the towns-folk are more loyal than candid, or my uncle is pretty well-liked around here. He's wealthy in real possessions, the house and land and the mines, but he doesn't have a huge amount of ready cash. The worst thing they had to say about him is that he's got a slight temper."

Holmes frowned and became more withdrawn as he listened to the praise. It told him nothing helpful. They eventually found the tall house again, and the neighbors gave a description that matched Moriarty to a T.

While searching the upstairs, Jane called to Holmes and said, "I found the room where Jenny was kept." She got down on the floor and examined every inch, finding a few crumbs that indicated the cupcakes Jenny told her about.

"Look," said Holmes, "a fine yellow hair." He picked it up from a couch cushion. "Come!" he said, heading down the stairs. "There is nothing else to be learnt here. This is where he kept her, and he intended us to know it. He even left crumbs for us to find. Now why was that, do you suppose?"

"Carelessness," said Jane, "and arrogance."

"No, Watson, no!" said Sherlock emphatically. "Moriarty is never careless. He has left them here for a reason. Let us find this barn. There is something . . . some clue, something done, or left undone, which will give us the key."

But Jane knew that Sherlock was speaking more in hope than knowledge. He would never admit it, but she had seen in him a streak of kindness that didn't always sit well with reason. Of course, she never said so to him.

There were only a few farms left in the area, and even fewer with barns. The most obvious one was just outside of town, but Holmes insisted that they first try the second most obvious, which was a little farther out.

The barn was just like Jenny described it. Holmes immediately entered to begin his search, but Jane was skeptical.

"Holmes," she said, "Do you really expect to find anything like footprints, hair, or whatever with all of this straw? We—"

Holmes cut her off with a triumphant shout as he held up a little white sock.

"What?" said Jane angrily. "So it's Jenny's sock. She was here. How exactly does this help us?"

Holmes responded by looking at his watch. "It is half past one already!" he said with desperate urgency. "We have no time to lose at all. Take us back to your uncle's house as fast as the car can go!"

Jane kept her foot on the gas the whole way back, and when they got inside, she saw on the clock that it was only a few minutes till two.

Holmes ran into Hunt's office, held up the sock, and yelled, "Bloodless! Tell me, what time does the ice-cream man play?"

Hunt looked at Holmes like he'd lost his mind.

"Believe me, sir," said Holmes fiercely. "I am deadly earnest! Your daughter will be perfectly safe until the ice-cream man comes . . ."

"You're nuts, kid!" yelled Hunt. "I've known Percy Bradford almost my entire life! He wouldn't—"

"With no intent," said Holmes. "It is the tune he plays. Look!" He held up the sock. "You see, it has no blood on it! This was left where Moriarty wishes us to believe he held her last night, and that this sock was somehow left behind. But it is not so. It is no doubt her sock, but taken from the *first* kidnap when you were not guarding her, having no reason for concern."

"What difference does it make?" asked Hunt.

"Send for the ice-cream man, and I will show you," said Holmes. "Have him come to the gates as is his custom, but immediately, now in daylight, and play his tunes."

While Hunt ran off to call Percy, Holmes grabbed Watson by the arm and moved for the staircase. "Come," he ordered. "I might need you, Watson."

About a half-hour later, Watson and Holmes sat in the nursery with Jenny, waiting for the ice-cream truck to begin playing. Finally, as it arrived, the lilting sound of "The Entertainer" began to fill the air.

Jenny suddenly became still, and sat as straight as a board. Her pupils dilated to the point where her irises almost disappeared. Finally, she got up and walked out of the room.

"Follow her," said Sherlock to Jane quietly, "but do not touch her. You may harm her if you do." Accompanied by Josephine, the three of them followed Jenny on tiptoes as she climbed up the stairs, into the attic, and finally stopped at a small cupboard. There, she wrapped a blanket around herself and closed the door.

Holmes turned to Josephine and said, "When the clock strikes eleven, I believe she will awaken and return to normal, confused but not physically injured. She will believe what she has been hypnotized to believe, that she was again taken by Professor Moriarty, as she was in truth the first time. No doubt he took her to several different places, and she will recall them in successive order, as he has told her. You will wait here so you can comfort her when she awakens and comes out, no doubt confused and frightened. Do not disturb her before that."

A few hours later, both Jane and Sherlock sat on the plane that would take them back to Seattle. Jane was tired, but she was also pleased with herself. She had managed to help Holmes score a decisive victory over Moriarty, and proved her worth, if only to herself, as a Baker Street Irregular.

"Tomorrow, Uncle Rob will issue a statement denying any rumor that he might sell his holdings in the mine," said Jane.

Holmes nodded and replied, "I had Mycroft advise him that, if he can raise the funds, it would be advantageous to purchase a slight amount of more stock. We must not allow Moriarty to imagine that he was won anything, don't you agree?"

"I do," said Jane. "Do you think Jenny will be okay?"

"Of course, my dear Watson," said Holmes, smiling. "A visit or two to a competent psychiatrist, and Jenny's mind will be purged of Moriarty's evil influence."

"Yeah," said Jane, yawning. "You did good, Holmes."

"No, Watson," said Sherlock. "*We* did good."

SHERLOCKS

BY AL SARRANTONIO

"Sherlocks," Al Sarrantonio's story set in the near future (it may be here before you read this), doesn't actually feature the great detective, but his legacy runs all through it; and an industry that named a nuclear submarine after Jules Verne's Nautilus *would almost certainly honor the World's Greatest Detective by christening one of Sarrantonio's devices after the great detective. No doubt the legendary John Henry would also approve of this story of Man vs. Machine.*

The hotel room smelled like rosewater. It was twelve foot by twelve foot square, with a few sticks of cheap furniture stuck in the corners, green wall-to-wall carpeting that curled up as it reached the walls, a rumpled bed with an open suitcase on it, and one small, dirty window that gave a good view of the metallic wall on the hotel a few yards away next door. A man lay on the carpeting in the center of the room. He was long and lean, with thinning blond hair and a youthful face with a lot of angles in it. There was a startled expression in his eyes, which were open wide. He lay on his stomach, with his head to one side, and there was a very large kitchen knife with a plastic handle standing straight up out of his back.

Lieutenant Henry Virgil, a small man who looked as much like a weasel as any creature that was not in fact a weasel possibly could, was circling the corpse nervously as his assistant Buckers bent over it. Virgil's black pebbly eyes stabbed this way and that, out through the doorway, daring anyone who stood out there, myself included, to enter the room.

I looked at the two old-line cops who were with me in the hall, waiting to photograph and bag the body, and they looked at me, and the three of us had the same look of resigned disgust on our faces.

Inside the room, Virgil said, "Well?" to Buckers, who then lifted the slim black tentacles of his sherlock from the body and checked the read-out on the flat box strapped to his shoulder that the tentacles led into. "The light's still green, sir," he said in a small voice. He was a large, square man, but was scared to death of Virgil. "It's still collecting." Virgil nodded briskly, and Buckers bent over the body again. Four other technicians, clean-shaven and efficient as whisk brooms, were minutely combing every inch of the walls, floor, ceiling, and furniture with their own machines.

I stood watching until I became uncomfortable, and then I shifted my weight against the doorjamb and said, in as pleasant a voice as I could, "The guy's dead, Virgil. Can't you go back to your computer room and let these poor fellows out here do their dirty work?" Virgil seemed to leap across the room at me. "That's it, Matheson," he said. "I agreed to let you up here on the condition that you didn't open your mouth."

He took me by the arm and pulled me towards the elevator. I didn't resist. I gave appealing looks to the cops in the hallway, but there was nothing they could do.

"I'd like to squeeze your arm right off," Virgil said. I tried to talk reasonably but he cut me off. "I don't want you bothering my people. Just because someone was stupid enough to hire you to look into this murder doesn't mean you can follow my crew around like a gawker with a bag of peanuts. I don't care how many old friends you have on the force. I want you to stay away from me." His anger subsided a bit as the elevator doors opened. I stepped into the car without saying anything. The doors were closing when Virgil stopped them with his hand. He shook his head in mock sadness and said, "I really feel sorry for you, Matheson. Why don't you stop playing detective and get yourself a job?"

He let the doors close.

He wasn't so far from the truth. I hadn't had a solid investigative job—even a wife-cheating assignment—in six months, and ever since the sherlocks had become commercially available two years before, my caseload had been down about sixty percent. Most of the big agencies were using the machines now, and almost all the younger PIs were using the things, coupled with a databank service. I was starting to feel old.

That morning, though, I'd suddenly found myself involved with a murder case when I'd got up to find a note pinned to the pillow next to my head and an open window where whoever had pinned it had entered and exited. The note had read:

$2000 HAS BEEN CREDITED TO YOUR ACCOUNT. FIND OUT WHO MURDERED VINDEBEER AT THE SEDGEWICK HOTEL.

There hadn't been any signature, but after checking with the bank and finding that the money had indeed been deposited, I'd decided there was nothing to do but put on some clothes and go down to the Sedgewick. There I'd found Virgil and his sherlockers, and a dead body, presumably named Vindebeer. And that's where I stood now.

It was getting dark by the time I reached home. I had a little haven in the middle of all the high-rise metal spires on 212th Street, because about seventy-five years ago, when all the forty-floor monsters were springing up everywhere, a gray-haired old lady named Mrs. Cornelius had refused to sell her two-floor Victorian. They built right up to the border of her eighth-of-an-acre plot, but she ignored them. I'd bought the place from her daughter about ten years ago and blessed Mrs. Cornelius every time I stepped through the gate.

I blessed her now, but when I stepped through, I noticed that the front door was wide open. No one was inside, but I found a folded note attached to my easy chair in the den. This one read:

GO TO THE NORTH DOCKS TOMORROW AT 2:30 PM AND STAND BY THE EAST TOWER ELEVATOR.

This one was also unsigned. I didn't really like the game with the notes, but there didn't seem to be anything to do about it at the moment. So I ate dinner, read a Perry Mason for a couple of hours, then went to bed.

In the morning I went down to the North Manhattan police station to see Jack Rutgers. I poked my head into the computer terminal as I walked by and saw that Lt. Virgil was pacing around nervously, shouting instructions to Buckers and his other assistants, leaping from panel to panel and adjusting the dials and reading meters. When he saw me he growled, so I hurried past.

Rutgers was a nearly bald man in his middle fifties. He wore an open vest, sweated a lot, and had a round, thoughtful face. He wore round spectacles, which he was always taking off and cleaning with his handkerchief. He was the only old-timer left who had any control at all over Virgil. He had been pretty friendly to me over the years. His office was cluttered with plants; when I walked in, he told me to move a couple aside and find a place to sit.

"I'm glad you're here, Phil," he said. He took off his spectacles. "I'd like to bat some ideas back and forth with you."

"I'm working on the Vindebeer case," I said.

His eyebrows shot up. "You know his name? Did Virgil tell you?"

"I don't think Virgil has thought of looking in the guy's wallet yet. Someone left me a note with the name on it, though." I told him about my anonymous client. "The only thing I was able to figure out from the short time I was at the hotel yesterday was that this fellow hadn't been there very long since he hadn't even bothered to unpack. Is there anything you can add to that?"

"Phil," he sighed, polishing his glasses, "you know damn well that the sherlock boys only tell me what I pull out of them. They just about run things here now. When I retire they will run things. I was able to find out that this Vindebeer boy was from Norway, though. He'd been in the country only six days, and spent very little time in the hotel. He'd been out looking for a job—he was some sort of technician. A couple of nights he went to a bar called The Norseman on 204th Street. We got all this from the doorman at the hotel who'd talked to him a couple of times. Seems he'd been kind of lonely. There were no fingerprints in the hotel room except for his own. No one suspicious was seen entering or leaving the hotel before or after the murder; nobody heard anything. One of the sherlocks found a brown hair that didn't belong to the victim. That's all there is now; Virgil says he's still running olfactory tests on a kind of rosewater scent the sherlocks detected." He paused. "You have no idea who broke into your place and left the notes?"

"Nope." I got up to leave, slowly, because I knew Rutgers didn't want me to go yet. He was rubbing his spectacles thoughtfully and I sat down again. I knew what was coming since we'd been through it before.

"Plants need watering, Jack," I said. "Look a bit dried out."

He stopped polishing, pointed his spectacles at me, and said, in a confidential sort of way, "You know, twenty years ago you and I would have hated each other's guts—in a respectful kind of way. The police captain and the sharp young detective, eyeball to eyeball." He shook his head. "I know it was never really like that, Phil, but still, the way it was was better than this. They think they can solve every crime with little sensors, data banks, and electric eyes. Well, I don't think they work as well as men do."

"I don't, either," I said. "But apparently the things work. And somebody above you thinks they're worth the investment. I may be old-fashioned, Jack, and I know I'll never use one of those things. But if someone else wants to use them that's fine with me. I'll still rely on my own wits, even if I go down trying."

"Yeah," he said, and then he was silent, cleaning his glasses. "Keep in touch, Phil."

"I will. Thanks for the information." And this time, when I got up, I left.

The docks of north New York City are nestled in a basin by Inwood. The Hudson River used to flow there before it was diverted inland into New Jersey, through and behind the cliffs. Don't ask me why the Hudson River was chopped up like a birthday cake and put back together somewhere else, because I don't really know. It was some sort of public works project, and the money was there, so it got done. I think there's an amusement park in Jersey on the banks where the river goes by now.

When the river was drained at Inwood, natural walls were left against the river banks, and the empty basin that was formed was coated with quickly constructed transport offices and launching docks and turned into a cargo port. The place looked nice in the beginning: thirty years later the better facilities in Philadelphia and Virginia had most of the shuttle cargo business and the Inwood docking area was pretty much a ghost port. Now a lot of it was abandoned, and the other parts were used by fly-by-night transporters. The surrounding neighborhood wasn't too nice, either.

I took the creaky east-end elevator down to basin level, staring up at the launch gantry and empty, dilapidated control towers. When the car finally wheezed to a halt at the bottom I threw the rusting metal caging back and stepped out.

A long block of shabby structures—abandoned travel offices, mostly—lay in front of me. The block stretched straight as an arrow to the west end of the docks, and I could make out the creaky framework of the other elevator from where I stood.

I checked my watch and noted that it was now two thirty. Fifteen minutes went by. No one used the elevator or came down the shabby lane to meet me. After a half hour my feet got tired; twenty minutes later I decided to give up. As I turned around to get back on the elevator I heard a shuffling noise behind me and then everything turned black.

Even though I don't use a sherlock, I do make certain concessions to modern technology. There was a piece of equipment which I wore that probably saved my head from being split open. It's a thin membrane of ultra-high-impact plastic, which fits skin-tight at the base of my skull and up around my ears. I can't feel it when it's there, and unless you look close it can't be seen. A friend of mine had sent it to me; one just like it had saved his head a couple of times from the poundings of annoyed husbands.

The impact of the blow knocked me down. I was staggering to my feet when suddenly everything went dark gray and I dropped out cold. Someone had used gas on me—and I wasn't wearing a nose filter.

I awoke in a small room. There was a tiny light bulb on the ceiling directly over my head that threw off sour light that hurt my eyes. There weren't any windows. When I tried to get up I discovered that my arms were tied to the bottom of the bed I was lying on.

Someone came and stood over me, cutting off the sour light. It was a young girl, with long, straggly brown hair and a small chin and a grim, set mouth. Not very pretty. She held her hair back with one hand and leaned over me.

"You're not groggy?" Her voice was throaty, hard-edged.

"A little," I said. "Would you mind telling me what's going on?"

She straightened up, and I saw what looked like a smirk on her face. "I think we'd better have this out now."

I just looked at her.

"I'll make this concise," she went on. "If you don't leave my father alone, I'll do anything I have to to stop you. You have no business with us."

"I'm sorry," I said, "but I really don't know what you're talking about. If you'll—"

"I've warned you," she said, and then she uncovered something in her hand, moving it close to my face, and the next thing I knew I was waking up in front of the east-end elevator.

I made my way back home. There weren't any notes waiting for me there. An hour later I had just settled into a warm bath when Jack Rutgers called to tell me that another young technician from Norway had been murdered.

This victim had lived in one of the nicer parts of town, a swanky apartment building in the lower 90s. The front of the place was sealed tight and operated by a voice print–activated computer that wouldn't let me in. There were no police outside, but I finally was able to get in when an elderly, wide-eyed couple, who had obviously just heard about the murder, left the building. Once inside I merely followed the line of uniformed policemen who had been dropped like peas along the route to the victim's apartment.

When I walked into the living room I found Buckers and Virgil bent over a woman on the couch. She'd been stabbed in the chest. Buckers was tracing the outline of her body with the tentacles attached to his sherlock; a few more men were crawling here and there, little black boxes in hand.

I got the woman's name, Ingri Hoffman, from one of the cops standing outside. After waiting around for a while I discovered that that was about all they knew. I stayed out of Virgil's way. I thought I smelled a hint of rosewater, but I couldn't be sure.

I stood watching the sherlocks work for a few minutes. I can't help it, I just don't like the little black boxes. They have retracting tentacles, electronic eyes, olfactory filters, and audio sensors; they collect data, sniff out criminal odors, study fingerprints, footprints, breathprints, collect bits of clothing and skin and strands of hair, beep, whiz, talk to each other, correlate information with a central data bank. And though the courts were still tied up in knots over whether the evidence presented via sherlock was admissible, it seemed that after eight long years they were slowly coming around to favor the little machines.

The last image I had in my eyes as I turned to leave was of Ingri Hoffman on the couch; and Buckers, bright and eager as a puppy, sliding the slender cold tentacles of his sherlock over her dead body.

The Norseman Inn was what I would call a gimmick bar. It was small, dark, and congenial, and everything in it was made of different-sized pieces of wood. The beer mugs and wine goblets were wooden, the tables were square slabs of wood, the bar itself was half a tree, sliced lengthwise and resting on huge wooden blocks. There were horned helmets and carved spears on the wall behind the bar, and though there was piped-in music, it was set low enough so that people could talk. Things were very carefully engineered: you could see and hear only the people in your immediate vicinity. There were a lot of young working girls.

I pulled a heavy wooden stool up close to the bar and motioned for the bartender to stay after he'd poured a beer for me. I asked him if he knew Helmut Vindebeer.

He thought for a moment, then shook his head and frowned. He was built like a Viking, of course, and the frown he made through his beard when I repeated the name told me he didn't know Vindebeer by name. I described the technician to him and his memory seemed to warm a little.

"I remember him," he said, the Viking persona dissolving into a Brooklyn accent. "He was in here three, maybe four nights in a row. That was about it. He looked like he belonged in the place, very Norwegian-looking, very naïve-looking too. I guess he came in because of the name, thought he'd meet a lot of Scandinavians, who knows. But I remember that the first time he came in it didn't take him long to meet a few people—there were one, maybe two people I remember him latching onto. As a matter of fact, they *were* Scandinavians. Wait here a minute."

He went to the other end of the bar, looking out over the crowd. He served a couple of customers down there, then came back.

"I think I found the two he was talking to: a guy and a girl. They're sitting at a table along the wall in the back. She's got a blue-and-white striped dress on, pretty good-looking. The guy has short black hair. Okay?" He smiled his Viking smile through the beard.

I thanked him and took my beer to the back room, threading my way through a lot of wooden tables and chairs.

The guy and the girl both had nice smiles, and they were sitting together on one side of a booth. They responded to Vindebeer's name when I asked if they knew him. The guy asked me to sit down on the other side of the table and I did so. His name was William Anderson—when he talked he sounded Scandinavian. So did the girl.

It turned out that they had met both Vindebeer and each other the first night Vindebeer had come into the bar. Vindebeer had been very shy, but friendly, and his accent had drawn them to him. Then Anderson told me that there had been another girl who had attached herself to their little group that night also.

"She was very animated, very bright," he said. He then went on to describe the girl I had seen dead an hour before.

They'd known about Vindebeer's death, but when I told them that the girl was dead too, they got a little upset.

"I don't understand," the girl, Helga, said after a few moments. She looked a bit older than she dressed, and she now held Anderson's hand tightly. "They both looked so happy. We were all so happy that first night. All of us had been alone, and then we all met at once."

I asked her if they'd gotten together with Vindebeer or the girl again.

"Yes," she said. "We met a couple of nights later, and once again the night after that. Helmut was very happy that last night because Ingri was going to get him a job."

"She was trying to get him a job," William corrected. "She worked for a research scientist, a well-known man, as his assistant, and was trying to get Helmut a job with his project. They were both technicians."

Neither could remember the scientist's name. I took a sip of my beer, which was now flat. "Did anything strange happen that night you were together? Did you meet anyone else?"

They both shook their heads.

"Did they say anything about the job Helmut was trying to get?"

"Not much," Anderson answered. "Just that this scientist needed another assistant. They mostly talked about how strange this scientist and his daughter were."

"Strange?"

The girl spoke up. "Ingri told us some very funny stories about the things these two people had done, how they were always complaining about being bothered, that people wouldn't leave them alone."

She looked down at her drink, and I looked down at mine. There was silence for a few minutes.

"Do you think someone would try to hurt William or me?" the girl said.

"I'm not sure, but I don't think so," I said. "Can I get you two another drink?"

"No, thank you," Anderson said. "I think we'll be leaving soon. Actually, we came here tonight to see if Ingri might come."

"I see," I said. "Well, is there anything else you can remember? Anything at all?"

There was another silence, this one longer. Then Helga said, and she was almost crying, "Only . . . that they looked very happy together. I thought they looked very happy."

On the way out I met Buckers coming in, who gave me a nasty look and passed on. Virgil was close behind him. I stepped in front of him so he couldn't avoid me.

"What's new, Lieutenant?" I said.

He scowled and made a motion to walk around me, then stopped. "I told you to stay out of this, Matheson."

"You know I've been hired to look into it."

"By who—the Man in the Moon?" He gave a short laugh. "You don't even know who your client is."

"Would you like to bet I get to the bottom of this before your sherlocks do?" I knew I was putting my foot in my mouth, but couldn't help it.

"You're on," he said. "Fifty bucks?"

"Fifty bucks it is, Lieutenant. See you around."

He walked back towards the bar, shaking his head.

I took a long walk home, and when I got there, there was another note from my anonymous employer waiting for me. This one was taped to the refrigerator door and read:

GO BACK TO THE NORTH DOCKS AT 9:00 TOMORROW MORNING.

I rolled it into a ball and threw it away. It was just about midnight. I grabbed a flashlight, made sure my neck guard was in place, put in my nose filters, and left for the North Docks.

To say the least, the docks were dark. I took the west-end elevator down, thinking it might be in better running order than the other one and make less noise, but if anything it groaned even louder. When I got to the bottom I could barely make out where I was, but flicking the beam of my flash this way and that soon told me what I already knew—that I was at the opposite end of the street bordered with travel offices that ran to the east end. I began to slowly make my way up one side of the street, pausing at each closed building with my flash off, trying to detect the least sound or possibly a flicker of light coming from inside.

When I'd gone about halfway up the block I thought I heard something close behind me, a footstep or a shifting in the dark. I stopped but nothing followed it; but as I turned to go on, someone rushed out at me from the darkened doorway I'd just passed and grabbed at me from behind.

I felt a little jab in the side and was down and out in about four seconds.

When I woke up there was one hell of a sore spot on my left side where a needle had been pushed in crookedly. I was trussed up again in the room with the sour yellow light.

"Your doing this twice to me is quite embarrassing," I said. The girl was standing off to one side, her back to me. It looked like she was going through my billfold.

"Keep quiet." She turned around, and I saw that she held a sherlock in her hand. She replaced my billfold in my breast pocket and then moved the sherlock slowly over my body.

"Where did you get that thing?" I asked.

She ignored my question. "You're a detective?" I nodded. "You're not who I thought you were," she said evenly. "Who sent you to look for my father and me?"

"I don't know, to tell you the truth." I told her about the notes to see what kind of reaction I'd get.

She finished with the sherlock and put it on a table behind her.

I said, "Is your father here now?"

"If he was anywhere near here you'd be dead."

She stood still for a moment, just staring at me, and then she left the room. When she came back she leaned over me.

I smelled rosewater, and my heart almost stopped.

She grabbed at something on a table against the wall. I was sure it was a knife, long-bladed and plastic-handled; but after the split second it took my eyes to tell my brain what it was seeing, I realised that it was a hypodermic. She plunged it savagely into my arm, and I quickly went under. When I swam up I found myself once again at the base of the elevator.

The next morning I called on Jack Rutgers to see if anyone had come up with anything on Ingri Hoffman.

"As a matter of fact," he said, "Virgil did come up with something. There was a partial print on the knife's handle this time, and also another strand of long brown hair, which was found on the rug near the body. The olfactory tests also showed a correlation on a type of perfume detected at the scene of the first murder. It's a kind of rosewater, from Scandinavia."

"Has anyone been able to find out who she was working for?"

"No. And we may have some trouble finding out because it now looks as though the girl was in the country illegally; Vindebeer wasn't but that doesn't help because he hadn't really started working for this fellow yet."

I told him about my two visits to the North Docks, and he listened in silence, polishing his glasses with his handkerchief. "You went there last night alone?"

I smiled sheepishly. "Sure it was stupid. But even though this girl's father is the scientist who hired Vindebeer and Ingri Hoffman, everything still doesn't fit. The girl may be the killer, but then again maybe she's not. And I still don't know who hired me, or why."

He sighed. "Well, looks like I can send some men out to the docks to flush the two of them out; at least we know the general area they're hiding from where you got ambushed last night. Why don't you sit tight for a little while, and I'll give you a call later."

"Sure," I said. "Sounds fair enough. And Jack."

His face had a probing look.

"Give those plants some water. They're starting to wilt."

He hesitated. "Right," he said.

I spent the rest of the day going through the last few days' junk mail and thinking. No matter how I twisted things around, everything always pointed back to whoever was leaving me those notes. There was a connection somewhere that I didn't have. And if the girl was the cat she seemed to be and eluded Rutgers's men, and if the note-man didn't reveal himself, the whole thing could stay very confused indeed.

As I was putting a late dinner on, Rutgers called. He had nothing to tell me on the girl and her father, but it seemed that Virgil wanted to talk to me, and that there might be the possibility of trading some information. I figured what the heck and headed downtown.

Halfway there I remembered I'd left the two front burners of the stove on and rather than burn my house down I turned back.

The front door had been opened, and as I reached the front porch the scent of rosewater hit my nostrils.

I edged the door all the way open and reached around to the umbrella stand where I kept a very heavy stick. It was pretty dark inside. I raised the stick in front of me and slipped inside.

I took two steps, then heard two sounds at once. There was a girl's scream from one side of the living room, and at the same time a lamp fell over as someone rushed at me from the other side. I could barely see but I could tell that it was a man and that he had an upraised hand with something in it. He ran into me and the hand swung down at my chest but I knocked it out of the way. He scrambled to his feet and pulled at the front door and ran out. Whatever he'd been holding fell to the porch behind him.

I lay breathing heavily for a moment. Suddenly someone turned on the hall light overhead. I was momentarily blinded, but I pushed my way to my feet and threw my arms out defensively, blinking fiercely. After a few seconds I was able to see that the girl with the light brown eyes stood before me.

I told her to stay away from me while I shut the front door and then walked over to my writing desk and took out a gun from the bottom drawer. There was a folded note taped to the desk and I pulled it off. I waved the gun at the girl, sat down in a chair, and told her to sit down in one opposite me.

She did as she was told—she was shaking like a leaf and looked dazed—and then I asked her what she was doing in my house.

"I . . . came here to bring you to my father," she managed to get out.

"Wasn't that your father who just tried to kill me?"

She shook her head no.

I ignored her for a minute and pulled open the note, which read:

YOU MUST RETURN TO NORTH DOCKS AND LOCATE SCIENTIST
AND DAUGHTER. 10:30 TONIGHT. CASE DEPENDS ON IT.
2000 MORE DOLLARS IN YOUR ACCOUNT.

"Hell," I said and showed the note to the girl. "Do you know who wrote this?"

She was really shook up for some reason but when she saw the look on my face and the way I held the gun she managed to open her mouth. "No."

"What's your name?"

"I . . . thought you knew. My name is Angela Beberger. My father is Edward Beberger."

"Edward Beberger?" I said, startled. Edward Beberger was the inventor of the sherlocks.

The girl began to talk, in a kind of stupor. "I came here because my father wants to see you. He thinks you can be trusted."

"What about the man who was here?"

"He was here when I came. He's the man who's been after my father and me all this time. He made me tell him where my father is . . ."

It all came into focus. I went to the front door and opened it, and there on the front porch was a pump sprayer, the kind you use to water plants. It was filled with rosewater. I showed it to Angela Beberger.

"He was spraying that all over when I came in. I only had three bottles. Two of them were stolen. They belonged to my mother when she was alive. She brought them from Norway—"

"Is your father alone now?"

"Yes."

I made a phone call to Virgil and then turned back to the girl. "Take me to him," I said.

When we got to the North Docks the floodlights were on and Virgil was waiting with his men.

"He's up on one of the rocket gantries," he said to me. "I wish I could kick you out of here and handle this myself, but he's got Edward Beberger with him, and he says he'll kill him if we don't let you go up."

I looked up into the bright lights and could just make out two figures perched on a gantry arm that swung out high above us. I told Angela Beberger to stay with Virgil and took a step towards the gantry. I stopped and turned back to Virgil.

"How close were you to finding out what was going on?"

It was an effort for him to tell me. "We thought for sure it was the girl, here. I owe you some money, Matheson."

I turned back to the gantry. I took the service steps up the side one by one, in silence.

"Hello, Jack," I said and I reached the top. He was on a small platform suspended between two girders about twenty feet away from me.

Below the platform was a drop of about a hundred meters. It was windy up there, and the floodlights gave everything a stark, black-and-white appearance.

Beberger was propped up against a steel canister with a plastic-handled knife in his chest. He looked dead.

Rutgers sat down on the platform with his feet dangling over the edge and began to polish his spectacles. "I had hoped it would take a lot longer for us to reach this point," he said calmly. "Things didn't go the way I planned, Phil."

"If you hadn't dropped that rosewater at my house tonight it might have taken me quite a while to figure things out."

"But the girl had decided to trust you. That was another thing I hadn't counted on. I thought I had the two of them too scared to trust God himself. That's why I had to get Beberger tonight."

"How long had you been harassing them?"

"A couple of months," he continued in a matter-of-fact tone. "It was easy. I started with anonymous phone calls; after a while I showed up at their place and said the police had received a threat against them. I picked up the rosewater, a few strands of hair, a kitchen knife with fingerprints on it—enough to throw the sherlocks off for a while. After I killed Vindebeer they didn't know what to think; it was obvious I was involved and since I was a cop, who could they turn to? I kept up the phone calls. Then they disappeared. I knew they were hiding down here at the docks somewhere, but I couldn't find them. That girl was smart. That's when I started leaving you notes."

"To get me to flush out Beberger for you?"

"That was part of it. The girl knew my face, but I thought that if she got a chance to get ahold of someone else who was possibly involved, I could track the two of them down. She was so careful, though; even though I found out where they were hiding, she moved her father right after getting rid of you. That's why I wanted you to go back, to give me another shot. But there was more to it than that, Phil." His voice rose a bit, and took on a bit of an hysterical edge. "You see, the whole idea was for you to come in cold and figure things out before the sherlocks did. The whole idea was for you to beat that damned machine."

"Like Paul Bunyan?"

"Yes."

"That's why you killed Vindebeer and Ingri Hoffman?"

"No!" He looked straight at me. "I killed the two of them because Beberger was expanding his research."

I gave a puzzled look.

"Come on, Phil! Don't you read the papers? He wasn't content with developing the god-damned black box Virgil is fondling down there. He was assembling a new research team to perfect the sherlocks; and eventually he was going to develop a centralized data bank that would replace almost all of the detective force in the city. *Ninety-five percent.* Most of the remaining personnel would be data computer experts, with only rudimentary police training. In one fell swoop, no more detectives. A way of life wiped out in a generation." I was silent while he rubbed at his glasses. Then I said, "What now, Jack?"

He put his spectacles down on the platform and looked at me with tired eyes. "I don't know, Phil. I suppose we could end this like an Alfred Hitchcock film with the two of us grappling on this little platform. Or I could sit here and start to weep like the crazy person I must be and let you lead me down to a squad car and a straitjacket." He paused. "I've been confused for a long time, Phil, and this whole thing ended too soon. But I guess you'll be the hero after." He sighed heavily, pointing at Beberger. "I didn't kill him. He's only unconscious; there's not a knife blade in the handle. Anyway," he smiled weakly, "there are other people carrying on the same type of research he's doing, so I guess it wouldn't have made much of a difference. Give me a hand down, will you?"

He took a step toward me with his hand out. I don't think it was the wind or that he slipped or that he didn't have his glasses on, but after one step he stumbled and fell from the platform, soundlessly hitting the concrete below hard. I looked down at his crumpled body, then at his spectacles lying on the platform. I picked up the spectacles and put them in my pocket.

Beberger was alive, as Rutgers had said, and when he came to I helped him down the steps of the gantry into the waiting arms of his daughter. I then waited solemnly as Virgil counted out five crisp ten-dollar bills into my hand. He wasn't happy about it.

"You know," he said, watching as Jack Rutgers's body was bagged and carried off, "I still can't believe a cop like that could do something like this. I knew he was a relic, but I didn't know he was a stupid relic."

I almost hit him then, but he quickly went on, seeing the look in my eyes. "Don't get me wrong, Matheson. I respected that guy. I knew he was like the old dog who can't learn new tricks, and I had every intention of forcing him out when I could, but, after all, we were all after the same thing, right? We just have different ways of doing it now, right?"

"Sure, Virgil. Whatever you say."

He seemed to want more, some kind of reassurance that what he was doing was worthwhile, but I left him to his little black boxes then; already a couple of his lab technicians were crawling up the gantry like sterile spiders to let their machines sniff what there was to be sniffed.

When I got up to street level and stepped out of the elevator I almost hailed a taxi, feeling the fifty dollars in my pocket already trying to leap out, but at the last moment I kept my hailing arm down and began to walk.

With the fifty dollars I renewed my investigator's license.

THE FIELD BAZAAR

BY SIR ARTHUR CONAN DOYLE

Sir Arthur Conan Doyle gave up the practice of medicine to become the most famous mystery writer on earth. "The Field Bazaar" was written for The Student, *the undergraduate publication of his alma mater, the University of Edinburgh. This sketch is an affectionate tour-de-force of Holmes's deductive method. It has rarely, if ever, appeared in collections of the Holmes stories.*

"I should certainly do it," said Sherlock Holmes.

I started at the interruption, for my companion had been eating his breakfast with his attention entirely centred upon the paper which was propped up by the coffee pot. Now I looked across at him to find his eyes fastened upon me with the half-amused, half-questioning expression which he usually assumed when he felt he had made an intellectual point.

"Do what?" I asked.

He smiled as he took his slipper from the mantelpiece and drew from it enough shag tobacco to fill the old clay pipe with which he invariably rounded off his breakfast.

"A most characteristic question of yours, Watson," said he. "You will not, I am sure, be offended if I say that any reputation for sharpness which I may possess has been entirely gained by the admirable foil which you have made for me. Have I not heard of debutantes who have insisted upon plainness in their chaperones? There is a certain analogy."

Our long companionship in the Baker Street rooms had left us on those easy terms of intimacy when much may be said without offence. And yet I acknowledged that I was nettled at his remark.

"I may be very obtuse," said I, "but I confess that I am unable to see how you have managed to know that I was . . . I was . . ."

"Asked to help in the Edinburgh University Bazaar . . ."

"Precisely. The letter has only just come to hand, and I have not spoken to you since."

"In spite of that," said Holmes, leaning back in his chair and putting his fingertips together, "I would even venture to suggest that the object of the bazaar is to enlarge the University cricket field."

I looked at him in such bewilderment that he vibrated with silent laughter.

"The fact is, my dear Watson, that you are an excellent subject," said he. "You are never *blasé*. You respond instantly to any external stimulus. Your mental processes may be slow but they are never obscure, and I found during breakfast that you were easier reading than the leader in the *Times* in front of me."

"I should be glad to know how you arrived at your conclusions," said I.

"I fear that my good nature in giving explanations has seriously compromised my reputation," said Holmes. "But in this case the train of reasoning is based upon such obvious facts that no credit can be claimed for it. You entered the room with a thoughtful expression, the expression of a man who is debating some point in his mind. In your hand you held a solitary letter. Now last night you retired in the best of spirits, so it was clear that it was this letter in your hand which had caused the change in you."

"This is obvious."

"It is all obvious when it is explained to you. I naturally asked myself what the letter could contain which might have this affect upon you. As you walked you held the flap side of the envelope towards me, and I saw upon it the same shield-shaped device which I have observed upon your old college cricket cap. It was clear, then, that the request came from Edinburgh University—or from some club connected with the University. When you reached the table you laid down the letter beside your plate with the address uppermost, and you walked over to look at the framed photograph upon the left of the mantelpiece."

It amazed me to see the accuracy with which he had observed my movements. "What next?" I asked.

"I began by glancing at the address, and I could tell, even at the distance of six feet, that it was an unofficial communication. This I gathered from the use of the word 'Doctor' upon the address, to which, as a Bachelor of Medicine, you have no legal claim. I knew that University officials are pedantic in their correct use of titles, and I was thus enabled to say with certainty that your letter was unofficial. When on your return to the table you turned over your letter and allowed me to perceive that the enclosure was a printed one, the idea of a bazaar first occurred to me. I had already weighed the possibility of its being a political communication, but this seemed improbable in the present stagnant conditions of politics.

"When you returned to the table your face still retained its expression and it was evident that your examination of the photograph had not changed the current of your thoughts. In that case it must itself bear upon the subject in question. I turned my attention to the photograph, therefore, and saw at once that it consisted of yourself as a member of the Edinburgh University Eleven, with the pavilion and cricket field in the background. My small experience of cricket clubs has taught me that next to churches and cavalry ensigns they are the most debt-laden things upon earth. When upon your return to the table I saw you take out your pencil and draw lines upon the envelope, I was convinced that you were endeavoring to realise some projected improvement which was to be brought about by a bazaar. Your face still showed some indecision, so that I was able to break in upon you with my advice that you should assist in so good an object."

I could not help smiling at the extreme simplicity of his explanation.

"Of course, it was as easy as possible," said I. My remark appeared to nettle him.

"I may add," said he, "that the particular help which you have been asked to give was that you should write in their album, and that you have already made up your mind that the present incident will be the subject of your article."

"But how—!" I cried.

"It is as easy as possible," said he, "and I leave its solution to your own ingenuity. In the meantime," he added, raising his paper, "you will excuse me if I return to this very interesting article upon the trees of Cremona, and the exact reasons for the pre-eminence in the manufacture of violins. It is one of those small outlying problems to which I am sometimes tempted to direct my attention."

THE DEPTFORD HORROR

BY ADRIAN CONAN DOYLE

Adrian Conan Doyle collaborated with suspense master John Dickson Carr on The Exploits of Sherlock Holmes, *a collection of "new" adventures. "The Deptford Horror," a story fully as harrowing as Sir Arthur's own "The Speckled Band," was written entirely by Adrian, who seems to have inherited a great deal more than just his father's name.*

I have remarked elsewhere that my friend Sherlock Holmes, like all great artists, lived for his art's sake and, save in the case of the Duke of Holdernesse, I have seldom known him to claim any substantial reward. However powerful or wealthy the client, he would refuse to undertake any problem that lacked appeal to his sympathies, whilst he would devote his most intense energies to the affairs of some humble person whose case contained those singular and bizarre qualities which struck a responsive chord in his imagination.

On glancing through my notes for that memorable year of 1895, I find recorded the details of a case which may be taken as a typical instance of this disinterested and even altruistic attitude of his which placed the rendering of a kindly service above that of material reward. I refer to the dreadful affair of the canaries and the soot marks on the ceiling.

It was early in June that my friend completed his investigations into the sudden death of Cardinal Tosca, an inquiry which he had undertaken at the special request of the pope. The case had demanded the most exacting work on Holmes's part and, as I had feared at the time, the aftermath had left him in a highly nervous and restless state that caused me some concern both as his friend and his medical adviser.

One rainy night towards the end of the same month, I persuaded him to dine with me at Frascatti's and thereafter we had gone on to the Cafe Royal for our coffee and liqueurs. As I had hoped, the bustle of the great room with its red plush seats and stately palms bathed in the glow of numerous crystal chandeliers drew him out of his introspective mood. As he leaned back on our sofa, his fingers playing with the stem of his glass, I noted with satisfaction a gleam of interest in those keen grey eyes as he studied the somewhat Bohemian clientele that thronged the tables and alcoves.

I was in the act of replying to some remark when Holmes nodded suddenly in the direction of the door. "Lestrade," said he. "What can he be doing here?"

Glancing over my shoulder, I saw the lean rat-faced figure of the Scotland Yard man standing in the entrance, his dark eyes looking slowly around the room. The police agent caught sight of us and pushed his way through the throng.

"He may be seeking you, Holmes," I remarked, "on some urgent case."

"Hardly, Watson. His wet boots show that he has walked. If there was urgency, he would have taken a cab. But here he is."

"Only a routine check," said Lestrade, drawing up a chair. "But duty's duty, Mr. Holmes, and I can tell you that I've netted some strange fish before now in these respectable places. Whilst you are comfortably dreaming up your theories in Baker Street, we poor devils at Scotland Yard are doing the practical work. No thanks to us from popes and kings, but a bad hour with the superintendent if we fail."

"Tut," said Holmes good-humouredly. "Your superiors must surely hold you in some esteem since I solved the Ronald Adair murder, the Bruce-Partington theft, the—"

"Quite so, quite so," interrupted Lestrade hurriedly. "And now," he added, with a heavy wink at me, "I have something for you."

"Ah!"

"Of course, a young woman who starts at shadows may be more in Dr. Watson's line."

"Really, Lestrade," I protested warmly, "I cannot approve your—"

"One moment, Watson. Let us hear the facts."

Lestrade continued: "Well, Mr. Holmes, they are absurd enough, and I would not waste your time were it not that I have known you to do a kindness or two before now, and in this instance your word of advice may prevent a young woman from acting foolishly. Now, here's the position.

"Down Deptford way, along the edge of the river, there are some of the worst slums in the East End of London but, right in the middle of them, you can still find some fine old houses, which centuries ago were the homes of wealthy merchants. One of these tumble-down mansions has been occupied by a family named Wilson for the past hundred years and more. I understand that they were originally in the China trade and when that went to the dogs a generation back, they got out in time and retired into their old home. The recent household consisted of Horatio Wilson and his wife, with one son and a daughter, and Horatio's younger brother Theobold, who had come to live with them on his return from foreign parts.

"Some three years ago, the body of Horatio Wilson was hooked out of the river. He had been drowned, and, as he was known to have been a hard-drinking man, it was generally accepted that he had missed his step in the fog and fallen into the water. A year later his wife, who suffered from a weak heart, died from a heart attack. We know this to be the case, because the doctor made a very careful examination following the statements of a police constable and a night watchman employed on a barge."

"Statements to what effect?" interposed Holmes.

"Well, there was talk of a noise that seemed to come that night from the old Wilson house, but the nights are often foggy along Thamesside and the men were probably misted. The constable described the sound as a dreadful yell that froze his blood in his veins. If I had him in my division, I'd teach him such words should never pass the lips of an officer of the law."

"What time was this noise heard?"

"Ten o'clock at night, the hour of the old lady's death. It's merely a coincidence, for there is no doubt that she died of heart."

"Go on."

Lestrade consulted his notebook for a moment. "I've been digging up the facts," he continued. "On the night of May seventeenth last, the daughter went to a magic-lantern entertainment accompanied by a woman servant. On her return, she found her brother, Jabez Wilson, dead in his armchair. He had inherited a bad heart and insomnia from his mother. This time there were no rumors of shrieks and yells, but owing to the expression on the dead man's face, the local doctor called in the police surgeon to assist in the examination. It was heart all right, and our man confirmed that this can sometimes cause a distortion of the features that will convey an impression of stark terror."

"That is perfectly true," I remarked.

"Now, it seems that the daughter Janet has become so overwrought that, according to her uncle, she proposes to sell the property and go abroad," went on Lestrade. "Her feelings are, I suppose, natural. Death has been busy with the Wilson family."

"And what of this uncle? Theobold, I think you said his name was."

"Well, I fancy that you will find him on your doorstep tomorrow morning. He came to me at the Yard in the hope that the official police could put his niece's fears at rest and persuade her to take a more reasonable view. As we are engaged on more important affairs than calming hysterical young women, I suggested that he call on you."

"Indeed! Well, it is natural enough that he should resent the unnecessary loss of what is probably a snug corner."

"Oh, there is no resentment, Mr. Holmes. Wilson seems to be genuinely attached to his niece and concerned only for her future." Lestrade paused, whilst a grin spread over his foxy face. "He is not a very worldly person, is Mr. Theobold, and though I've met some queer trades in my time, his beats the band. He trains canaries."

"It is an established profession."

"Is it?" There was an irritating smugness in Lestrade's manner as he rose to his feet and reached for his hat. "It is quite evident that you do not suffer from insomnia, Mr. Holmes," he said, "or you would know that birds trained by Theobold Wilson are different from other canaries. Good night."

"What on earth does the fellow mean?" I asked, as the police agent threaded his way towards the door.

"Merely that he knows something that we do not," replied Holmes dryly. "But, as conjecture is as profitless as it is misleading to the analytical mind, let us wait until tomorrow. I can say however that I do not propose to waste my time over a matter that appears to fall more properly within the province of the local vicar."

To my friend's relief, the morning brought no visitor. But when, on my return from an urgent case to which I had been summoned shortly after lunch, I entered our sitting room I found that our spare chair was occupied by a bespectacled middle-aged man. As he rose to his feet, I observed that he was of an exceeding thinness and that his face, which was scholarly and even austere in expression, was seamed with countless wrinkles and of that dull parchment yellow that comes from years under a tropic sun.

"Ah, Watson, you have arrived just in time," said Holmes. "This is Mr. Theobold Wilson, about whom Lestrade spoke to us last night."

Our visitor wrung my hand warmly. "Your name is, of course, well-known to me. Dr. Watson," he said. "Indeed, if Mr. Sherlock Holmes will pardon me for saying so, it is largely thanks to you that we are aware of his genius. As a medical man doubtless well versed in the handling of nervous cases, your presence should have a most beneficial effect upon my unhappy niece."

Holmes looked at me resignedly. "I have promised Mr. Wilson to accompany him to Deptford, Watson," said he, "for it would seem that the young lady is determined to leave her home tomorrow. But I must repeat, Mr. Wilson, that I fail to see in what way my presence can affect the matter."

"You are overmodest, Mr. Holmes. When I appealed to the official police, I had hoped that they might convince Janet that, terrible though our family losses have been in the past three years, nevertheless they lay in natural causes and there is no reason why she should flee from her home. I had the impression," he added, with a chuckle, "that the inspector was somewhat chagrined at my ready acceptance of his own suggestion that I seek your aid."

"I shall most certainly remember my small debt to Lestrade," replied Holmes dryly as he rose to his feet. "Perhaps, Watson, you would ask Mrs. Hudson to whistle a four-wheeler, and Mr. Wilson can clarify certain points as we drive to Deptford."

It was one of those grey, brooding summer days when London is at its worst and, as we rattled over Blackfriars Bridge, I noted that wreaths of mist were rising from the river like the poisonous vapors of some hot jungle swamp. The spacious streets of the West End had given place to the great commercial thoroughfares that resounded with the stamp and clatter of the dray horses, and these in turn merged at last into a maze of dingy streets. As we followed the curve of the river, I noted the neighbourhood grew more and more wretched the nearer we approached to that labyrinth of tidal basins and dark evil-smelling lanes that were the ancient cradle of England's sea trade and of the Empire's wealth.

I could see that Holmes was listless and bored to a point of irritation and I did my best, therefore, to engage our companion in conversation. "I understand that you are an expert on canaries," I remarked.

Theobold Wilson's eyes, behind their powerful spectacles, lighted with the glow of the enthusiast. "A mere student, sir—but with thirty years of practical research," he cried. "Can it be that you too—No? A pity! The study, breeding and training of the Fringilla *canaria*—a rare species I have helped develop—is a task worthy of a man's lifetime. You would not credit the ignorance, Dr. Watson, that prevails on this subject even in the most enlightened circles."

"Inspector Lestrade hinted at some special characteristic in your training of these little songsters."

"Songsters, sir! A thrush is a songster. The Fringilla is the supreme ear of nature, possessing a unique power of imitation which can be trained for the benefit and edification of the human race. But the inspector was correct," he went on more calmly, "in that I have put my birds to a special effect. They are trained to sing by night in artificial light."

"Surely a singular pursuit."

"I like to think that it is a kindly one. My birds are trained for the benefit of those who suffer from insomnia and I have clients in all parts of the country. Their tuneful song helps to while away the long night hours; only the dousing of the lamplight will terminate the concert."

"It seems to me that Lestrade was right," I observed. "Yours is indeed a unique profession."

During our conversation, Holmes, who had idly picked up our companion's heavy stick, had been examining it with some attention. "I understand that you returned to England some three years ago," he observed.

"I did."

"From Cuba, I perceive."

Theobold Wilson started and for an instant I seemed to catch a gleam of something like wariness in the swift glance that he shot at Holmes. "That is so," he said. "How did you know?"

"Your stick is cut from Cuban ebony. There is no mistaking that greenish tint and the high polish."

"It might have been bought in London since my return from, say, Africa," Wilson suggested.

"No, it has been yours for some years." Holmes lifted the stick to the carriage window and tilted it so that the daylight shone upon the handle. "You will perceive," he went on, "that there is a slight but regular scraping that has worn through the polish along the left side of the handle, just where the ring finger of a left-handed man would close upon the grip. Ebony is among the toughest of woods and it would require not only considerable time to cause such wear, but also a ring of some harder metal than gold. You are left-handed, Mr. Wilson, and wear a silver ring on your ring finger."

"Dear me, how simple. I thought for the moment that you had done something clever. As it happens, I was in the sugar trade in Cuba and brought my old stick back with me. But here we are at the house and, if you can put my silly niece's fears at rest as quickly as you can deduce my past, I shall be your debtor."

On descending from our four-wheeler, we found ourselves in a lane of slatternly houses. So far as I could judge, for the yellow mist was already creeping in, the lower end of the lane sloped down to the river's edge. At one side was a high wall of crumbling brickwork, and set in it was an iron gate through which we caught a glimpse of a substantial mansion surrounded by its own garden.

"The old house has known better days," said our companion, as we followed him through the gate and up the path. "It was built in the year that Peter the Great came to Deptford to study shipbuilding."

Usually I am not unduly affected by my surroundings but I must confess that I was aware of a feeling of depression at the melancholy spectacle that lay before us. The house, though of dignified and even imposing proportions, was faced with blotched weather-stained plaster which had fallen away in places to disclose the ancient brickwork that lay beneath, whilst a tangled mass of ivy covering one wall had sent its long tendrils across the high-peaked roof to wreathe itself around the chimney stacks. The garden was an overgrown wilderness, and the air of the whole place reeked with the damp musty smell of the river.

Theobold Wilson led us through a small hall and into a comfortably furnished drawing room. A young woman with auburn hair and a freckled face, who was sorting through some papers at a writing desk, sprang to her feet at our entrance.

"Here are Mr. Sherlock Holmes and Dr. Watson," announced our companion. "This is my niece Janet, whose interests you are here to protect against her own unreasonable conduct."

The young lady faced us bravely enough, though I noted a twitch and tremor of the lips that spoke of a high nervous tension. "I am leaving tomorrow, Uncle," she cried, "and nothing that these gentlemen can say will alter my decision. Here there is only sorrow and fear—above all, fear!"

"Fear of what?" asked Holmes.

The girl passed her hand over her eyes. "I—I cannot explain. I hate the shadows and the funny little noises."

"You have inherited both money and property, Janet," said Mr. Wilson earnestly. "Will you, because of shadows, desert the roof of your fathers?"

"We are here only to serve you, young lady," said Holmes with some gentleness, "and to try to put your fears at rest. It is often so in life that we injure our own best interests by precipitate actions."

"You will laugh at a woman's intuitions, sir?"

"By no means. They are often the signposts of providence. Understand clearly that you will go or stay as you see fit, but perhaps, as I am here, it might relieve your mind to show me over the house."

"An admirable suggestion!" cried Theobold Wilson cheerily. "Come, Janet, we will soon dispose of your shadows and noises."

In a little procession, we trooped from one over-furnished room to another on the ground floor.

"I will show you the bedrooms now," said Miss Wilson as we paused at last before the staircase.

"Are there no cellars in a house of this antiquity?"

"There is one cellar, Mr. Holmes, but it is little used, save for the storage of wood and some of Uncle's old nest boxes. However, this way, please."

It was a gloomy stone-built chamber in which we found ourselves. Logs were piled against one wall, and a potbellied stove, its iron pipe running through the ceiling, filled the far corner. Through a glazed door at the top of a flight of steps, a dim light filtered down upon the flagstones. Holmes sniffed the air keenly, and I was myself aware of an increased mustiness from the nearby river.

"Like most Thames-side houses, you must be plagued by rats," he remarked.

"We used to be. But since Uncle came here, he has got rid of them."

"Quite so. Dear me," Holmes continued, peering down at the floor, "what busy little fellows!"

Following his gaze, I saw that his attention had been drawn by a few garden ants scurrying across the floor from beneath the edge of the stove and up the steps leading to the door. "It is as well for us, Watson," he said, pointing with his stick at the tiny particles with which they were encumbered, "that we are not under the necessity of lugging along dinners thrice our own size. It is a lesson to us."

Mr. Wilson's thin lips tightened. "What foolery is this!" he exclaimed. "The ants are there because the servants would throw garbage in the stove to save themselves the trouble of going to the dustbin."

"And so you put a lock on the lid?"

"We did. If you wish, I can fetch the key. No? Then, if you are finished, let me take you to see the bedrooms," said Mr. Wilson.

"Perhaps, Miss Wilson, I may see the room where your brother died?" requested Holmes as we reached the top floor.

"It is here," replied the girl, throwing open the door. It was a large chamber furnished with some taste and even luxury, and it was lighted by two deeply recessed windows flanking another potbellied stove. A pair of bird cages hung from the stove pipe.

"Where does that side door lead?" asked my friend.

"It opens into my room, which was formerly my mother's," she answered.

For a few minutes, Holmes prowled around listlessly. "I perceive that your brother was addicted to night reading," he remarked.

"Yes. He suffered from sleeplessness. But how—"

"Tut, the pile of the carpet on the right of the armchair is thick with traces of candle wax. But hullo! What have we here?"

Holmes had halted near the window and was staring intently at a section of the wall up near the ceiling. Then, mounting the sill, he stretched out an arm and, touching the plaster lightly here and there, sniffed at his fingertips. There was a puzzled frown on his face as he climbed down and commenced to circle slowly around the room, his eyes fixed upon the ceiling.

"Most singular," he said.

"Is anything wrong, Mr. Holmes?" asked Miss Wilson.

"I am merely interested to account for these odd whorls and lines across the upper wall and ceiling."

"It must be those dratted cockroaches dragging the dust all over the place," exclaimed Wilson apologetically. "I've told you before, Janet, that you would be better employed in supervising the servants' work. But what now, Mr. Holmes?"

My friend, who had crossed to the side door and glanced within, now closed it again and strolled across to the window. "My visit has been a useless one," said he, "and, as I see that the fog is rising, I fear that we must take our leave. These are, I suppose, your famous canaries?" he added, pointing to the cages above the stove.

"A mere sample. But come this way," Wilson led us along the passage and threw open a door. "There!"

Obviously it was his own bedroom, yet it was unlike any bedroom that I had entered in all my professional career. From floor to ceiling it was festooned with scores of cages, and the little golden-feathered singers within filled the air with their sweet warbling and trilling.

"Daylight or lamplight, it's all the same to them. Here, Carrie, Carrie!" he said and whistled a few liquid notes. The bird took them up into a lovely flow of song.

"A skylark," I cried.

"Precisely. As I said before, the Fringilla if properly trained are the supreme imitators."

"I confess that I do not recognize that song," I remarked, as one of the birds broke into a low rising whistle ending in a curious tremolo.

Mr. Wilson threw a towel over the cage. "It is the song of a tropic night bird," he said shortly, "and, as I have the foolish pride to prefer my birds to sing the songs of the day whilst it is day, we will punish Peperino by putting him in darkness."

"I am surprised that you prefer an open fireplace here to a stove," observed Holmes. "There must be a considerable draft."

"I have not noticed one. Dear me, the fog is indeed increasing, and you have a bad journey before you."

"Then we must be on our way," said my friend.

We descended the stairs and, whilst Theobold Wilson fetched our hats, Sherlock Holmes leaned over towards our young companion. "I would remind you, Miss Wilson, of what I said earlier about a woman's intuition," he said quietly. "There are occasions when the truth can be sensed more easily than it can be seen. Good night."

A moment later we were feeling our way down the garden path to where the lights of our waiting four-wheeler shone dimly through the rising fog.

My companion was sunk in thought as we rumbled westward through the mean streets whose squalor was the more aggressive under the garish light of the gas lamps that flared and whistled outside the numerous public houses. The night promised to be a bad one and already, through the yellow vapor thickening and writhing above die pavements, the occasional wayfarer was nothing more than a vague hurrying shadow.

"I could have wished, my dear fellow," I remarked, "that you had been spared the need to waste your energies which are already sufficiently depleted."

"Well, well, Watson. I fancied that the affairs of the Wilson family would prove no concern of ours. And yet"—he sank back, absorbed for a moment in his own thoughts—"and yet, it is wrong, wrong, all wrong!"

"I observed nothing of a sinister nature."

"Nor I. But every danger bell in my head is jangling its warning. Why a fireplace, Watson, why a fireplace? I take it that you noticed that the pipe from the cellar connected with the stoves in the other bedrooms?"

"In one bedroom."

"No. There was the same arrangement in the adjoining room where the mother died."

"I see nothing in this save an old-fashioned system of heating flues."

"And what of the marks on the ceiling?"

"You mean the whorls of dust?"

"I mean the whorls of soot."

"Soot! Surely you are mistaken, Holmes."

"I touched them, smelled them, examined them. They were speckles and lines of wood soot."

"Well, there is probably some perfectly natural explanation."

For a time we sat in silence. Our cab had reached the beginnings of the city and I was gazing out of the window, my fingers drumming idly on the half-lowered pane, which was already befogged with moisture, when I was startled by a sharp ejaculation from my companion.

He was staring fixedly at the window. "The glass," he muttered.

Over the clouded surface there now lay an intricate tracery of whorls where my finger had wandered aimlessly.

Holmes clapped his hand to his brow and, throwing open the other window, he shouted an order to the cabby. The vehicle turned in its tracks and, with the driver lashing at his horse, we clattered away into the thickening gloom.

"Ah, Watson, Watson, true it is that there are none so blind as those that will not see!" quoted Holmes bitterly, sinking back into his corner. "All the facts were there, staring me in the face, and yet logic failed to respond."

"What facts?"

"Here is a man from Cuba, he not only trains canaries in a singular manner but knows the call of tropical night birds, and he uses the fireplace in his bedroom. There is deviltry here, Watson. Stop, cabby, stop!"

We were crossing a junction of two busy thoroughfares, and the golden balls of a pawnshop glimmered above a streetlamp. Holmes sprang out. After a few minutes he was back again and we recommenced our journey.

"It is fortunate that we are still in the City," he chuckled, "for I fancy that the East End pawnshops are unlikely to run to golf clubs."

"Good heavens . . ." I began only to lapse into silence whilst I stared down at the heavy niblick which he had thrust into my hand. The first shadows of some monstrous horror seemed to rise up and creep over my mind.

"We are too early," exclaimed Holmes, consulting his watch. "A sandwich and a glass of whisky at the first public house will not come amiss."

The clock on St. Nicholas' Church was striking ten when we found ourselves once again in that evil-smelling garden. Through the mist, the dark bulk of the house was broken by a single feeble light in an upper window. "It is Miss Wilson's room," said Holmes. "Let us hope that this handful of gravel will rouse her without alarming the household."

An instant later there came the sound of an opening window. "Who is there?" demanded a tremulous voice.

"It is Sherlock Holmes," my friend called back softly. "I must speak with you at once. Is there a side door?"

"There is one to your left. But what has happened?"

"Pray descend immediately. Not a word to your uncle."

We felt our way along the wall and reached the door just as it opened to disclose Miss Wilson. She was in her dressing gown, her hair tumbled about her shoulders and, as her startled eyes peered at us across the light of the candle in her hand, the shadows danced and trembled on the wall.

"What is it, Mr. Holmes?" she gasped.

"All will be well if you carry out my instructions," my friend replied quietly. "Where is your uncle?"

"He is in his room."

"Good. Whilst Dr. Watson and I occupy your room, you will move into your late brother's bedchamber. If you value your life," he added solemnly, "you will not attempt to leave it."

"You frighten me!" she whimpered.

"Rest assured that we will take care of you. And now two final questions before you retire. Has your uncle visited you this evening?"

"Yes. He brought Peperino and put him with the other bird in the cage in my room. He said that as it was my last night at home I should have the best entertainment that he had the power to give me."

"Ha! Quite so. Your last night. Tell me. Miss Wilson, do you suffer at all from the same malady as your mother and brother?"

"A weak heart? Why, yes, I do."

"Well, we will accompany you upstairs where you will retire to the adjoining room. Come, Watson."

Guided by the light of Janet Wilson's candle, we mounted silently to the floor above and thence into the bedchamber where Holmes had found the markings on the walls. Whilst we waited for our companion to collect her things from the adjoining room, Holmes strolled over and, lifting the edge of the cloths which now covered the two bird cages, peered in at the tiny occupants.

"The evil of man is as inventive as it is immeasurable," said he, and I noticed that his face was very stern.

On Miss Wilson's return, having seen that she was safely ensconced for the night, I followed Holmes into the room which she had lately occupied. It was a small chamber but comfortably furnished and lighted by a heavy silver oil lamp. Immediately above the tiled stove there hung a cage containing two canaries which, momentarily ceasing their song, cocked their little heads at our approach.

"I think, Watson, that it would be well to relax for half an hour," whispered Holmes as we sank into our chairs. "So kindly put out the light."

"But, my dear fellow, if there is any danger it would be an act of madness!" I protested.

"There is no danger in the darkness," Holmes said.

"Would it not be better," I said severely, "that you were frank with me? You have made it obvious that the birds are being put to some evil purpose, but what is this danger that exists only in the lamplight?"

"I have my own idea on that matter, Watson, but it is better that we should wait and see. I would draw your attention, however, to the hinged lid on the top of the stove."

"It appears to be perfectly normal."

"Just so. But is there not some significance in the fact that an iron stove should be fitted with a tin lid?"

"Great heavens, Holmes!" I cried as the light of understanding burst upon me. "You mean that this man Wilson has used the interconnecting pipes from the stove in the cellar to those in the bedrooms to circulate some deadly poison to wipe out his own kith and kin and thus obtain the property. It is for that reason that he has a fireplace in his own bedroom."

"Well, you are not far wrong, Watson, though I fancy that Mr. Theobold is rather more subtle than you suppose. He possesses the two qualities vital to the successful murderer—ruthlessness and imagination. But now, douse the light like a good fellow and for a while let us relax. If my reading of the problem is correct, our nerves may be tested to their limit before we see tomorrow's dawn."

Lying back in the darkness and drawing some comfort from the thought that ever since the affair with Colonel Sebastian Morgan I had carried my revolver in my pocket, I sought in my mind for some explanation that would account for the warning contained in Holmes's words. But I must have been wearier than I had imagined. My thoughts grew confused and finally I dozed off.

It was a touch upon my arm that awoke me. The lamp had been relighted and my friend was bending over me, his long black shadow thrown upon the ceiling. "Sorry to disturb you," he whispered. "But duty calls."

"What do you wish me to do?"

"Sit still and listen. Peperino is singing."

It was a vigil that I shall long remember. Holmes had tilted the lampshade, so that the light fell on the wall with the window and the tiled stove with its hanging bird cage. The fog had thickened and the rays from the lamp, filtering through the window glass, lost themselves in luminous clouds that swirled and boiled against the panes. My mind darkened by a premonition of evil, I would have found our surroundings melancholy enough without the eerie sound that was rising and falling from the canary cage. It was a kind of whistling, beginning with a low throaty warble and slowly ascending to a single note that rang through the room like the peal of a great wineglass. As I listened to the song's uninterrupted repetition, my imagination seemed to reach out beyond those fogbound windows into the dark lush depth of some exotic jungle. I had lost all count of time, and it was only the stillness following a sudden cessation of the bird's song that brought me back to the present. I glanced across and, in an instant, my heart gave one great throb and then seemed to stop beating.

The lid of the stove was slowly rising.

My friends will agree that I am neither a nervous nor an impressionable man but I must confess that, as I sat there gripping the sides of my chair and staring at the dreadful thing that was clambering into view, my limbs momentarily refused to function.

The lid had tilted back a few centimetres or more and through the gap this created, a writhing mass of yellow sticklike objects was clawing and scrabbling for a hold. And then, in a flash, it was out and standing on top of the stove.

Though I have always viewed with horror the bird-eating tarantulas of South America, they shrank into insignificance when compared with the loathsome creature that faced us now across that lamplighted room. It looked to be bigger in its spread than a saucer, and it had a hard smooth yellow body surrounded by legs that, rising high above it, conveyed a fearful impression that the thing was crouching for a spring. It was absolutely hairless save for tufts of stiff bristles around the leg joints and, above the glint of its great poison mandibles, clusters of beady eyes shone with a baleful iridescence.

"Don't move, Watson," whispered Holmes, and there was a note of horror in his voice that I had never heard before. The sound roused the creature and, in a single lightning bound, it sprang from the stove to the top of the bird cage, and then, reaching the wall, it whizzed around the room and over the ceiling with a swiftness that the eye could scarcely follow.

Holmes flung himself forward like a man possessed. "Kill it! Smash it!" he yelled hoarsely, raining blow after blow with his golf club at the shape racing across the walls.

Dust from broken plaster choked the air and a table crashed over as I flung myself to the ground when the great spider cleared the room in a single leap and turned at bay. Holmes bounded across me, swinging his club. "Keep where you are!" he shouted and even as his voice rang through the room, the thud—thud—thud of the blows was broken by a horrible squelching sound. For an instant the creature hung there and then, slipping slowly down, it lay like a mess of smashed eggs with three thin bony legs still plucking at the floor.

"Thank God that it missed you when it sprang!" I gasped, scrambling to my feet.

He made no reply and glancing up I caught a glimpse of his face reflected in a wall mirror. He looked pale and strained and there was a curious rigidity in his expression. "I am afraid it's up to you, Watson," he said quietly. "It has a mate."

I spun round to be greeted by a spectacle that I shall remember for the rest of my days. Sherlock Holmes was standing perfectly still within two feet of the stove and on top of it, reared up on its back legs, its loathsome body shuddering for the spring, stood another monstrous spider.

I knew instinctively that any sudden movement would merely precipitate the creature's leap and so, carefully drawing my revolver from my pocket, I fired point-blank.

Through the powder smoke I saw the thing shrink into itself and then, toppling slowly backward, it fell through the open lid of the stove. There was a rasping slithering sound rapidly fading away into silence.

"It's fallen down the pipe," I cried, conscious that my hands were now shaking under a strong reaction. "Are you all right, Holmes?"

He looked at me and there was a singular light in his eyes. "Thanks to you, my dear fellow!" he said soberly. "If you—but what is that?"

A door had slammed below and, an instant later, we caught the swift patter of feet upon the gravel path.

"After him!" cried Holmes, springing for the door. "Your shot warned him that the game was up. He must not escape!"

But fate decreed otherwise. Though we rushed down the stairs and out into the fog, Theobold Wilson had too much start on us and the advantage of knowing the terrain. For a while we followed the faint sound of his running footsteps down the empty lanes towards the river, but at length these died away in the distance.

"It is no good, Watson. We have lost our man," panted Holmes. "This is where the official police may be of use. But listen! Surely that was a cry?"

"I thought I heard something."

"Well, it is hopeless to look further in the fog. Let us return and comfort this poor girl with the assurance that her troubles are now at an end."

"They were nightmare creatures. Holmes," I exclaimed, as we retraced out steps towards the house, "and of some unknown species."

"I think not, Watson," said he. "It was the Galeodes spider, the horror of the Cuban forests. It is perhaps fortunate for the rest of the world that it is found nowhere else. The creature is nocturnal in its habits and, unless my memory belies me, it possesses the power to actually break the spine of smaller creatures with a single blow of its mandibles. You will recall that Miss Janet mentioned that the rats had vanished since her uncle's return. Doubtless Wilson brought the brutes back with him," he went on, "and then conceived the idea of training certain of his canaries to imitate the song of some Cuban night bird upon which the Galeodes fed. The marks on the ceiling were caused, of course, by the soot adhering to the spiders' legs after they had scrambled up the flues.

"It is fortunate for the consulting detective that the duster of the average housemaid seldom strays beyond the height of a mantelpiece. Indeed, I can discover no excuse for my lamentable slowness in solving this case, for the facts were before me from the first and the whole affair was elemental in its construction.

"And yet to give Theobold Wilson his due, one must recognize his almost diabolical cleverness. Once these horrors were installed in the stove in the cellar, what more simple than to arrange two ordinary flues communicating with the bedrooms above. With the cages hung over the stoves, the flues would themselves act as magnifiers of the bird's song and, guided by their predatory instinct, the creatures would invariably ascend whichever pipe led to the bird. And Wilson knew, having devised some means of luring the spiders back again to their nest, that they represented a comparatively safe way of getting rid of those who stood between himself and the property."

"Then its bite is deadly?" I asked.

"To a person in weak health, probably so. But there lies the devilish cunning of the scheme, Watson. It was the sight of the things rather than their bite, poisonous though it may be, which he relied upon to kill his victims. Can you imagine the effect upon an elderly woman, and later upon her son, both suffering from insomnia and heart disease, when in the midst of a bird's seemingly innocent song this appalling spectacle arose from the inside of the stove? We have sampled it ourselves, and we are healthy men. It killed them as surely as a bullet through their hearts."

"There is one thing I cannot understand, Holmes. Why did he appeal to Scotland Yard?"

"Because he is a man of iron nerve. His niece was instinctively frightened and, finding that she was adamant in her intention of leaving, he planned to kill her at once, in the same way.

"Once done, who should dare to point the finger of suspicion at Master Theobold? Had he not appealed to Scotland Yard and even invoked the aid of Mr. Sherlock Holmes himself to satisfy one and all? The girl had died of a heart attack like the others and her uncle would have been the recipient of general condolences.

"Remember the padlocked cover of the stove in the cellar and admire the cold nerve that offered to fetch the key. It was bluff, of course, for he would have discovered that he had 'lost' it. Had we persisted and forced that lock, I prefer not to think of what we would have found clinging around our collars."

Theobold Wilson was never heard of again. But some two days after his disappearance, a man's body was fished out of the Thames. The corpse was mutilated beyond recognition, probably by a ship's propeller, and the police searched his pockets in vain for definite identification. They contained nothing, however, save for a small notebook filled with jottings on the brooding period of the Fringilla *canaria*.

"It is the wise man who keeps bees," remarked Sherlock Holmes when he read the report. "You know where you are with them, and at least they do not attempt to represent themselves as something that they are not."

BEFORE THE ADVENTURES

BY LENORE CARROLL

Lenore Carroll, gifted in both the mystery and historical western fields (her Annie Chambers *is a gritty, moving chronicle of the life of a frontier prostitute), here offers a refreshing new take on our favourite subject, in an autobiographical letter written by Watson to his publishers. Holmes purists may take umbrage at the central revelation, but the Watsonians among us will greet Carroll's courageous, intelligent physician with open arms.*

May 6, 1881
Mr. H. Greenhough Smith
Editor, *The Strand Magazine*
Burleigh Street, The Strand,
London

Dear Mr. Greenhough Smith:
Many thanks for your kind letter. Your warm response to the story I submitted to your magazine is indeed heartening. I have had two short novels about my detective character published, one in *Beeton's* and one in *Lippicott's*. But they were by only a very small response, and I feared this "scandalous" orphan might find no home. So I am delighted that you see a series of these stories, and am greatly encouraged to continue.

Let me assure you that the principal characters (aside from the detective and his friend) have no counterparts in real life to my knowledge. I created them by stitching together bits and pieces of real life into a patchwork fiction. I trust the results are seamless.

It is true, however, as you suggest, that there are actual people who inspired the story's protagonist and his narrator friend. And it is flattering for you to ask how I came to write these tales. I must confess that I, like my narrator, am a trained physician; and at one time I had no thought at all of ever becoming an author. I entered the Army Medical Department after receiving my degree, and eventually found myself in India as an Army surgeon. I had determined to make my career in Her Majesty's service, and had looked forward to making a good start.

My career was cut short, however, when I was gravely wounded during service in the Afghan war. And when I was invalided out of the Army, I found the rain-soaked greenery of my native island, for which I had longed heartily while residing in the brown desert, only aggravated the wounds I had sustained. An irony to add to the irony of a surgeon sent to heal being hurt in the fray. I had taken one Jezail bullet in the shoulder and another penetrated my leg at the fatal battle of Maiwand.

I began limping about despite the pain, as soon as I was able, thinking that improved circulation of blood to the region would aid its healing. At first I ventured in the immediate vicinity of the hotel where I had taken lodgings. As I regained my health, I roamed further afield to escape the dreary hotel. On the streets of the great metropolis of London I found human beings of every description—prosperous businessmen, ladies of fashion, street Arabs, gin-sodden bawds, stevedores from the docks, Roman clergy like so many ring-necked blackbirds, well-dressed children accompanied by uniformed nannies. When my distress at having my career in India cut short got me in the dumps, I would take to the streets, learning each avenue, lane, and mews as I once learnt the arteries of the body while studying medicine at the University of London. I learnt the textures and humour of the city as I spent day after day stumping the streets, my stout cane in hand. I walked through drizzle and fog, some days from mid-morning until the lamps were lighted at dusk.

My legs and eyes were well occupied and my self-prescribed cure worked very satisfactorily, but I cast about for some similarly healthy occupation for my brain. I am not a person of great imagination, nor am I prone to be in exceedingly high spirits or low, but when left with no occupation, memory returned again and again to the horror of battle. Over and over my thoughts recalled the heathen cries of the attackers, dust obscuring the charge, red blood soaking redcoats, pounding hooves, and the piteous cries of the wounded. I would not have escaped but for the action of my orderly, who threw me across a packhorse and brought me safely to the British lines.

Thus I revived my youthful habit of composing verse in my head. My Bohemian proclivities (which had nearly prevented my taking a degree) came to the surface in aid of my practicality. As I walked, I occupied my mind with rhyme, metre, form, and syntax. Nothing equals verse in its demands on the writer. After several hours I would return to my hotel and transcribe the lines into my journal, another therapeutic aid to maintaining sanity. I passed several months and regained my health to a large extent, although my shaken nerves would not bear disruption or rows.

I continued to walk as if in the streets of my beloved London I would find direction for my future. I had neither kith nor kin in England and no money, my wastrel brother having squandered the little our father had left him. I needed to rouse myself to recommence the practise of medicine, or resign myself to a limited existence on half-pay. But when the weather turned cold and rain poured down daily, the soot-coloured fog seemed to penetrate even my lodgings. I would prop my bad leg on a cushioned chair and sink into a brown study. Although my wound did not prevent me from walking, it ached wearily at the change in the weather. The thoughts that filled those grey days in my rooms were of money—how could a surgeon on half-pay find the capital to buy a London practice? I had proceeded to Netley after taking my degree and went through the course prescribed for Army surgeons. To what use could I put that knowledge in London?

And what girl, or rather, woman, would ever condescend to share my life under these circumstances? What woman could look upon my wounds, though fading from scarlet to a politer pink, without repugnance? I was still in my twenties, and while I counted myself not bad looking in a sandy, freckled way with my imposing new moustache, I could not rely on charm or dash to carry my suit. Rather, common sense, respectability, and application were my virtues. I had no fear that my Bohemian penchant would interfere with married life. My mentor at university, Dr. Averill, described it as a response to boredom. Loyalty and not so many brains as to be likely to get myself in trouble was his estimation of me.

It was on one of my rambles near the Thames that I made the acquaintance of Budger.

I was negotiating the cobblestones outside the saloon bar of the George & Dragon when my cane slipped on the muddy surface. My bad leg gave way when the unexpected weight of my body fell upon it. I lay on the stones for a moment to catch my breath and ensure no serious damage had been done. Before I could right myself, however, I felt a helping hand reach over my shoulder and help me up.

"This ain't Afghanistan, Doc," said a man's voice as he heaved me to my feet. I turned to thank him and beheld a miniscule Cockney, whose strength belied his size, a bowler tilted to a raffish angle and hands already back in his pockets.

"How did you know I was a doctor?" I asked.

"Are ye, now? What a lucky guess, I'm certain." (I will not try to set down his Cockney dialect exactly. The transliteration is tedious for the writer and even more tiresome for the reader to decipher. I will try only to capture some slight indication of his colourful manner of speaking.)

I rummaged in my now-muddy trousers for a coin with which to reward him.

"No charge, Doc, glad to oblige."

"Would you do me the favor of sharing a pint with me?" I indicated the George which I had just quitted.

"Don't mind if I do," he replied, and took my elbow as if he feared I might come a cropper again. He steered me into the public bar and

I ordered our pints. We introduced ourselves and he told me his name was Budger.

Again I asked, "How did you know I was a doctor? And that I had been in Afghanistan? Do you refer to everyone as Doc? Surely a lucky guess would not have been so accurate."

"To tell yer the truth, Doc, I *know* what I know, but damme if I can learn *how* I know it. Fer instance, take that man at the window table. He's a railroad worker, probably a ticket agent, who works at Waterloo. He's stopped in here for a pint afore he goes home. He's got to stop and pick up sothin' fer dinner and take it home to the missus."

I gaped in astonishment.

"Now it wouldn't do, would it, Doc, to disturb the man's privacy and ask if it was true, but we can follow him out and after he runs his errand, ask him for directions and say he looks like a ticket agent of our acquaintance from Waterloo. Are ye game, Doc?"

"Yes, certainly. But try to think of how you knew I was a physician."

"There's yer mustardy-colour complexion, if you'll fergive my mentionin' it. That says you've been in Hindia or Afghanistan or one of them places probably, most likely with the Army, as you don't have the look of the sugar merchant about you. More military-like in the way you walk, despite yer limp. Now if you was a gentleman, you would be exercising on horseback; if you was a foot soldier, you'd rather be drawn and quartered than walk. Since yer neither fish nor fowl, I'd taken you for an Army doctor. With yer limp and the faded look of yer skin I'd say yer were invalided out three months ago, give er take a week. 'Ow's that?"

"That's remarkable!" I exclaimed. "You guessed within a week of how long I had been back."

"Well, now, I *can* study as to how I know these things," he said with a touch of surprised pride.

At that moment, the man arose from the window table and left the George. We followed him from a slight distance and, true to Budger's prophecy, saw him stop at a green grocer and come out in a few minutes with a parcel. "He's getting on fer 'ome," said Budger after a few blocks. We picked up our pace and overtook him at the next corner.

"Pardon me, guv'nor," said Budger, in his engagingly cheeky manner. "Is this the way to Nelson Square?"

"Why no," our quarry responded. "You must go in the opposite direction to find it."

"Sir, you put me in mind of an agent I've boughten tickets off of," said Budger.

"That may be true," said our anonymous friend, "I have a cage at Waterloo, although I hope I shan't offend you if I say I do not recognize you."

"Notter tall, sir," said Budger, "and thankee for the directions." He winked as he rejoined me, pleased with his success. We waited until the ticket agent had turned down the street, then I besought Budger to explain his "lucky guess" this time.

"Well, got a whiff of him as we came in and he 'ad the smell of the coke they use for steam engines. If you spend much time at a train station, it gets into yer clothes and hair. There were a worn place on the front of his waistcoat where he must rub against the edge of the counter and red stamp-pad ink on his fingers from stamping the tickets." He cocked his head to see if I followed his drift. I nodded him to continue. "Then Waterloo was a guess. Victoria's on the other side of the river and if he lives hereabouts, why the George is halfway between it and where he's headed 'ome, and handy fer a nip. He was scowling at a piece of paper, probably a note from the missus. What should it be but sothin' he fergot she wants him to fetch and he ain't too happy, neither."

I gaped at him, astonished. Truly, he *knew* better than he could explain.

When weather permitted, I found myself drawn by curiosity to the George, where Budger could usually be found at midday for tiffin and a pint. He continued to announce his speculations on his fellow tipplers with surprising accuracy, occasionally winning a bet from doubting persons not yet familiar with his peculiar gift.

We became friends in a way. I sadly lack a firm sense of class consciousness. I frequently wonder who I am and who I presume to be, and to which class I would most familiarly fit. I am a physician by training and inclination, but the rigid restrictions of my time and place frequently weigh heavy on me. Often I wish for the camaraderie of the officers' mess, the openly sensuous women of the East who are not bound by convention, as exemplified by our beloved sovereign. Every woman I saw in London was encased in that cage of whalebone which symbolized these conventions. It was deemed necessary for beauty, but was nearly disastrous for muscle tone and adequate breathing (although it did aid some back disorders and those of posture). The frequency of fainting could probably be laid at the door of the corsets necessary for fashion.

Budger, with the delightful cheerfulness of his rank and class, was also a maverick, in his own way. He treated me like an old chum from the docks rather than as a proper professional man. My rather shabby though genteel clothes and penchant for unconventional experiences gave him leave to take what liberties he might.

Budger seemed always to have enough money to while away his afternoons at the George. If my powers of observation had been as acute as his, I would have made note of his coming and going there. He moved from his own table and talked briefly first to this man, then another. So expert was his sleight of hand, scarcely ever did I note money and information changing hands.

One brisk day as the winter sun endeavoured to pierce the yellow pall of fog that hung over Bankside where we strolled, I put it to him.

"How," I asked, "do you make your living, Budger? Now tell me straight. We've known each other for several months and I have yet to see you short of funds, yet you are daily at the George. No common labourer, office clerk, or delivery man could spend his time so freely. Tell me, what is it you do to support yourself?"

We had stopped and Budger gave me a sharp look from under the rim of his bowler. He was so short and I so tall that it was better to converse while sitting. He had once remarked as we strolled out of the George together that he looked like my pet that I was walking off the lead, so vast was the difference in our respective sizes. He did not answer at once, but turned his glance from me and began strolling again. "Well, Doc," he said at length, "I know there's no malice in yer intention, but it's for the best yer don't know too much. Wotcher don't know can't hurt ye, don't yer know."

"But surely you have some visible means of support," I remonstrated.

"Doc, ye must take this much and not worry me fer more: I'm in the way of being a private accountant. I hold money while my foolish friends bet, taking a percentage for my profit. I'm apt to run errands for solicitors and other toffs who don't wish to be seen digging for information for their cases among the low life. If a gentleman is looking for a coachman, likely I can find an out-of-work chap who's fill the bill. I do a bit o' this and a bit o' that, and one way and another I make enough to stay ahead of me creditors. If you must, call me a private agent, but an agent of what, I couldn't say."

I mused over this information for a bit, and then commented, "You are putting to use your remarkable gifts of judging people."

"Coo! I guess I am," he replied in amazement. "I never thought it like that, Doc. It must be good for sothin'."

We turned away from London Bridge and retraced our steps to the George, and after a bit I ventured, "It occurs to me that you could make yourself wealthy, putting this gift to great use."

"Wadder yer mean, Doc?"

"Why, you could go upon the musical comedy stage and astound the audience with your divinations, or, with a little backing, go into a business where your knowledge of human nature could be turned to profit."

"Aye, yer on the track, Doc. But there's sich a thing as telling people more than they want to hear, isn't there? A little bit of it now and again is fun, and people says 'How amazing!' and 'Wadder yer know!' But tell a man he's 'ad a fight with his missus that morning, that he must have got dressed in a real rush because his socks don't match, and his boots ain't been cleaned nor his hat brushed, and he won't thankee for it." We walked in silence for a bit as I slowly recognized the truth of what he had said, and then he continued: "Tell a lady she takes belladonna at night, laces her stays too tight because her figger ain't wot it uster be and uses powder to cover the circles under her eyes, and she won't thankee. Lucky you'll be if she doesn't throw a 'ysterical fit and pretend to faint. Add to that that she not only knows what a mattress is for but has enjoyed the time spent there, and she'll fall into a brain fever and take three month to recover. Too much o' the truth is frightenin' to folks."

"I fear you are correct, Budger, and my suggestion was ill-put. I was only trying to find recompense in measure equal to your gifts."

"I know that, Doc, and think the world o' ye fer it."

"I dare say you could have told me more about myself that first day you hauled me from the kerb, had you less diplomacy. Of course, I feel an open book to you now."

"Yes, Doc, I could. I could've told ye yer were in a bad way for occupation, and getting low on money."

"Really, now!"

"'Tis true, 'tisn't it?"

"Yes, I must admit you are accurate as usual. I do not like to burden my acquaintances with my own troubles, but rather to deal with my problems in private. I do not wish to appear a weeping sister to my friends," I replied, somewhat stiffly.

"Come offen it, Doc. Yer livin' on half-pay and there's not a situation in sight. Yer leg's 'most healed, as well as it ever will, and ye haven't had a woman since ye left Hindia."

I started to draw myself up and remonstrate Budger for his liberties. But I knew in my heart that he read me accurately and that any objections on my part would only further prove his statement that people didn't want too much truth. "Alas, Budger, you are correct," I replied. "Now, pray tell me, what am I to do about my circumstances? And don't tell me any more about myself for the time; I've heard as much as I can bear."

"Doc, I can only indicate. It's yer life to lead and I'd like to give you a leg up, if I could. Yer going back to doctorin', I suppose?" He raised his voice to indicate there might be some doubt, but it was a statement of fact, not a question. Yes, I would return to work as a physician, by some means or another. But I told him that I lacked the capital at present to buy a practice in London, and hesitated to ask for a situation at a hospital where the staff physicians worked long days for little remuneration.

"Wotcher need is an old doc who's getting on in years and thinkin' about retiring. One who's got a good practice now, hasn't let it slip too much, and who's got a little put by for a rainy day."

I admitted that that was the kind of situation I should like to acquire.

"Then I'll keep my eyes peeled, won't I now?" he said.

"But now . . . where . . . can you . . . ?" I sputtered.

"Never you mind, Doc, just leave me at it," he said with a wink, and we parted company for the day.

Inclement weather kept me indoors for several days. When next I sought the George, I found Budger fairly bursting with excitement. After a hasty pint, he led me out and we repaired immediately to Harley Street.

"I think I've found ye a likely situation," he boasted, as we hurried along the street.

"Surely I could be counted on to know that all the best doctors reside in Harley Street," I answered with impatience.

"Just yer wait, Doc, and we'll see what we'll see, won't we now?"

Budger drew to a halt in front of a prosperous residence-*cum*-surgery. A brass plate with the name Morestone was reflecting the midday sun.

"There she is, Doc," he said proudly.

"There what is? Now, see here, Budger, what is this all about? Why drag me along here to see another doctor's prosperity? Have I not enough to plague me?"

"Now, now, Doctor, take it easy. First, I said to myself, we needs to find a older doc, one that's taken kindly to some assistance (that's you). So's I spent a little time hereabouts chattin' up the drivers and butlers and some of the prettiest parlourmaids in London. This bloke"—he indicated Morestone—"seems the likeliest prospect."

"But how do you know?" said I, ever the naïf where the machinations of Budger's mind were concerned.

"First, there's his steps. The stoops hereabouts was laid when the houses was built, but this one is more worn than many another. Tells me he does a thrivin' practice. He keeps a brougham and a driver, three maids, a butler, a cook, a scullery maid, and a page, all just for him and his daughter, Mary. Not bad at all!"

"And just how did you learn all this, this . . . intelligence?"

"Same way I pick up stuff for the solicitor toffs. Hanging about, liftin' a few at the nearest pubs, keeping me eyes open and puttin' two an' two together. You know better'n I how I do it. You studied it; I just do it."

Lest he think me unappreciative of his efforts, I murmured, "Carry on."

"Morestone's got rheumatiz pritty bad. And he don't do much surgery no more, on account of his 'ands is all crippled up. His brain's as sharp as ever, but the old machine is wearin' out. He looks like a man who could use a rest, but he's probably giving a thought to his daughter, isn't he? He needs to stay active until she's taken care of, married or provided for, one way or another . . . One more but I found out, Doc," said Budger, his pale eyes dancing with secret amusement. "He put in some time as an Army surgeon when he was a young 'un. He might take a shine to ye."

I told Budger that I appreciated his efforts on my behalf, and despite his disappointment, I hurried away from Harley Street determined to forget his presumptuous arrangements for me.

However, my resolution did not withstand my curiosity. After a day or so, I began casual inquiries of my own and discovered Budger had made an excellent choice, by his lights. I repaired to the George and apologised for my brusque treatment of him. He took it well and allowed as how people didn't like to have their lives arranged for them by an outsider. I did, however, have a question for him. Assuming I decided the situation was desirable, how was I to go about ingratiating myself to Dr. Morestone? This put Budger at a loss, but he said to leave it to him, he'd think of something, hadn't he always?

In the meantime, I arranged a proper introduction to Dr. Morestone through my former mentor, Dr. Averill. It was at a reception for the new director of Lambeth Hospital, with the cream of London medical society present. I doubt I impressed him very strongly as there were many young doctors there, ready to make themselves agreeable in hopes of future notice by their betters.

One morning as I sat over a cooling pot of breakfast tea, I received a note from Budger. His writing was not educated, but the message was clear: I was to meet him at Dr. Morestone's address in Harley Street at 12:20 promptly.

I wondered what adventure was afoot, as I dressed with more than usual care.

I appeared at the corner at 12:15 and started towards the doctor's address. Budger's bowler-topped head appeared from behind the steps of the house opposite and he waved me back. I stopped at the corner and looked around for a few minutes, wondering what Budger wanted of me. I checked my watch, and found that the appointed hour had arrived. I looked up as I slid it into my waistcoat pocket to see Budger's arm motion me forward. As I started towards the address, a young lady came down Morestone's steps and entered a brougham which had been waiting apparently for her. My brief glance had told me the woman was comely and well dressed. I assumed her to be one of Dr. Morestone's patients.

No sooner had the carriage pulled into the street than I noticed Budger's signal again from the corner of my eye. I looked about me wondering what I was supposed to do, when a boy with a handcart darted in front of the brougham. The driver reined in the horses to avoid collision and the horses shied. The urchin escaped, but a loud noise from across the street alarmed the horses further and they began galloping in my direction. The driver could not control them and they were gaining speed as they approached me. I limped desperately towards the horses, grabbed the harness of the one nearest me, and pulled with all my weight. With the aid of the driver we stopped the animals and brought the brougham to a halt.

My next thought was for the lovely occupant. I pulled open the door and found her sitting bolt upright, her face pale and her hands gripping the seat so that the knuckles showed white from the strain.

She took one look at me and her eyes slid up as she fainted. I hoped it was from the shock and not my appearance. I propped her up in the seat and called to the driver that I was a doctor, that she had fainted, and that I wished to take her home. He answered that she was Miss Morestone and that she had just come from her residence. Rather than wait until he had turned the vehicle around, I swept her into my arms and carried her down the street to her father's house.

The door opened as I climbed the steps. A maid evidently had seen what had happened and was waiting for us. She showed me into a parlour, and I laid the still insensible Miss Morestone on a horsehair sofa. Her father hurried in, his stethoscope still dangling from his neck. He pushed me aside (I had been beside Miss Morestone, taking her pulse), and examined her for himself. I sat on my heels and waited. He held smelling salts under her nose and presently she came around.

"Oh, Papa," she said. "The most dreadful thing happened!" She then looked about her and noticed that she was in her own parlour and that I was present. She gasped and said, "This gentleman rescued me when the horses bolted. How did I get home?"

"There, there, now, you've had a fright," the old physician replied. "You're safe and sound."

As if to prove his words, Miss Morestone sat upright and looked at me. "And you, sir, is it to you I owe my thanks?"

So abashed was I in the presence of her beauty, I merely nodded my head, not trusting myself to speak normally. I realised that I had held her in my arms in a moment of need, and would never again have that privilege.

"So I, too, have you to thank," said Dr. Morestone. He extended his hand and we rose (me helping him slightly) and shook. "Who are you, sir? And how did you happen to be in Harley Street today?"

"I, too, am a doctor, and was coming to meet a friend." In the excitement I had totally forgotten about Budger.

"In that case, perhaps we should not impose any further upon your time," he responded. But a glance from Miss Morestone told me that she did not wish me to depart.

"My friend had not arrived," I temporized, "so I am completely at your disposal."

Tea was ordered and the doctor took a few minutes from his surgery to make my acquaintance again. I mentioned that we had met, and at his urging told him a little about myself. He then left me with Miss Morestone. Our conversation was commonplace—weather, health, and the current debate of Parliament. If eyes could speak, mine would have poured out the entire sonnet series of Shakespeare, so smitten was I with Miss Morestone's charms. She seemed not immune to whatever charms I may have displayed. Before I left, I had secured an invitation to tea two days hence.

I scarcely remembered leaving and was halfway down the block on my way back to my lodgings when a familiar voice reached my ears. "Dropped yer stick, Doc." Budger! I had completely put him out of my mind. It was now over an hour past our appointed time!

"Oh, Budger, my friend! I have completely forgotten you in the excitement! Did you see me take the lady into Dr. Morestone's house? That was Miss Morestone, and a lovelier lady I have yet to meet. What were you doing by those steps? And what happened to the boy with the cart?"

Budger looked up at me quizzically and did not reply. Slowly the realisation came over me! Budger had arranged my "heroic" rescue of Miss Morestone!

"Budger, did you have anything to do with what happened today?"

"Now, how could I have anything to do wif an act of God, like an accident?" he said with a twinkle in his eye. I gave him a hard look and he gave me a cheeky grin and nothing more was said.

My visits to the George became more infrequent in the following weeks. I called on Miss Morestone as often as she would allow. I had progressed to dinner invitations and then to driving out with her (in her father's brougham, alas). The old doctor took to me, and my fondest wish was granted on the evening he took me into his private study.

"You wish to marry my daughter?" he asked bluntly.

"More than anything in the world," I replied.

"And what will you live on?"

"I receive half-pay from the Army and hope to find a suitable situation, perhaps with a hospital as a resident physician, so that I can support her."

"I see. What would you think of coming here as my assistant?"

My mouth fell open and I did not trust myself to reply.

"The hours would be easier and I could use some help," he continued. "If you're not completely an idiot, you should be able to take over my practice so I can retire in a few years and enjoy my grandchildren."

I could think of no suitable reply, but simply grabbed his arthritic hand and shook it until he winced. My problems were solved and my life better arranged than I had dared hope, and all thanks to Budger.

The ensuing months sped by. Miss Morestone and I were soon married, and I moved into the house on Harley Street. I began by taking overflow patients, and after a few months was seeing all but his oldest patients, whom he reserved for himself for old-time's sake. In a year, I could scarcely remember the trying time when I stamped the streets of London, wondering bleakly what the future would be.

I retained, however, my friendship with Budger. He had declined to be my best man, saying it would not be seemly, and I'm sure Mary was relieved when I sorrowfully told her his admittedly garish checked suit would not stand up with us. He did sit in a place of honour, grinning like a cat who swallowed a complete aviary of canaries, remembering his part in our happiness. We met almost weekly after that at the George for a pint and a "natter," as he put it. It felt good to escape my stuffy surgery and the busy round of patients for an hour or so. He continued to astound me with his gifts of acute observation. At his suggestion, I wrote some of them down and submitted them to the weekly magazines, but with little luck.

One afternoon, Budger asked what was sticking out of my coat pocket. It happed to be a story returned by an editor with polite regrets. He read it through slowly, then sat staring out of the windows of the George, lost in thought. "Wotcher need," he said at last, "is some interesting blokes in yer story. You've got the action right enough, but the people don't come through."

I was astonished that an unlettered Cockney would have the temerity to criticize my literary efforts but as he continued I realised he had a good idea. I borrowed his stub of a pencil and made notes in the margins incorporating his suggestions. He added touches of behaviour that illuminated the characters in a way that I would never have thought of. I put aside my wounded pride as a neophyte author and revised the story along the lines he had suggested. The tale was accepted, and I shared the modest payment with Budger when we met. As time went on, our weekly meetings were spent working on other stories I had written. We had a certain indifferent success, until one fateful day when Budger said: "We're too smart by half, I fancy."

"What do you mean, Budger?" I asked.

"Instead of bein' God and tellin' all there is to tell, have the der-tecktive tell 'em," he replied. I had observed that Budger had a goodly share of mother wit, and while he was unlettered, in the sense of formal education, he was not unread. "Why, folks don't want yer to be too subtle wif 'em, do they now?" he continued. I hadn't been aware that he knew the word.

"What do you mean?" I asked.

"Like sayin' the man who ruined the girls was handsome. People like their villains to look bad. And the dertecktive studying who done it—you gotter give the readers a little show-off stuff, show 'em how 'is mind works, so's they can see how 'e does it, not just spring to the answer on the last page."

"Carry on. I think I see what you're getting at."

"Like that jewel thief. He collects art, he dresses well, and the ladies like him. When yer finds out he's the crook, yer disappointed. Better make him despicable in some way. Or the boxer in t'other story. You'n me know that the bigger the fellow, the gentler he is. A big bruiser knows his strength and isn't so apt to throw his weight around as some feisty little chump like me. In real life an ugly man can have a heart of gold, but it's confusing in a story, isn't it? But people expects the bad 'un to be nasty and pushy.

"And take the lady in the story who lied about the jewels. We both know that people can lie without turnin' a hair, like the patients who come to yer surgery and don't tell you everything, but expects yer to cure 'em in spite of what they're holding back. Best let her give herself away a bit, or the end don't seem ter hang right."

I acknowledged the truth of that.

"In a story there's got ter be sothin' to give 'em away, so that yer reader feels good when the dertecktive solves the crime. Like me, I can't tell a body too much about hisself or he'll be up in arms and I'll never get anywhere. But give 'em a bit to attract their curiosity, and they're eatin' outer my hand."

I nodded with increasing excitement.

"Can ye fathom my meaning, Doc?"

"That I can, Budger! Let me mull this over, and I'll bring you a story every editor in London will want to publish!"

True to my word, I returned in a fortnight with a new tale for Budger to look at. We altered some few lines together on my foolscap draft, then pronounced it finished. We drank a pint of mild to celebrate. "Doc, I think yer on the way to bein' a spellbinder." Better praise I never earned.

The story was accepted by *Beeton's Christmas Annual*, and it opened a new chapter in my life. It began with a brief description of the narrator, then picked up a character Budger and I had put together. He had polish and education and a different physical appearance, but he had Budger's gift of reading a person from slight clues. A show-off, but in an agreeable way with enough quirks of personality to be interesting. We created him without interest in money or women so as to be incorruptible. The narrator, who somewhat resembled myself, was self-effacing in the extreme and nearly colourless, but the protagonist achieved some popularity.

His first words were similar to the first I heard from Budger: "You have been in Afghanistan, I perceive."

"How on earth did you know that?" asks the narrator in astonishment, ever the naive but willing foil for the genius with whom fate had cast him.

It was all really elementary.

SONS OF MORIARTY

A SHERLOCK HOLMES NOVELLA
BY LOREN D. ESTLEMAN

Loren D. Estleman published his first Sherlock Holmes novel, Sherlock Holmes vs. Dracula, or The Adventure of the Sanguinary Count, *in 1978, and it has rarely been out of print; 1979's* Dr. Jekyll and Mr. Holmes *pops up nearly as frequently.* "Sons of Moriarty," *a full-length novella pitting Holmes against the Mafia, appears here for the first time.*

CHAPTER I.

THE ASSASSIN'S DAUGHTER

To commence this narrative, I shall tell you, dear reader, that even now, nearly twenty years after the events I intend to relate, I keep the windows shut in my second-storey bedroom on the sultriest of summer evenings. I take no comfort from a sheer drop of some sixty feet, with no purchase offered to a nocturnal visitor. I would rather swelter the night through than be discovered in the morning with my throat cut from ear to ear.

It all began early in 1903. I was in semi-retirement from my London practice, attending only those long-time patients who would not countenance the idea of treatment by anyone else, and half-heartedly corresponding with a publisher about the prospect of writing my memoirs; a project I viewed with suspicion, as a way of obtaining that which had been withheld by another: the life and intimate remembrances of Mr. Sherlock Holmes.

At the desk in my consulting-room, I recalled Holmes's own ideas on the subject.

"As out-of-favor as he has unfortunately become," said he, "I stand with Oscar Wilde on the subject of the posthumous biography: It brings a new terror to death."

"But writing about oneself is not posthumous."

"It would be, in my case. In that, I stand with Mark Twain, who has directed that his memoirs be suppressed until he has been dead one hundred years. You know very well, Watson, there is dynamite in that little tin box of yours."

He was referring to the dispatch-case I keep under lock and key at Cox & Co., bankers, containing my notes on such cases as the unconvincing conviction and the strange business of the American snapping turtle.

Smiling at the memory of this conversation, I drew out the ledger-book in which I record various reminders to myself and began to write.

"I quite agree," barked a familiar voice at my back. "That turtle alone could overturn civilization. Better her story is left to the next century, when, no doubt, the species will be bred for racing as well as soup."

I started, spoiling the page with my pen, and spun round to face my old friend lounging in the doorway, wearing the shapeless canvas hat and bulky ulster he put on when he wished to wander about the city incognito. This attire quite changed his famous profile; I might not have recognized him straightaway had I not known the clothing.

"Holmes!" I sprang to my feet and wrung his hand, upsetting the delicate operation of rolling a cigarette in the American fashion, a habit he'd acquired after reading the reminiscences of Frank Harris. We hadn't seen each other in months.

Then I backed away. "Really, this is sorcery! How could you know I was thinking of adding that codicil to my will? I only now just thought of it."

He brushed the spilled tobacco from his coat, chuckling in his dry fashion, and proceeded to build another smoke. "I envy you, dear fellow. How refreshing it must be to wake up in a new world each morning. I know you will never grasp my methods, but I shan't give up expecting you someday to understand them."

"Nor I, the opportunity to bring you amusement."

"You must indulge me. I have none to needle since Lestrade was promoted beyond my ken. You were lost in thought, and did not notice that I have been standing here some minutes. I am never idle. There upon the drawleaf of your desk is the letterhead of a publisher—not your own, but the same one who stopped hounding me at last about spraying my wisdom like a delouser throughout the stalls. It was clear the persistent rascals had taken their case to you. I watched you place it there after reading it, doubtless not for the first time, then send your gaze about your immediate vicinity. It lit, first, upon the square patch on the wallpaper where hung until recently your framed inscribed copy of the playbill featuring poor Wilde's *Lady Windermere's Fan*, then shifted abruptly to your Mark Twain set in the glazed book-press, easily eight feet away. Surely the thought of one led immediately to the thought of the other.

"Whereupon," said he, striking a match off the seat of his trousers and setting fire to the finished cigarette, "I recalled our discussion of last Easter and the references I'd made to those two authors. Certainly I can think of no circumstance in which two such disparate artists would be paired otherwise. When, resolute, you opened your ledger-book and began to write, I took a leap—of supreme self-confidence, if not of faith—and made my pronouncement."

"You might let a fellow know you're in town. The last wire I received was from Leicester."

"I had a courier send it. I was digging in Bosworth Field to learn who killed the Princes in the Tower."

"Richard the Third, of course. Every British schoolboy knows that."

"Every British schoolboy has grown up on the Bard, who we mustn't forget introduced modern-day clocks to Caesar's Rome. I rather think the former Duke of Gloucester has been wrongly used in this instance."

He pulled a wry face. "This is what I'm reduced to, Watson; the greatest criminal expert in Europe, burrowing in the rubbish bins of history in despair of uncovering sinister genius in his own time. Our brave new century is an arid desert of common footpads, pickpockets, cardsharps, mugger-snatchers, and spivs. If I cannot have a Burke, give me a Hare, at least, and a Richard if not a—"

"Don't say the name," I broke in. "You made a resolution."

"So I did."

I bade him sit, but he shook his head and put out his cigarette in the human marrow-bone I used for an ashtray. "Another time. I'm off to the Tower."

"They won't let you in there with a spade."

"How well you know me, if not my *modus operandi*. I wish merely to pace the grounds. If there are two feet of wall space unaccounted for, that may be where my investigation ends, with two frail skeletons and Richard damned in my books as well as in Lamb's Shakespeare. Failing that, I shall scrutinize a pair of mysterious noble cousins who founded the first legal firm in Glasgow. It was established in 1485, not long after the princes vanished." He became suddenly keen. "It's nearly eight; are you expecting a visitor?"

"All but one of my friends is dead, or else residing abroad, and I've seen my last patient for this week. I didn't hear the tread on the stair."

"You did not hear mine. In this case it's forgivable, if it's as light as the scent she is wearing."

He snatched open the door. Ever since the adventure I have made public as "The Final Problem," he kept the habit of surprising unannounced callers before they could surprise him.

Here he succeeded beyond measure. The young lady poised to tap on the panel with the handle of her parasol was so startled she nearly fell through the opening.

Holmes, reflexes sharp as always, caught her by the elbow. "I beg your pardon, miss. I hope I haven't contributed to the effects of your crossing. Gibraltar's tortuous in all events, but this time of year it's torturous as well."

The expression on the woman's face was perplexed, though I could not tell whether it was because of his precise knowledge of the niceties of English vocabulary or his assumption of the route she'd taken to my door. Certainly there was a foreignness about her that suggested a tenuous association with the King's tongue; her plain coat, cloth hat, and boots were not of local manufacture, and her handsome oval face was olive-hued. I judged her to be younger than twenty.

She confirmed my assessment regarding her origins when she spoke, in a husky voice with a heavy accent. "However did you know, sir, from where I have travelled? I know I could never pose as English, but I'm told many of my countrymen reside here."

"I decided first to disregard your clothing, which may be purchased many places in our cosmopolitan city, in order to concentrate upon the scent you're wearing: an Egyptian blend with a touch of turmeric, which has just become available here, but the tariff compels our shopkeepers to charge a price too dear for one who cannot afford furs this time of year. It's imported through Italy, where it can be obtained for a few lira. That you made the voyage fairly recently is evident by the stitching on your coatsleeve where the price marker was freshly removed. It's just the thing for the North Atlantic and England this season, but would be an unnecessary expenditure in the Mediterranean climate."

"*Meraviglioso!*" She clapped her tiny hands in woolen gloves. "But how can you, a man, know of such things as *profumo*? You are, perhaps a merchant, and not—?" Her lively face registered disappointment.

"*Negazione, signorina.* Merely considering a monograph on women's chemical enhancements, can Piccadilly but slow down their proliferation long enough for me to write it."

"Then I have not been misdirected, and you are the Sherlock Holmes. I am so—so—"

"Watson!"

When it comes to medicine, my own reflexes are not so far inferior to the detective's. Scarcely had she swooned into his arms than I poured a glass of medicinal brandy. He carried her to my old leather couch and picked up her parasol for examination as I lifted her head and placed the glass between her lips.

When at present she came round, a deep flush spread beneath the dark pigment of her skin. She stirred, as if to rise, but I entreated her to lie still.

She obeyed. "Your pardon, *signors*. You were right, Mr. Holmes, about my recent crossing. I arrived in London only this afternoon, and made haste to your rooms, where the *signora* told me I might find you here. I've come all the way from Palermo just to see you." She cast a doubtful glance at me; but Holmes put her mind at ease, and the parasol aside. The time for parlour tricks had passed.

"You've come to the home and workplace of Dr. Watson, my friend and confidant, who has given you this restorative. His discretion is as good as his cellar. Now that you know us, perhaps you will return the favor, and we shall all have been properly introduced. I know the quaint customs of your island and the regard in which a woman's honour is held. We shan't want any vendettas waged on our behalf."

This witticism had the opposite effect of the one intended. Her face paled and her teeth chattered. Fearing a seizure, I came forward once again with the brandy. But she waved it away and sat up, peering anxiously at Holmes.

"My name is Magdalena Venucci, and I have come to beg for your help, as I have no one else to whom I can turn. My father, *Signor* Holmes, was Pietro Venucci. Perhaps you remember the name."

He shook his head. "I fear you've been reading the doctor's panegyrics with an unjaundiced eye. Most of my memory is stored not in my cranium, but in my commonplace books. I have concluded some seven hundred seventy-three cases in England, a score or more on the continent, and one in America. I can recite the details of but a hundred. As for those I *failed* to conclude—"

"There is no need to explain. The man was dead when first you heard his name, and he was but slightly involved with the—what is your word?—*case* you were working upon at the time. It was the affair of *Il Seis Napoleoni*, and for a time Scotland Yard believed he was central to the solution. One cannot fault them for arriving at that conclusion. You see, my father was—was—oh, *come si chiama in inglese?*"—Two tiny fists pounded the leather upholstery in her frustration—"*uccisore, assassino—*"

"Killer," Holmes said grimly. "Assassin. You remember the business, Watson? The ritual destruction of the six plaster busts of Napoleon the First." He was watching our guest from beneath lowered lids; a certain sign that she'd aroused his attention. "Your father was a mercenary, paid to commit murder for the Mafia."

CHAPTER II.

THE GRAVEDIGGER'S STORY

As yet, the adventure I have called "The Adventure of the Six Napoleons" had yet to appear in print, although some of the particulars had been reported in the press, and evidently contained sufficient interest to have been appropriated by foreign papers, or our comely visitor would have known nothing of the case.

Inspector Lestrade had enlisted Holmes's aid in getting to the bottom of a series of bizarre crimes in which a number of inexpensive plaster busts of the French Emperor had been stolen and smashed to pieces. It developed that the infamous black pearl of the Borgias, missing for some time, had been secreted in one of the *objets d'art* before the plaster had set in order to avoid arrest, and the thief responsible had been forced to track them down to their purchasers and eliminate them one at a time. The last of the six had turned out to contain the item, which Holmes, with his passion for theatrics, had been privileged to extract himself before an appreciative audience.

One Beppo, a known associate of the Italian secret society known as the Mafia, was the culprit. He had slain the assassin Venucci in a struggle to obtain it, and for a time Lestrade had suggested closing the case as an example of an Old World vendetta.

Such had been our one-and-only brush with that sinister organisation. We'd thought it to be our last.

Holmes, needless to say, was elated. Here at last, it seemed, was a reprieve from the *ennui* that plagued him whenever his gifts were in idle, and to see him rub his hands, eyes bright, like an artist seized with sudden inspiration, quite heartened me.

Would that I had not been so naive; but to attempt to dissuade him *in medias res* would have been as futile as trying to stop a charging train by standing on the tracks with arms upraised.

"Watson, I think your patient has recovered to the point where we may treat her as a guest."

"I agree."

Presently, we had repaired to my sitting-room, contentedly arranged in my worn but comfortable old upholstered chairs, Holmes and I with whiskies-and-sodas. Miss Venucci, her colour restored by another draught of brandy, declined further refreshment.

"And now, young lady," said Holmes, curled up like a cat with his legs crossed beneath him and his long fingers tented, "kindly proceed with your predicament."

Her account was brevity itself. She had a better command of our language than she proclaimed, a mystery she herself explained almost at the start.

She had never known her father. Her mother, the daughter of the owner of a tiny vineyard outside Palermo, Sicily, had died giving her life, and in his grief and ignorance of child-rearing, her father had remanded her to the care of the local sisters of charity, who had included lessons in English, Spanish, and Greek in addition to her native tongue. Although they would tell her nothing of her father, some of the other girls in the orphanage were better versed in the ways of the world, and through them she learnt that Pietro, a local gravedigger, had fallen in with the Mafia when the local *don* had paid him handsomely to dig an extra few feet and bury some inconvenient corpses beneath the legitimate residents interred above.

Venucci, it developed, possessed the gift of discretion: "*Omerta,*" his daughter injected at this point. "You know this word?"

Holmes nodded. "The oath of silence. A sacred thing, in that culture—enforced, of course, by the threat of death to the transgressors. In its way, it's the key to criminal success, as valuable as confession is to the Catholic, albeit it less conscionable. Do I interpret it correctly?"

"*Sì,*" said she, clearly impressed. (This was personal approbation; despite his disparagement, I had not exaggerated the detective's phenomenal resources of memory in regard to the *demimonde* in which he was as comfortable as in our own respectable class. I forbore to point it out, in keeping with my pledge never to distract him in the course of interviewing a potential client.)

In time, this ability—and Venucci's greed—led to his trial by fire: murder for hire. His first victim was a tailor who'd refused to share his profits with "the order" (for such it was euphemistically called; also *la cosa*—"this thing"—and various other terms of refinement designed to confuse the authorities). The details were unknown, but from the results, the gravedigger's prowess with a stiletto matched his skills with a spade. He was thereupon promoted to that elite society comprised of thugees, *hashashim*, and Destroying Angels that has plagued mankind since Cain slew Abel.

Just how Venucci came to emigrate to England, she could not supply. Possibly one of his assignments had led to complications with the authorities, and it was deemed wise that he set sail for cooler climes.

"I can tell you nothing more of him," his daughter concluded, "as I heard nothing until the circumstances of *Il Seis Napoleoni* appeared in the local journals. I was eighteen years old at the time, and the nuns encouraged me to take the vows. 'It's your calling,' Sister Maria Immaculata insisted. I was cheeky—this is a word, *sì*?"

"It is a word, yes," said Holmes. "I pray you not to bog down your interesting narrative with unnecessary asides."

"Very well. I was cheeky enough to reply, 'Tell them I'm out.' She slapped my face, as you may well imagine, and locked me in my cell on a regimen of bread and water. But she overlooked the rotted wood in which the latch of the window was secured. I absconded, and—"

"—made your way in the world, through this means or that," Holmes finished. "I am neither your judge nor your biographer, *signorina*. Tell me those circumstances that brought you into my sphere."

"I shall; although I must tell you there was nothing disgraceful in the life I led. Degrading, perhaps; demeaning, certainly. But I would not follow my father's example into a life my mother would find repugnant. She was by all accounts a decent woman, who had she the opportunity might have directed my father into a life far more noble than the one he fell into. I acknowledge that he was a weak man. Such men may be evil or noble, given the fates that befall them."

"I'm unpersuaded; but I may be prejudiced, based upon my observation of human nature at its most inhumane and unnatural. Now that I know the sum total of your father's travels, I would know yours."

Her dark eyes flashed fire. I can think of no more original way to describe what happens when Mediterranean features register rebellion. I envy the tropical races their range of emotion. A British woman of breeding might have distended her nostrils a tenth of a centimetre, and there's little romance in it.

"I seek the restoration of my family," she said. "I want to remove my father's remains from the depths of degradation and return them to his homeland, the last place that offered him a chance at redemption.

"I know not, had my mother survived, whether he would have continued to lead a decent life. Our opportunities are limited, compared to yours; just as your own class system is constrained by the standards of American liberty and equality, you must admit. We shall never know now. But I believe, as strongly as I have faith in anything, that if I am to make something of myself in this new century, I must begin by returning my father's remains to hallowed ground."

She sat back, her hands gripping the arms of her chair; and in that moment I recalled, in a flash, the same attitude assumed by my dear departed Mary, challenging Holmes to make right her own paternal legacy. Codger that I was, entering the final phase of an adventurous existence, I wondered if there might perhaps be someone out there yet who could rescue me from a lonely old age.

Holmes, I could tell, was moved. His heavy lids flickered. He untented his hands and folded them across his stomach, still spare after all these years (I envied him his wizard metabolism).

"It's a simple matter, after all," he said. "Petition Scotland Yard for an order of disinterment, suffer a season of hemming and hawing, and sign the document when it arrives. *Semplicità*."

"Not so simple, *Signor* Holmes. Your own country has refused directly to surrender the body."

"Bureaucratic incompetence."

"I have written Scotland Yard three times. Each time they have given me a different excuse."

"One hand knows not what the other is about."

"I wrote your Home Secretary. An assistant-to-an-assistant assured me my request was in the files and would be attended to."

"Passing it on."

"A man who identified himself as an inspector with Scotland Yard advised me not to pursue the matter, for reasons of international relations."

"Xenophobia. What was the inspector's name?"

"Lestrade."

The detective smiled thinly. "Dear me. If the world grows any smaller we'll be drawing lots to stay aboard."

"Holmes," I said, "that hardly sounds like Lestrade. He's obstinate and barely competent, but I've never known him to be deliberately obstructive."

"Perhaps his recent promotion has him flying too close to politics. Well, if his motives were to pique my interest, he's succeeded. I haven't had a good match with authority since that Dreyfuss business. I shall look into the matter, *Signorina* Venucci."

"Splendid!" Then she looked troubled. "I can pay but little. I saved enough for passage both ways, lodging, victuals, and the cost of disinterment, but—"

"*Prego.*" He held up a hand. "I no longer hide from my creditors. I shall ask no more compensation than to see your father's coffin loaded aboard—*The Mother Cabrini*, is it not? No matter; my passion for the shipping columns is hardly unique. I await that day with pleasure."

She rose. When he returned her parasol, her hand touched his. "*Molto grazie, Signor* Holmes." She gave him the address of the rooming house where she was staying in Poplar. We saw her to the door, and soon there was nothing of her left in the room but her exotic scent.

"Amazing young woman," said Holmes. "To brave the North Sea in February, leave behind the only home one has ever known, and plunge into the heart of wicked London at such a tender age is either the height of valor or the depth of folly."

"Rather more of the latter, I should think. I would allow no daughter of mine to take shelter in a place like Poplar."

"And with the West End so very accommodating to the penniless refugee," he replied, with some asperity. "The time has come, my dear fellow, to rescue you from the clutches of the middle class."

"I resent that. I voted for Churchill."

"My mistake; you're positively an anarchist. How is your schedule?"

"I'm free as air."

"Excellent! Meet me at our old digs first thing in the morning."

"How shall I dress?"

"Respectably, as we'll be calling upon Scotland Yard. Sturdily, as we may be in for a bit of grave-robbing later."

CHAPTER III.

LESTRADE IN EARNEST

Bright and early, I found Holmes, silk-hatted and carrying his stick, waiting for me in the entrance to 221B Baker Street, and we took a cab to New Scotland Yard, built upon the foundations of an opera house that could never have known more drama than the construction that now occupied the site.

G. Lestrade—now assistant to the chief inspector, with an office down the corridor from his immediate superior—greeted us warmly and bade us sit down opposite a desk piled high with documents. A bit less wiry than of old, but every bit the bull terrier in features as well as temperament, he snatched a paperweight from atop a stack and offered it to Holmes, asking him what he made of it.

My friend examined the object, which appeared to be nothing more interesting than a three-sided piece of granite with a sort of spine down the middle.

"Early Cenozoic," he pronounced. "Pre-Clovis, but effective enough in stopping three—no, *two* specimens of the species *Mammuthus imperator*; this third mark is but a chip, not a notch, and much more recent than the others; some careless handler, no doubt." He stroked an edge with the ball of his thumb.

"Nothing else?" Lestrade sat back and hooked his thumbs inside the armholes of his waistcoat, looking pleased with himself.

"Apart from the fact it was employed as a weapon within the past twelve hours—fatally, I'm bound—not a thing." He returned the item to the inspector's desk.

"Gad!" Our host lunged forward and pounded the desktop with both fists. "The hounds gave me their word they wouldn't go to press with it until this evening! I might have known you'd be up with the early-bird edition!"

"Good inspector, I haven't seen a paper. The grey-matter adhering to the spearhead is scarcely dry, and apart from some certain police officials—present company excepted—I've yet to meet the man who could spare so much and live. Women are a horse of a different colour, as they seem quite capable of thinking without brains."

"I'll thank you to spare me your conjurer's tricks until I've broken my fast. Sometime around midnight, a watchman in the British Museum surprised a burglar emerging from the curator's office with a satchel full of money from the safe where the donations are kept. The thief snatched the nearest object, a property from the Primitive Man exhibit, and bludgeoned the poor sod to death. It wasn't the watchman's night, nor for that matter his murderer's; he bolted out the door straight into the arms of the constable on patrol. I rather thought I had you this time, but I'd forgotten your sharp practices."

"Watson, next time we set out for the Yard, be good enough to fetch me a smart rap on the *medulla* with the mallet you use to test a patient's reflexes. It's the responsibility of a good guest to level the playing field."

Lestrade sighed. "I take it from your genial conversation you've come for a favor."

Holmes explained the purpose of our mission. The other man stiffened at mention of Pietro Venucci.

"As I told the young lady, it's impossible. The body is in Stranger's Field, where they bury indigents, executed criminals, and convicts who die behind bars in cases when no one has come forward to claim them. It's situated atop a section of Roman catacombs, and the Home Secretary has banned all excavation on behalf of the Royal Historical Society, to preserve the artefacts from destruction."

"It's one grave. I shall apply for a variance."

"Apply away, but you'll find the grave impossible to locate. Most of the records were destroyed last spring when the river overran its banks and flooded the basement where they were kept."

"I shall examine those that survived."

"You'll need the permission of the courts. Miss Venucci's relationship with the deceased must be confirmed, and that can take months."

Holmes's smile was sinister. "An embarrassment of riches, Inspector. I might have accepted one excuse, possibly even two. But you continue throwing boulders at me in desperation, like blind Polyphemus. I believe we'll stroll down to Stranger's Field and chat up the caretaker." He began to rise.

Lestrade leaned across the desk and gripped his wrist, stopping him. The inspector's expression was stern, but not aggressive.

"Sherlock, I'm speaking to you as a friend, and not as an official. This is one investigation that must remain closed."

It was a rare event to see my companion puzzled. In all the years we'd known him, Lestrade had never before addressed him by his Christian name.

"You cannot leave it there," he said. "If you know me well enough to call me friend, you know too I shan't be warned away without an explanation as to the nature of the danger, and why it's necessary."

For a moment I thought Lestrade would refuse. I was sufficiently familiar with that stubborn expression to expect him to take that course. However, he released his grip on Holmes's wrist and sat back again with his palms resting flat on the desk.

"The assassin's shell is of no account. No one cares about the nationality of the worms that feed off it. But with you involved, any action is sure to find its way into the press. It's best for all concerned that Venucci remain forgotten, along with his old associations.

"I'm not threatening you," he said. "Neither the Yard nor Whitehall would press any charges against you. Thanks to Dr. Watson and his busy pen, the prime minister himself could introduce into evidence a photograph of you strangling King Edward and no jury in England would vote for conviction. But your sudden loss, through disappearance or worse, could never be repaired; this government could not survive it.

"I ask you," he concluded, "who is to solve the murder of Sherlock Holmes?"

CHAPTER IV.

STRANGER'S FIELD

"A bleak place, is it not, Watson? Yet I feel more at home in such surroundings than in Covent Gardens."

Looking out upon the Isle of Dogs, I could not say that I shared his enthusiasm. That geographical second thought, fashioned by an abrupt twist in the Thames, was a conglomeration of hovels built from wrecked vessels, patched when needed by planks pilfered from the West India Docks, and reeked of foreign dishes from many lands, each of which might have been quite delectable when experienced separately, but which crowded together in such close quarters created the evilest of stenches. It was as if the river, coming upon them, had crossed the entire neighbourhood just to escape.

"Miss Venucci's address is just the other side of the docks," said I. "Surely she chose this wicked place just to be near her father."

"More likely it was an economic decision. I've stayed here as long as a month on less than you'd pay for four nights at Claridge's."

"It would be worth that to stay anywhere else." I stopped at a kerb to scrape some unidentifiable offal off the sole of my boot.

We came at length to Stranger's Field. No sign pointed it out; just a cleared section of raw earth with numbered stakes pounded into it at intervals and the caretaker's shack, a tumbledown affair with a slant roof pierced by an iron stovepipe. Holmes tapped his stick against the door, which opened to reveal a brute in tobacco-stained overalls with a mop of uncombed black hair and a leather patch over one eye.

"Good morning, Latch. How are your knees?"

"Like sin, Mr. 'Olmes. They can't seem to adjust to my h'elevated circumstances."

"Latch was a first-cabin gravedigger when we met," Holmes told me. "You might say he started at the bottom and worked his way up. He suffers from rheumatism, a common hazard of the profession. I seek a plot, my old friend."

"Sickly?"

"It is not for me. The one I have in mind is occupied already, by an aristocrat: a member of your own guild, named Venucci."

The caretaker's visible eye widened. His chin wobbled. He brought his hand up as if to steady it. "We 'aven't anyone of that name."

"Hundreds of graves and you know the names of all those in them. You've missed your calling, Latch. I've never seen better, and I know a memory artist who's toured three continents, providing mental inventories of the contents of a dozen ladies' handbags and the kings of England in reverse."

"It's my business, Mr. 'Olmes, and I'll thank you to go on about yours and leave mine to me." The door slammed.

Holmes appeared bemused. "We live and learn. I've always held a graveyard to be the one establishment where one couldn't be thrown out."

"He wasn't being rude, Holmes. The man was terrified. Venucci's name was enough to make him so. Perhaps Lestrade was right. This is one case we should let alone."

"Dear Watson. It's I for whom you fear. You've faced Jezail bullets, poisoned darts, and the threat of imprisonment and ruin, and asked only if we might make the last seating at Simpson's. I can do no less. We should, however, confer with our client. If we are in danger, so is she, and the decision is hers to make."

We had, however, gone fewer than a hundred metres when he stopped suddenly and produced his watch. After studying it he snapped shut the lid and returned it to his pocket.

"How many?" I asked; for I knew well what that action signified.

"Two. One medium and well-dressed, one short and slovenly. The first fancies himself a billiards savant; his companion sets pins in a bowling alley. There is so much more to be got from a watch than just the time, if you keep the inside of the lid well polished. My instincts remain as bright."

"Shall we challenge them?" I fingered the revolver in my pocket.

"They would deny everything, and we should have tipped our hand. Let them think themselves clever for now. Whoever they are, we must not lead them to the *signorina's* door."

We strolled in the direction of the underground station, swinging our sticks and paying no attention to our followers.

"I assume the tall fellow bore traces of coloured chalk, which this time of the morning would suggest an overaffection with a billiards parlour," I said. "I can't fathom how you arrived at pin-setter in the case of the short man."

"Chalk, and callosities upon his left thumb and forefinger, which he calls attention to by rubbing them together. The yellow-oak stain on the other's trousers is peculiar to the varnish used on bowling lanes, and I could smell fresh perspiration at a distance of nearly a square. It's a strenuous job, especially when the Rotherhithe Rollers are hosting the Netherlanders for the international championship. I've been following the scores in the *Telegraph*."

"What can such fellows want with us?"

"I refuse to speculate without facts, but grown men who play games in broad daylight frequently work at night. Whoever said there's nothing in the dark that wasn't there in the light knew nothing of the ways of the transgressor. Not yet, Watson. Patience is the mother of discretion."

We had descended a flight of steps to the railway platform, and continued our conversation while the train approached. It had stopped, but as I stepped forward, he caught my sleeve. We waited in silence while others boarded. Then Holmes gave my back a gentle pat and we strolled back towards the entrance to the underground. The train blew its whistle and started forward.

"Now, Watson! Sharp!" Holmes clawed open the door of the nearest car and shoved me from behind. I literally stumbled up the step. He leapt aboard and yanked the door shut behind him as the train picked up speed. Watching through the window, I caught my first glimpse of our followers running along the platform, shouting for the train to stop. The tall one wore a striped suit and bowler hat at a jaunty angle, his companion a lumpy worn woolen coat over dirty duck trousers.

"Could they be connected with another investigation?" I asked, once we'd found a seat.

"Doubtful." Holmes fished out his brier and dilapidated tobacco-pouch. "Unless Richard the Third has enemies whose blood is still hot enough to prevent me from clearing his name. Of late I've been involved with nothing that would interest so unscholarly looking a pair of scoundrels."

"Then we must fall back upon Lestrade's admonition by default. Now that we've thrown the dogs off the scent, will we double back to Poplar and warn Miss Venucci?"

"We'll wire Lestrade and press him to put a man on her door. That's a precaution only. If Mr. Billiards and Mr. Ten-Pin are associated with the Mafia, they must have followed her to your door, and received instructions to direct their attentions to us. Knowing or suspecting what she's about, they could have slain her any time prior, believing that dead women are no more likely to bear tales than dead men. The fact that she survived long enough to consult me suggests they'd rather avoid desperate measures until they're unavoidable. Now that she's spread her intelligence to us, she's relatively safe."

He got his pipe going, broke the match, and flipped it out the open window. "Now comes the test. Holmes and Watson are on the scent, raising the bar. Shall it be bribery, intimidation, or the simple act of murder?" He blew smoke into the locomotive exhaust streaming past the window and exposed his excellent teeth. "Observe, Watson; are not all your senses acutely alive at this moment? The smell of burning coal, the stations whirling past in a blaze of colour, the sound of your heart keeping time with the drive-rod? How I've missed it, the clear razor-edge between Mrs. Life and Mistress Death. When I think that cocaine could serve in its place"—he sat back, shaking his head and drawing smoke—"O, that I had the pen of a poet, that I may make others feel as I do at this moment!"

"*The Journals of Lewis and Clark*," I muttered.

"Elucidate."

"They were excerpted in *Harper's Weekly*, the American journal. You know how much I enjoy stories of adventure."

"In lieu of the real thing, yes."

"The explorers filled page after page with gleeful anticipation of their first encounter with a grizzly bear, about which they'd heard many fantastic stories."

"I sympathize."

"Weeks later, after a string of near-fatal encounters with that hellish creature, Clark wrote—I paraphrase—'We find that our curiosity has been satisfied as to the nature of this beast.' I fear, Holmes, that our own curiosity will be satisfied in short order."

This put him in a reflective humour. At length he rapped his pipe against the sill, emptying the dottle into the slipstream.

"A grizzly is not a man," said he, "but as there is an excellent specimen of *Ursus horribilis* in the British Museum, stuffed and mounted in threateningly erect position, but no less dead for it, I daresay I must make space in our dear old sitting-room for a specimen of *Mafiosus scaribilis*."

"Your Latin is execrable," I grumbled, "as is your healthy sense of caution."

"I muddle on nonetheless. The finest tenor of our time is performing *Pagliacci* tonight at Albert Hall. Be a good fellow and see if you can get us decent seats. I find that *Doctor* is nearly as effective in such circumstances as Minister of the Exchequer; probably more so, as everyone has some notion of just what services are performed by a physician."

CHAPTER V.

THE CLOWN FAILS TO LAUGH

At the time of our conversation aboard the Underground, I thought Holmes was playing the *dilettante* once again, diverting its serious course towards the trivial. I was to learn differently, when we made the personal acquaintance of the greatest tenor of his or any other generation.

I confess I am no fan of Grand Opera. When I prize myself into a stiff shirt and cummerbund, wedge a tile onto my head, and distribute gratuities from the overdressed doorman down to the fellow who directs me to my seat—which is clearly numbered and easily claimed without help—I'd sooner anticipate an audience with the king than suffer through hour upon hour of human hippopotami singing at the top of their lungs with a rapier transfixing their livers; but that may be the medical specialist in me, obstructing the necessary suspension of disbelief. It was worth all the bother to see Holmes in complete repose, dreamily weaving his slender fingers with the music as if he could feel the very notes with the tips. Apart from his hellish decades-long flirtation with the demon cocaine—relegated, I prayed, to the dead past—I never saw him so completely offered up on the altar of bliss.

The star player, I must admit, was superb. Even my limited knowledge of Italian could not obstruct the pathos of his clown who laughed outwardly while grieving inside. His tenor was as clear and clean as a silver bell ringing on a cloudless dawn. I say without shame that I cried during his aria, which brought to the surface all the pain I'd sought to inter with my dear wife Mary.

Holmes affected not to notice; and when we joined the house in rising to our feet at the curtain call, he leaned close and whispered in my ear: "The great man has agreed to meet us in his dressing-room. I spared his favourite prompter from a prison sentence in a matter too trivial to recount, and he hasn't forgotten the favor. When you've performed the same role a hundred times, it's useful to have a fellow who will prevent you from jumping from Act One to Act Three because some fool of a librettist repeated a cue. Surely you know the danger, Watson; most often it's the experienced swimmer who drowns, and the celebrated surgeon who stitches an overlooked pair of forceps inside an appendectomy patient. Familiarity breeds carelessness, if not precisely contempt."

I made no remark, even to question the invitation. My friend, who had refused an audience with an emperor, was scarcely the type to meet with an entertainer, even one he admired. How often had I heard him say, "The gifted are invariably disappointing upon acquaintance. They leave everything on the canvas, the stage, and the leaf. Why shatter the illusion by learning they perspire and belch like the rest of us?"

Working our way through the maestro's admirers reminded me of Afghanistan, and the press of bodies in retreat from the field of disaster, where my patients awaited aid. In this case, they were all in full charge; dowagers, stage-door Johnnies, critics from the provinces, and that class of female that attaches itself like a pilot fish to the latest and shiniest of shark and dolphin, pressed together in a humid horde. I was all for giving the thing up when the man at the door, a hulking presence in a suit of clothes that could have been made only to his measure—and that staked out as for a tent—broke into a wreath of smiles at sight of my companion.

"*Mis*ter Holmes! I heard you was killed."

"They were right every time," said my friend. "Is Himself in a position to receive visitors?"

"If he ain't, he can go looking for another'n to look after his best interests. I'll be with you directly."

Contemplating this freshly closed door, I said, "Is there anyone in this city you *don't* know?"

"None of social consequence, I must own. The gentry have bred themselves out of everything useful to my practice."

Presently the fellow opened the door. "He will see you for five minutes."

"Tell him he'll see me for as long as it takes or not at all."

The big man smiled. "I told him you'd say something like that." He swung the door all the way and stepped aside.

"Greasepaint!" said Holmes, breathing in the atmosphere. "Hold your breath, Watson, I implore you. It's a thousand times worse than lotus."

He hadn't exaggerated; although there was nothing in that heavy air to make me trade my stethoscope for a cap and bells. It was larded with turpentine, perspiration, and that combination of terror and exhilaration that accompanied every theatrical endeavour since Aristophanes. My friend, consummate amateur player that he was, was more affected. I'd always held that the theatre lost a Booth when criminal science gained a Holmes.

We followed the doorman through a narrow aromatic hall to a door upon which hung a gold-painted star. One rap, and we were in the presence of a short barrel of a man, wearing a paper bib over his white clown's tunic, scrubbing the makeup off his face with cold cream. Seated before a three-sided mirror, he was shorter than he'd appeared on stage, and a good deal fatter; but I was heartened to note that his speaking voice was as cultured as the one with which he sang on stage; indeed, every phrase fell as if it had been written by a composer and delivered for the benefit of the last row.

"*Mamma mia!* I have a stone in my stomach! Is there not a chef in England who can make a decent lasagna?"

"There is an excellent one in Deptford," said Holmes. "His establishment seats only five, and reservations must be made months in advance, but I've a hunch he'll make an exception in your case, if you'll pose with him for a photograph."

"Leave the name with Bruno at the door. You are the detective, yes?" He was watching our reflections in the mirror.

"And you are Enrico Caruso, the greatest singer in the world."

"*Sì.*"

"Take note, Watson. As you know, I regard false modesty as no better than an idle boast. I am here, *signor*, to discuss your experience with *Il Mano Negro*."

The tenor stopped his movements abruptly. The bare spots on his face were nearly as white as the makeup that remained. "*Dio mio*," he whispered, crossing himself. "Do not say that name so loud. I have paid them in Rome, in Naples, in Paris, and in New York City. I thought perhaps here I would be safe."

"Have they approached you in London?"

"Yes."

"What are the terms?"

"The amount varies; in New York it was nearly twice as much as in Rome, which was the highest. If I fail to pay—Splash! Acid in my face. These devils, they know one's greatest weakness. The face, it is the mask through which the notes are pushed. It would be the same as if my throat were slit."

"Have you been to the authorities?"

"I was warned against it. But what purpose would it serve? The police cannot be with me every hour of every day. Even were such a thing possible, it takes but a second to carry out the threat and flee. No one can be prepared for that. So I pay." He resumed sponging his face. "I wasn't aware that my predicament had been published."

"Nor am I, but very little of a criminal nature takes place anywhere without coming to my attention. I've come to you, *signor*, for any details you may provide."

"I'm at sea, Holmes," said I. "I thought we came to discuss the Mafia. What is *Il Mano Negro*?"

"Forgive me, Watson. Like many major concerns, the society has several branches. The one that specializes in extortion translates as the Black Hand."

CHAPTER VI.

THE BLACK HAND

"Not very subtle, these fellows," said Caruso. "The warning is always the same; someone bumps against me in a crowd, *i guardare*! I discover in a pocket a square of paper upon which someone has traced his own hand, filled it in with black ink, and written, '*Pagar o morir.*'"

"'Pay or die.' What they lack in finesse they make up for in brevity. No mention of acid?"

"That comes later, in the form of a telephone call to my home or hotel, the voice disguised as a whisper. I have changed my number six times, but they always seem to find it somehow. Is it any wonder I take the threat seriously?"

"Have you ever seen any of these men?"

"*Sí*, here. I had barely alighted from the ship in Southampton. The fellow who jostled me asked my pardon and vanished into the crowd, beside a companion. He spoke in a whisper. I thought nothing of it until I saw the note."

"Would you know them again?"

"But of course. The man who spoke was a squat, swarthy fellow, roughly dressed. His friend was tall and wore a striped suit."

"Have you paid on this occasion?"

"Not yet. I expect a call anytime with instructions. In the past, we have arranged for me to leave the money in a parcel at some public place. I am enjoined not to linger, and I have obeyed, as to see who retrieved it would surely mean my life, as that might lead to their apprehension and prosecution." He shrugged. "One cannot, after all, press charges against someone for bumping into one in a crowd."

"*Signor* Caruso," said Holmes, "I would be grateful if, when you have received that call, you would wire me the particulars at this address." He produced a card.

"I could not do that. I don't fear for myself, *capisce*? My conscience would not bear the result if you were to meet with disaster."

"We are old acquaintances, disaster and myself. And yet here I stand. Pray, fear not for me, as at any moment I might encounter an enemy from one of a hundred venues. I must insist," he pressed, when our host began to protest. "By this action, you may spare another soul anguish."

Caruso agreed, albeit reluctantly, and we took our leave, with thanks for his cooperation; but not before he gave us words of advice: "I entreat you, *signores*; if you ever receive a communication such as I have described, obey."

Holmes invited me to the quarters we once shared in Baker Street, where I made myself comfortable in my old armchair, whisky-and-soda in hand. He stood by the bow-window, smoking his clay.

"Progress, of a sort," said he. "We know our two-man entourage are with the Mafia, and that they've emigrated to England."

"What if Caruso reneges upon his promise? He was anything but certain."

He smiled at the window. "Finding them won't take much detecting skill. I'm looking at one of them right now."

I began to rise; but he made a slashing movement with one hand, blocking the gesture with his body. "Let us not give him a reason to repeat his vanishing act. Like a good pigeon, I've returned to my roost, where no doubt they came after losing our trail. Or at least one has; our friend the billiards player seems to be absent."

"Shall we give chase?"

"That would compound our chances of discovery by one hundred percent. Make yourself at home until I return, and please be good enough to get up from time to time and walk past the window. I'm recruiting you to take the place of the ingenious wax bust that led to Colonel Sebastian Moran's current circumstances. Mind you, Watson," he said gravely, "at all times present a moving target. We know not whether these gentlemen be messengers or angels of death."

He changed quickly from his *boulevardier* attire to a homely one of ear-flapped cap and inverness, his uniform of choice whenever he wished to blend into the cosmopolitan crowd of our sprawling metropolis, armed with his stout leaded Penang lawyer—and, doubtless, his trusty Eley revolver in its custom-reinforced pocket—and left without another word.

Holmes was gone three-quarters of an hour, and I should not look forward to another such interval. As advised, I left my seat from time to time, ostensibly to recharge my glass from the siphon, conquering the urge to look through the window. For a time, lighting a cigar, I attempted to involve myself in the day's edition of the *Times*, but I could not have provided a phrase of what I read, and finished my vigil in contemplation of the events of the day. But I'd learnt from bitter experience not to try to ape my friend's powers of deduction, as I could make neither head nor tail of precisely what they signified or where they would lead.

The Lestrade business had unsettled me. Journeyman detective that he was, unhindered by genius or imagination, he had never until now advised inaction in a criminal matter. What were our chances, mere *dilettantes*, when officialdom throws in its hand?

When I heard Holmes's characteristic tread upon the stair—taking the steps two at a bound, as if the laws regarding time and geography were a personal affront—I rose in time to see him burst through the door. His eyes were as bright as a bird's and his cheeks were in high colour.

"Whisky, Watson! It can hardly impair these faulty faculties. The devil must be part Cassandra, for no sooner had I sought shelter in a doorway from which I could observe his movements than he quit his post, and proceeded double-time towards the Baker Street Station, where he lost me in the crush. Several trains left in close succession, and I'll be bound if I knew which one he took, or if he scorned them all and departed by way of a pedestrian exit. It serves me well for underestimating him based upon his oafish attire. They're well trained, this lot; George Gordon might have drilled them before overstepping himself in Khartoum."

"Worse luck!" said I.

"Luck is the refuge of the incompetent. I'm less concerned with how he eluded me than with what became of his companion. For all I know he was shadowing me, even as I was shadowing the pin-setter. Such is the state into which this business has plunged me, to question my own skills in detecting whether I am pursuer or quarry." He flung himself into his basket-chair without pausing to doff his outerwear, and drank deeply from his glass.

"We still have Caruso. If indeed we have him."

"We must perforce hope. Mrs. Hudson met me at the door with Lestrade's reply to my telegram. I have at least his word that Miss Venucci will be under the protection of London's Finest. Say what you like about the turtle-like workings of a constable's mind, he's a regiment of fusiliers when it comes to protecting the innocent. In any case, I believe her to be safe from assault, if only because the Mafia's attentions have been redirected from her to us."

"Justice has one thing in its favor," I said, "apart from the diligence of the policeman on the pavement. It has Sherlock Holmes."

He smiled without mirth.

"And John H. Watson, let us not forget. I should not have asked anyone else in the universe to spend the hour you have just now." He fingered his glass. "What did you think of *Pagliacci*? I saw the maestro perform in Rome and Milan, and thought him a gift from Olympus; but I never saw a British audience so borne away by an artist as I saw tonight."

"It was diverting, though I prefer my clowns to be surrounded by a circus, with trained elephants, lion tamers, and a high-wire act."

"Patience, dear fellow. We may know all three before this account is closed."

CHAPTER VII.

THE DROP

I accepted Holmes's invitation to spend the night, and was heartened to learn that my old room had not been touched, except to provide a fresh razor, soap, and a dressing-gown that still bore the imprimatur of the finest tailor in Piccadilly. I slept well, having expended my reservations about our current endeavor during those forty-five minutes alone in the sitting-room; we'd retired late, and it was nearly eleven when I turned out. After a wash-up and shave, I was privileged to sit down to one of Mrs. Hudson's homely but hearty breakfasts, accompanied by the strongest coffee this side of Turkey. Holmes, as was his wont, had risen after only a few hours' rest and dined already. He slammed shut the hefty volume he'd been studying as I finished my kippers.

"I procured the book this morning from my favourite stall in the Strand," he said; "Yes, I've been out and about while you slept the sleep of the virtuous. It was published privately in Naples, and is quite a fine account of the history of the Mafia from ancient times to our own. The name is an acronym, derived from the slogan *Morte alla Francia Italia anela*, meaning 'Death to the French is Italy's cry,' and dates back some five centuries, to when the Medieval Angevins of France engaged in the oppression of that country. My Italian is rusty, but evidently the society considered itself too well established to disband after the Angevins abandoned the practice, so it turned—as warriors often will, once the object of their training in battle has become obsolete—to crime; specifically to wrest tribute from the landed gentry, and eventually to hire itself out as mercenaries upon its behalf. At this point it arrogated the methods of oppression for its own ends, victimizing peasants, who could only be expected to buy it off through tribute earned at the sweat of their brow."

"Appalling," said I, "but hardly shocking. Force will find its way, and it's usually the path of least resistance."

"Excellent reasoning. Interestingly, the Mafia is regarded in some rural provinces as an improvement upon the local authorities, who are either unqualified by their lack of experience to deal with certain criminals, or corrupted by bribery, to provide sufficient service and protection to the populace. In such cases—for a price, Watson, always for a price—the society offers security not only from itself, but from independent interlopers. If a rough or a footpad who is unaffiliated with the Order preys upon those who have paid for protection, he's dealt with summarily, and without the bother of a sluggish legal system. When Giovanni Public has a grievance, he applies to the local *don*, who sees to the matter without demanding further recompense: Unregulated brigandry represents a personal insult, and is dealt with."

"Machiavellian!"

"Just so; but it helps to explain how so unprincipled a culture has managed to survive throughout half a millennium. It's the difference between a privateer operating under an unofficial seal of approval and a common pirate. However, I'm more interested in a brief interview herein with a policeman of Italian birth, who's pledged his efforts to eradicate the Black Hand in America. That glorious republic has offered shelter to hordes of Italian immigrants, who are prime targets for the Mafia's methods of extortion. Even to apply for a lowly job paving the streets requires intervention by the neighbourhood *don*, who helps himself to a healthy portion of the wretches' wages in return for finding them employment."

"I despair of the race."

"This policeman does not. He's made it his personal responsibility to free it of this yoke. Giusseppe Petrosino is his name, and in his position as a detective in New York City, he appears to have learnt more about the Black Hand and its activities than anyone else, in the Old World as well as the new. He intrigues me. Were I more egocentric than I am, I'd suspect him of studying my own methods and applying them to an astounding degree. The tropical races, Watson, are capable of demonstrative emotion, but also of single-minded determination to set things right. He is unhampered by wife and family, and therefore in my own position of absolute devotion to his duty."

"I daresay he's no prospect for a life policy."

"That he has lived long enough to answer this author's queries indicates an extraordinary capacity for precaution. I quite like this fellow, based upon what I've read. He appears to know the dense quarter of New York City called Little Italy as well as I know London."

"Jealousy?" For I knew how to prick my friend's vanity.

"Call it admiration of a colleague." He scooped the bowl of his brier into the worn Persian slipper he used to store his tobacco. "Idle speculation, at this point. Let us see what our pet tenor has to contribute beyond dusty scholarship."

As it developed, we hadn't long to wait. Presently Mrs. Hudson tapped at our door, and was admitted bearing a silver tray upon which lay a telegram in its distinctive yellow envelope.

Holmes thanked her, and read it upon her withdrawal. "The tenor writes!" He compared his watch to the clock on the mantel. "Two minutes' variant. We still have half an hour to respond. More coffee?"

"Thank you, no. Two cups of this brew will keep me awake for a week."

"It may be needed. I'll fetch a cab while you dress. I regret your attire may be a bit formal, but we haven't time to visit your lodgings. The Royal Guard will upstage you in all events."

I knew better than to press Holmes in his pawkish mood; all would be revealed in the course of time. But as our cab neared Buckingham Palace, and we elected to walk the rest of the way as our path was blocked by pedestrian traffic, I heard the brump and crash of a military band, and knew that we were in for the daily Changing of the Guard at the king's palace.

Like most Londoners, I had come to regard the spectacle as a massive waste of the treasury. No serious attempt had been made upon the life of a British monarch since the assassination of Charles I, and the sight of tall young men in scarlet tunics and tall bearskin shakoes straddling prancing white steeds to the air of "God Save the King" embarrassed me somewhat, and made me think of better ways to spend the inland revenue, such as settling the Irish Question and bringing certain unscrupulous foreign publishers to task for violating authors' copyrights; in this last, I admit, I had a personal interest, with both the Americans and the Russians making free with my chronicles of Holmes's adventures, translated onto the page by the sweat of my brow.

However, when in the presence of the mighty revue, watching tourists from abroad craning their necks and snapping their Kodaks as those fine, straight-legged young men went about their business to precision, an Englishman would have to be made of stone not to feel his chest spreading with patriotic pride.

Holmes, however, was interested in things more prosaic.

"The Americans, in their superior idiom, refer to this exchange of cash for mercy as a 'drop.' Vulgar as it sounds, it's most descriptive. Pray you, put not your faith in princes or their pomp, and look to the mundane: a streetsweep or some such invisible menial, attending to his office with somewhat more zeal than the common. He may come away with more in his homely canvas sack than a cigar-stub."

He compared the face of his watch to the palace tower. "By now, friend Caruso has done his bit, placing a parcel inside that telephone box upon the corner. They proliferate; giving unintended succor to the extortionist. Clever of these fellows to choose this hour for the transaction. Who will notice so ordinary a thing in the presence of majesty?"

We chose a corner directly opposite the box, but it was a near enough thing with spectators shifting to and fro for a glimpse of the ceremony. Thrice at least I thought I saw our man creeping towards the "drop," and said as much to Holmes; but he was impatient with my report.

"If I understand this type, they won't creep, but march boldly to the prize, like any honest citizen simply wishing to use the facility for its intended purpose. Mark you," he said, gripping my sleeve; "speak of the devil, and he shall avail himself."

He was, as usual, right personified; for in that moment, the vagabond with varnish stains on his canvas trousers advanced to the box, hands sunk deep in his pockets and lips pursed, undoubtedly whistling some air from the concert halls. With a furtive look up and down and across the street, busy as it was with mounted grenadiers, he tugged open the door and ducked inside.

My heart races still when I recall that dash, passing as close as we did to those arrogant horses to feel their hot breath upon the back of my neck, and an uncharacteristic "Cor, blimey!" from a rider in the saddle as he drew rein to avoid running us down. Betimes I awake in the middle of the night to the shrill sound of a constable's whistle, seeking to stay us from our course. But Holmes would not be waylaid. He caught the fellow by the back of his collar just as he was quitting the telephone box.

"What is this?" The man's accent was heavily Mediterranean. "Let go me."

"I would see that parcel beneath your arm," said Holmes; "Failing that, you will see oblivion." He shook the heavy leaded head of his stick in the man's face.

The whistle blew again. I saw the constable making his way across the street, obstructed by the consistent traffic of well-groomed horses boarded by guardsman similarly well treated.

Holmes said, "The choice is yours: Surrender the parcel or yourself to the red-faced fellow in uniform."

"*Dio mio! Sì!*" He transferred the item, in brown paper wound with string, to Holmes's hands, and prepared to leave. But my friend's grip on his shoulder stayed him.

"Come away, and you will be safe from arrest. We seek information only."

"*Dio mio!*" said he again. "*Prego, signor*; anything but that!"

Holmes increased his grasp. The pin-setter (for I shall always think of him thus) struggled frantically, actually managing to free himself from his coarse overcoat, and sprinted away, weaving a path through the mass of spectators and leaving Holmes holding only his outer garment.

Whereupon the constable, panting and florid of face, accosted us. Before he could speak, Holmes said, "This gentleman demonstrates all the symptoms of accelerated circulation. Do you concur, Doctor?"

"I do indeed," I said, catching his meaning. "When was the last time you were examined by a physician?"

"If you please, sir—" He was too short of breath to press the point.

"My name is Dr. Watson. This is my friend, Sherlock Holmes. We have at times been of assistance to Scotland Yard. I implore you, sir, to consult your department physician at once. We can't have an officer of the public peace succumbing to apoplexy on the job."

We left the fellow pressing his fingers to his jugular. Holmes chuckled. "The underworld lost a fine pair of confidence men when we threw in with the law. How do you feel, Watson? Confess: You're experiencing that same rush of adrenaline that comes to those who have just performed well onstage."

"I shan't disagree. However, I don't wish to repeat the experience until I've checked my own circulation. How much did we get?" I added archly.

"A born thief, had you but the necessary disadvantages." We'd turned a corner into a deserted neighbourhood, although one well enough illuminated by gaslight to discourage the common purse-snatcher. He opened the parcel, thumbed through the notes inside, and emitted a low whistle. "A thousand pounds. Caruso must be doing well indeed, to be able to afford such a tribute. We must be discreet in the matter of returning it. No hint of welshing must adhere to him."

"You are the soul of discretion, Holmes. Congratulations upon a job well done."

He held up the coat the extortionist had left behind.

"Would that it *were* done. I'd pledge the same amount from my own small savings to have the man who belongs to this garment."

CHAPTER VIII.

THE PRICE OF FAILURE

"Good news, Holmes! We've nabbed the fellow."

Lestrade, in a better humour than I'd seen him in since the last time he thought he'd stolen a march on Sherlock Holmes, was smoking an uncommonly fine cigar in his office; that it was a gift from the chief inspector no detective need deduce. We'd been summoned there by messenger, the day after our adventure before the palace.

"You found my description helpful?" asked Holmes.

"That, and the garment you were so thoughtful to leave with us. We traced the laundry mark to a place in the Tottenham Court Road, and from there to the customer, who resided above a butcher's shop in Blackwall, square in the foreign quarter. Would you care to know his name?"

"Luigi Pizarro. I spoke with the laundryman on my way to the Yard with the overcoat. I had faith you'd apprehend him without my assistance."

"Your faith was well placed. He's in the cooling-room, assessing his chances. I find it helpful to let these fellows contemplate the error of their ways in private until they're ripe to pluck. Would you care to have a go? Being interviewed by a citizen with no authority sometimes yields encouraging results."

"I would, if Dr. Watson is allowed to accompany me and record our conversation."

"Consider him invited. Not long ago we lost a prosecution because the stenographer couldn't spell. I've read a thing or two of the doctor's in *The Strand*, and found nary a participle misplaced."

"I'm blessed with able editors," said I, not displeased by this praise, and somewhat surprised by his knowledge of the technicalities.

Holmes appeared to agree. "I have always said, Inspector, that the College of English at Oxford is much the worse for your decision to enforce justice."

"Yes; well." Lestrade seemed uneasy as to his intent. "We'll see that Mr. Caruso is reunited with his thousand quid. Quite the state of affairs when a canary can part with such a sum while those of us who put our lives on the line to see to his well-being make do on twenty a month."

"If only life were as fair as fiction; but if you heard this particular canary trilling, you might surrender the point."

"Likely not. Mrs. Lestrade says my ears are hammered from lead." He consulted his turnip watch. "Room B, second floor. Fifteen minutes?"

"Ample."

The chamber was furnished with only a yellow-oak table upon which many initials had been carved and three straight chairs. A framed print of our late queen, still wreathed in black crepe, provided the sole decoration.

"A fine portrait," said Holmes. "I met the lady in the flesh, and observed that same obsidian gaze, overseeing an empire four times greater than Alexander's. *Parla inglese?*"

"Better, Guv'nor, than I warrant you speak *Italiano*." Our charge, sitting hunched at the table with his hands resting palms-down on the top, kept his gaze on his thick and broken nails. Deprived of his bulky coat, he was slight, wearing a dirty shirt without a collar and a silver crucifix winking at his throat. His speech was Cockney, with a decided foreign accent.

"I concur. I've never grasped just where to place the verb, and imagine I must sound to a native like a street merchant newly arrived from Milan extolling his wares to the passersby. You remember me, I think."

"*Sí.* I miss my overcoat. Your London winters are misery."

"It's safe, and will be returned to you; not that you'll be in a position to enjoy the outdoors for a season. Who directed your efforts?"

"Myself. When I see one of my own countrymen pulling down by the week more than my father made laying brick in his lifetime, I give myself virtuous airs."

"Humbug." Whereupon Holmes launched into an extended soliloquy in Italian so rapid I could not hope to capture it in my notebook even phonetically. I have but two languages, if you regard my pidgin understanding of the Afghani tongue among them, but I had the distinct impression he spoke the wretch's native *lingua* as one to the manner born.

Pizarro's reaction bore me out; his swarthy features assumed an expression equal parts astonished and terrified. It's no small thing, once one assumes a kind of immunity based upon his own encoded speech, to find that his interrogator is wise to its every *nuance*. He crossed himself, muttered something I could not catch, in whatever language it was couched, and met Holmes's gaze for the first time.

"*Scusamenti, signor.* If I was to answer your questions, my life wouldn't be worth a penny-farthing."

"The Yard can protect you. These walls have never been breached. The charge as it stands against you is a trifle; we seek bigger game, and a word in that direction will make you a witness rather than a defendant, entitled to the full force of the Metropolitan Police in your preservation."

Holmes, seated across from him, leaned forward, seizing his left wrist. He tugged it free of its cuff, exposing a crude tattoo etched in blue ink: OMERTA.

"A foolish oath, *signor*; etched recently. I know something of body art, and the time it takes for the scab to fall away; I've written upon the subject for publication. Your responsibility to the human race goes back generations. Surely the latter must claim precedence over a wop with a dirty needle."

This hideous reference to the man's heritage I found repugnant, and hesitated an instant before I set it down on paper. It was a gambit: Holmes's only prejudice was directed against those who violated the laws of man and nature. He sought through crudity to draw the man out.

"*Diavolo!*" Pizarro wrenched his wrist from Holmes's grasp. He entwined the fingers of both hands in a wringing movement. Beads of sweat glittered on his forehead. "It's death, I say! Do you really think your cumbersome machinery of justice is any defence against the stiletto, *la pistola*, the garrote? Men more prominent than Caruso have been slain in broad daylight, in a public place, and the *politziotto* made base clowns of in chasing the assassins. You British are children when it comes to *Il Mano Negro*! Take me to my cell, and to the devil with your promises! Life in prison is life, at least. There is no appeal from eternity."

Lestrade was waiting for us, hands in pockets, when we emerged. He was detective enough to read the result upon our faces. "A stone, what? These dregs will put their self-styled honour before their own self-interest. Daft."

"He was frightened," said Holmes. "Anyone can be, under circumstances far less pressing. How long can you keep him in custody?"

"Not long. There's no crime in possessing a large sum of money; although with the singer's testimony we may prosecute him for extortion."

"I doubt Caruso will oblige. He hasn't the advantage of our system, and will in all likelihood consider himself fortunate to have gotten off so cheaply, without inviting further mayhem from his predators. He may even forfeit the return of his money, lest it invite another attempt, and one more costly given the extra trouble. Merely informing us of the details of the 'drop' was out of character."

"Then Pizarro will be free in twenty-four hours."

"Pray, Lestrade, keep him a bit longer. Vagrancy is out of the question, given the sum of money he possessed; it may develop that you're forced to return it to him, with an apology for detaining him."

"I'd sooner resign my position. The legality of his residency may be an issue we can turn to our advantage. The Home Secretary may elect to deport him."

"Knowing the tortoise nature of our government system, I'd venture to say *Signor* Pizarro will be the ward of the state a fortnight at least. That should give his superiors pause; has he peached? Is he being held as a material witness? He must be aware these questions will be asked. Another interview in a day or so may yield a better harvest."

Lestrade studied him. "You're cold as ice, Holmes, when push comes to shove. He'll suffer hell's own torment in twenty-four hours."

"I cannot disagree. It may be I'm responsible for it, but I can't say that I'll lose a moment's sleep over the matter. *Signor* Caruso may cough up the sum of two years' wages for the common man without complaint, but I shouldn't wish to ask the common man his opinion on the situation were it turned his way. For him, a shilling is so big he can scarcely see round it.

"Twenty-four hours, Lestrade," said he, tugging on his cap. "The Crown is kinder to its detainees than anywhere else on earth, but I can think of no worse penalty than to leave a dishonest man alone with his thoughts."

In this, for once, Sherlock Holmes was naive; but even he could not foresee every event.

I slept in my old room that night, at Holmes's invitation; it was closer to Scotland Yard than my present arrangements, and I tired more easily than in earlier days of our adventurous partnership.

How long I slept I know not; it was still dark when Holmes shook me by the shoulder. He was dressed for the street, and his face was pale as death. "Disaster, Watson. Dress quickly. I'll explain on the way."

Fifteen minutes later, unshaven and wearing yesterday's soiled and wrinkled clothes, I listened to my companion's account. He'd received a curt wire from Lestrade, who'd been knocked out of bed himself by news from Scotland Yard.

"Pizarro is dead. The gaol-keepers insist he hanged himself in his cell, using his own trousers, but I'm unsatisfied. That a man who only a few hours ago so feared death he'd sooner face prison than answer our questions should suddenly decide to take his own life, flies squarely in the face of my reading of human nature."

"No man can know for certain what's in another man's heart," I said. "You can't blame yourself."

"Whom else, if not me? Faster, man!" He thumped the roof of the hansom with his stick. A whip cracked and the horse broke into a canter.

Soon we found ourselves in Bow Street, home of the police-court and of much of the history of law enforcement in our ancient city. Lestrade met us within, looking every bit as ill-groomed as I, and conducted us down a whitewashed corridor to one of a series of reinforced oaken doors with iron gratings set into them through which the prisoners could be monitored. A lantern had been left burning in the cell, and I saw the man's shadow before I saw him, dangling with legs obscenely bared from his makeshift noose. His eyes bulged sightlessly and his mouth was agape.

"Normally in such cases we cut them down immediately, in case a spark of life remains; but it didn't take a degree in medicine for the keeper to determine our guest could trim the place for a year as well as a minute, and the result would not be different."

I concurred; for in the flickering light the fellow's face was as wine-dark as Homer's sea. I examined his fingernails. They were a shade of purple that quite settled the question.

"Thank the fellow for me, Lestrade," said Holmes. "It's a rare civil servant who respects the scene *in situ*."

"Surely the only foul play is the hiding the Yard will take from the press. When a man commits suicide in custody, that event is as predictable as Tuesday."

"Let us leave the cart and horse where they are at present, Inspector."

Holmes extracted from the folds of his caped overcoat a bull's-eye lantern, and adjusted the louvers until the shaft fell full upon the hideous countenance of the dead man. It lingered there but briefly, then shifted round the cell, stopping at last with a self-satisfied intake of air on the detective's part. "What do you make of it, Watson? Inmates have been known to decorate their bleak surroundings in an effort to cheer them up, but this particular ornament may be unique."

I stepped close to the masonry wall, studying the object upon which the shaft of light fell, fixed to the mortar between the stones by means of a square nail driven through it. It was horseshoe-shaped. "It appears to be a scrap of leather; the end of a belt?"

"Use this." He handed me his pocket lens in its leather sheaf.

I unfolded it and scrutinized the object through the powerful glass. "Good Lord," I whispered, lowering the lens. "It's a human tongue. Dried and puckered from its exposure to the air, but a tongue just the same."

"I thought as much. A man's trousers do not serve the same merciful purpose as a hangman's coils, which snap the third cervical vertebra immediately, causing instantaneous death—more or less. This poor devil strangled. In such cases, the tongue swells and protrudes between the lips, but I observed at once that while the mouth was wide open, that appendage had not made its appearance. It must be somewhere, said I to myself, and so it is. What do you think of your suicide theory now, Lestrade?"

"Blown, like my recent promotion. I shall consider myself fortunate to rattle doorknobs in Whitechapel when this gets out. Murder, certainly; but what can it mean to cut out a man's tongue and nail it to a wall?"

"It means my disgrace, as surely as yours. I thought detaining Pizarro would force him to reconsider his silence, lest his comrades suspect him of informing against the society; that they would act so swiftly to prevent him was an alternative I didn't foresee. It's a message, Lestrade: To talk is to die, and the symbolic amputation of the chief instrument of speech removes all ambiguity."

"I shall issue a warrant for the arrest of the man in the striped suit. Either he did this thing, or he knows who was responsible. Simultaneously I shall authorise a complete investigation into the characters of the personnel who oversee these cells. That door wasn't forced; whoever opened it had a key, and we don't leave them around like candy in a dish. Money changed hands, depend upon it."

Holmes lowered the lantern, returning the cell to its murky twilight. "I'm sorry, Lestrade. For what it's worth, I'll welcome whatever onus you may shift to me."

The inspector shrugged. "It's just as well. The closer one gets to chief inspector, the greater the likelihood of unemployment next time the government changes. Perhaps my past record will allow me to return to my old duties. Give me my passion-killers and second-story men, and the Empire can assign the right good profile of the Metropolitan Police to the politicians."

"A good fellow," said Holmes, as we drove away from that grim scene. "I beg you, Watson, if your works are ever collected, to edit out certain disparaging remarks I've made in regard to that capital man."

"What now?"

"I shall leave Mr. Billiards to Lestrade; whether he was the instrument of Pizarro's death, or merely the messenger, the lesson itself will make him a vault of secrets, lest it be repeated." He brightened. "What say you to a voyage abroad? Will your practice survive a holiday of a month or so?"

"My practice has shrunk to old men with lumbago and old ladies with the vapors; whatever they are. They'll be there when I return. I've always wanted to visit Italy. The pope is a sight to see, they say, upon his balcony, and the Swiss Guards nearly the equal of Coldstream."

"Perhaps you shall, although not this season. I speak of a pilgrimage to New York City, and an audience, not with the pontiff, but with Detective Giusseppe Petrosino, who has dedicated himself to the eradication of the Mafia, and knows them as a hunter knows his prey. Pack pullovers," he added. "I'm told the winds off the harbour blow cold as Valley Forge through those corridors of brownstone."

CHAPTER IX.

LITTLE ITALY

On the morning of our departure we met upon the dock. Holmes smiled at my luggage.

"Two trunks," said he, "and I recall when you travelled with only a razor and a fresh collar."

"Both optional, back then." For I was in a bright mood, and would not be needled. In the excitement of packing I had realised how much I'd missed the hurly-burly of shucking off months of inaction and taking to the high seas as on a whim. "Do not fear that I've become a clothes horse. I stuffed the second trunk with authors I've been meaning to catch up on: Stevenson, Clark Russell, Conrad, Jack London, the American writer. Is that *all* your gear?" I nodded towards his carpetbag.

"The clothes I'm wearing, tweeds for warmth, a dinner jacket, and sundries." Items shifted heavily inside when he hefted the bag. I knew them well: brass knuckles, a cosh, his revolver—the "sundries" he'd mentioned.

"No reading material? Won't you be bored?"

"I place my trust in the mortal equation. Six hundred souls living in close proximity for a fortnight will provide entertainment for an ageing detective, or the race is lost irretrievably."

Without going into detail, I shall report that he was proven right our first day out, when a number of our fellow passengers complained to the crew that their staterooms had been entered in their absence and certain items removed: a wooden comb, two small sewing kits, a battered pewter flask, and a tobacco pouch. It was but the work of two days to connect the pilferage of these varied and relatively worthless items to a pet marmoset belonging to the assistant purser, who had adopted the monkey during a stopover in Brazil and was unaware of what the animal was about while he was engaged in his duties. Objects and their owners were reunited and little Mono was placed in Holmes's temporary custody at his request, "for observation." By the time we passed the grand lady holding a torch in the harbour, he'd drafted a monograph concerning the difference between willing thievery and innocent curiosity in our fellow primates.

"*Signor* Holmes! Welcome to America!"

No sooner had we reclaimed our luggage than a sturdy party in brass buttons and a peaked cap ploughed his way through the passengers and well-wishers on the dock. He was clean-shaven, with a broad square face and a gold shield pinned to his breast.

But before he could reach us, a group of men in long overcoats in need of brushing and bowler hats touched up with bootblack intercepted him, charging our way with pencils and notebooks in hand. Holmes looked pained. "The American press. Aggressive fellows. I fear we're in for a proper grilling."

We were saved, however, when a whistle shrilled and what seemed a regiment of men in uniforms similar to the first man's double-timed their way across the dock, shoving aside the crowd and inserting themselves between us and the gang of journalists. A chorus of middle western twangs, Irish brogues, and pidgin English assailed them as the officers sent them into retreat with wooden bludgeons prominent.

"Lieutenant Joe Petrosino, sirs, at your service." The first man pumped Holmes's hand and then mine, using a two-handed grip I still feel in my wrist and fingers when the weather is damp.

Holmes saw me wince. "Be grateful, Watson. Imagine how it must feel when those fingers grip a miscreant's shoulder in the middle of his crime. I cabled the lieutenant from aboard ship, and was pleased to receive a positive response. I hardly thought you would take the trouble to greet us," he told Petrosino, "much less throw yourself between us and our interrogators. And in the full array of your office."

The Italian's smile was abashed. "I haven't had it on since Columbus Day. These fellows are the salt of the earth, but I knew they could not resist an interview with the great Sherlock Holmes come hell or high water, short of a show of force on my part. Have you arranged accommodations?"

"The Brevoort Hotel. If we may prevail upon your hospitality even more, we'd be grateful if you would send on our bags and take us to your office straightaway."

"Splendid! I, too, cannot wait to confer with you."

Petrosino made the necessary arrangements with a porter—paying him despite our protests—and led us to a black contraption with red trim that resembled a London growler, albeit with four pneumatic tyres and no team in sight. "You know the motorcar, certainly," he said.

"I've yet to experience one at firsthand. Still feeling adventurous, Watson?"

"Don't bother looking round for me, Holmes. I'll be there." I could not wait to climb aboard.

Petrosino cranked the machine into sputtering life and we squeezed in beside him on the stiff leather upholstery. Our contraption appeared to attract little attention from passersby; plainly, the citizens of the New World had accepted the presence of horseless carriages in their midst as a rite of Yankee passage. Our pilot depressed a pedal, pulled a handle, and soon we were whirring along the macadam at a dizzying 24 kilometres an hour, all of us holding on to our hats.

"It belongs to the chief," Petrosino shouted above the chugging motor. "When I told him the great Sherlock Holmes was coming to consult the department, he insisted you be greeted in style. I talked him out of sending along a brass band. That would have attracted every reporter in five boroughs. He is a good enough fellow, but no policeman."

I was astonished at the number of motor vehicles we passed: touring cars nearly as long as omnibuses, lorries stacked with cargo, and two-wheelers operated by men in dusters and goggles growled, grumbled, and clanked between the kerbs, exciting little interest from pedestrians or horses. Holmes, of course, followed the path of my thoughts.

"This century will belong to America. One can only hope that Great Britain will cede it with grace."

We crossed a dozen squares in a short space of time, passing, it seemed, through as many countries, identified by shop signs in Chinese, Cyrillic, Hebrew, Spanish, German, and finally Italian, coming to a stop before a squat building erected of unprepossessing sandstone, with electric globes flanking the entrance, each marked POLICE.

"It is even uglier inside," said Petrosino, "but it has the advantage of being too far from City Hall for the politicians to visit."

When we alighted, he summoned two officers who were smoking on the front steps to guard the automobile. "It is Little Italy, after all," he confided to us, "and while most of my compatriots are honest and decent, one cannot expect the overworked customs officers on Ellis Island to filter out all the undesirables."

As we accompanied him up the steps, a sharp crack rang out. Instinctively, the lieutenant slapped at the revolver in a holster on his belt; but as he wheeled in the direction of the noise, a lorry loaded heavily with what appeared to be kegs of beer thundered past, expectorating a ball of black smoke from a pipe mounted at the rear with an ear-splitting report. Petrosino chuckled and scabbarded his weapon.

"In time, I suppose, we will be so accustomed to backfires we will be able to distinguish between them and gunshots."

Holmes and I withdrew our hands from the pockets containing our own firearms. "Yet another theme for a monograph," said he. "Our brave new world threatens to turn me into a full-time scholar."

The interior, railed and wainscoted in oak, smelled of cigars, chewing tobacco, and furniture oil. A brass cuspidor greeted us on all three landings and lined the narrow dim corridor that led to a door with LT. J. PETROSINO lettered on pebbled glass. He unlocked it and led us into a corner room with windows overlooking his domain to the south and west. It contained a battered desk, four wooden chairs, a telephone box mounted upon one wall, and framed portraits of various dignitaries, including the American President Roosevelt and a fierce-looking fellow in a foreign uniform. Holmes nodded towards the last.

"An excellent likeness. I met *Generale* Garibaldi in Victor Emmanuel's court while hiking across the Continent. Before your time, Watson."

"At last I know where you learnt to speak Italian."

"I envy you," said Petrosino. "Garibaldi is a god in this neighbour-hood. Welcome to the Italian Squad, gentlemen. This is the oldest precinct house in Manhattan. When the squad was formed, I was offered a modern office at headquarters, but—"

"Politicians," Holmes finished. "They're the same all over. I turned down a knighthood for fear it would lead to an earldom and the House of Lords."

Someone knocked on the door. Petrosino barked an invitation. A bull-necked man with stripes on his uniform sleeves asked if anything was needed. The lieutenant looked at us. "Refreshment?"

We declined, with thanks. Petrosino dismissed the man, waved towards the chairs, and seated himself behind the desk. Instantly he ceased to look like an immigrant in uniform. His genial expression became stern with authority.

"And now, my friends, I beseech you to abandon your plans to stop at the Brevoort."

"We were told it's one of the best hotels in the city," I said.

"It is fine, very fine. However, I assume you made arrangements by cable, which involved two telegraphers at least, a messenger, and any number of hotel personnel. That is a small army of strangers who know where you can be found."

"The danger is that profound?" Holmes asked.

"Perhaps not. But the object of your investigation has large ears and long arms. Its pockets are deep and its methods of intimidation are infamous, especially in Little Italy. As your host, I must offer what advice I can to ensure your safety during your stay in my adopted country."

"Good Lord!" said I. "You make the Mafia sound like a criminal East India Company."

Petrosino put his finger to his lips. "It's best not to invoke the devil's name in his own backyard. No, it is not so large as that. An organisation extending across many nations must call attention to itself, and invite scrutiny. This one is feudal in nature, consisting of small groups, each commanded by the local *don*. The level of cooperation that exists among them is unique in the underworld: Uncle Umberto in Messina sends a cable to Cousin Giovanni in Brooklyn, and *poof*! Brother Carlo is discovered floating in the East River with his throat cut and his *salsiccia* stuffed in his mouth." He smiled suddenly, showing perfect white teeth. "You must agree that would be a most inhospitable act in the present circumstances, and a source of division between the British Empire and the United States."

Holmes lit a cigarette. "Ingenious and simple. The local authorities cannot hope to apprehend Umberto; in most cases they are unaware he exists. The best they can hope for is to track down the man who put Carlo in the river."

"Even that event is rare. *Omerta* is a shield as well as a sword."

CHAPTER X.

CROWN OF THORNS

"Where do you recommend we put up?" Holmes asked. "Mind you, we're easily pleased. Watson is an old campaigner, and I've spent as much as a month in places where the landlords thought clean linen was a myth spread by the *bourgeoisie*."

"Then you'll be pleased. Constance L'Azour operates a boarding house in Greenwich Village in which I would not hesitate to place my sainted mother. She will not thank you to address her as *Madame*. The house was a notorious brothel in its day, and she one of the most successful managers in the city. Since finding the Lord, she's become quite respectable. It's convenient to this precinct, and as the denizens of the neighbourhood are artists by and large, none will think it strange that a pair of visitors from London should reside there. I shall be glad to take you there when this meeting is finished."

"That won't be necessary. I spent part of our voyage studying recent maps of all the boroughs. I look forward to testing my education."

Petrosino frowned.

"It is old New Amsterdam, and laid out at random, not like our orderly blocks to the north. I have informed you of the potential dangers. I should not enjoy investigating your murders should you wander down some blind alley with death at the end."

"We'd be of scant use to you if we spent our stay avoiding phantom hazards. We cut our teeth, as you Americans say, on Whitechapel and Spitalfields, where I daresay some of your worst element would pause to navigate without a regiment of assassins in tow."

"As you wish. You are armed?"

"We are."

The lieutenant unshipped a pewter watch from inside his tunic and studied the face. "You will want to rest after your journey. I shall see personally that your bags are transferred from the Brevoort, taking all necessary precautions."

He put away the timepiece and leaned forward, lacing his blunt fingers on the desk.

"Take care, I pray you. I have dedicated myself to erase this foul stain upon my heritage, but there are others who would act as vigorously to maintain it. Wop, dago, guinea, ginzo, spaghetti-bender, greaseball; you are aware of these filthy names?"

"Tragically, yes," said Holmes. "The Irish are similarly wronged."

"And yet the Irish are white, and only a prime ass would object to one's existence in principle. You have heard, perhaps, that the Eskimos in Alaska have some fifty words for 'snow'?"

"I've heard there are twenty."

"A hundred, here," I interjected.

"Less than all of those, I should wager. But whatever the true number, I would bet as much that they are not as many as there are intolerable names for my people. Every day this scum remains at large to prey upon the innocent ensures their proliferation. Our ancestors conquered the known world, invented running water, paved roads, and the democratic system that furnishes the spine of the American Experiment. A thousand years were spent in the effort. It has been the work of but ten on the part of these *furfantes* to brand us as villains: lazy, shiftless, utterly unworthy of trust. I would gladly surrender my life if it meant their destruction.

"It is five o'clock," Petrosino said. "Shall we meet here at eight o'clock tomorrow morning, and plot our course?"

"We shall be here upon the stroke." Holmes stood and thrust his hand across the desk.

The lieutenant, standing, accepted it. I could see by his reaction that the detective's grip was the equal of his own. "*Dottore?*" said he, disengaging and pushing his hand my direction.

I accepted it with reluctance, pushing my fingers deep into his palm to avoid further injury. Coming away, I fervently hoped that

Mrs. L'Azour's establishment provided plenty of hot water to soak out the ache.

Greenwich Village was as complex an arrangement of streets and ancient buildings as advertised, with street artists hawking their daubs on every corner and an industrious Levantine creating a remarkably faithful rendition of *The Last Supper* on the pavement in coloured chalk. Gaggles of immodestly dressed young women passed us, chattering about theatrical engagements and appointments to model for what I assumed were tableaus even less acceptable to Victorian eyes. It was a dizzying quarter, worse than our own Soho, but Holmes led us deftly past bewildering street signs to our destination without so much as pausing to consult one of the maps I knew he carried upon his person.

I confess that I spent that excursion with one hand gripping my old service revolver in its pocket. Joe Petrosino had impressed me as a serious man, not given to melodrama. Every suspicious passerby—and there were many, some attired inconsistently in opera capes and ladies' picture hats, others shuffling along with eyes on the ground and hands thrust deep in the pockets of overcoats in deplorable condition, muttering to themselves; still others dressed in striped suits like our billiards-loving friend in London, straw boaters tipped at arrogant angles and swinging bamboo canes that could double easily as singlesticks—set my fingers to cramping on my weapon of self-defence.

Holmes, needless to say, traversed the whole way with bright eyes taking in the scenery, whistling some public-house tune, seemingly unawares. I, who knew him as well as anyone could make that claim, suspected he was acting the part of the staked goat. I really think he was disappointed when we arrived at the aforementioned boarding house without event.

The landlady proved to be a wiry woman not a centimetre above five feet, with her hair in a bun, a simple frock that reached to her ankles, and a man's stout leather slippers on her rather large feet. A ponderous brass crucifix hung upon her bosom from a chain round her neck. She'd been forewarned of our arrival, and showed us immediately to what she called a "second-floor" room (first, in the British tradition of medieval castles where the ground floor was given over to livestock).

It was pleasant in appearance, bearing out the spotlessness of the foyer and staircase, with twin beds on brass steads done up in cheery quilts and goosedown pillows, a writing desk, two upholstered chairs, pictures in gilt frames, and a bright window, which overlooked a neighbourhood of bookshops, bicycle-repair emporia, and a Queen Anne house advertising piano lessons in the ground-floor window.

"Two dollars the week," said she, chin outthrust, as if we might argue the amount. "Over St. Patrick's my rates go to six."

"Ah, yes; the annual bacchanal." Holmes pressed upon her a ten-pound note. "We may keep odd hours. I hope this will compensate for the inconvenience."

She snapped the note between her hands, held it up to the light, grunted. "Seeing's how you're gentlemen—I've an eye, sirs, it's served me in good stead these forty years—Agreed." Her brow creased. "You're not—?" She waggled a hand, a gesture that brought heat to my cheeks.

"Anarchists?" finished Holmes, with a playful expression. "Rest assured, I'm a bachelor in every meaning of the term, and my friend a widower, who wears the conquests of three continents upon his belt."

She appeared unsatisfied; but shrugged her bony shoulders. "Petrosino says you're all right, which is good enough for now. Will you be dining downstairs? Fifty cents' extra, the week, if you take your meals in this room."

"Neither, I fancy. We're pilgrims to this country, eager to sample all its wares."

She left us. When her tread retreated upon the stairs, Holmes and I looked at each other and laughed, with the abandon of schoolchildren left suddenly alone.

"Trust a reformed sinner to see to the niceties," he said, when we'd exhausted ourselves. "Mark you that picture. I await your judgment."

There were two: a steelpoint engraving of Washington crossing the Delaware and a portrait of Christ wearing His crown of thorns, which when one altered his angle of view appeared to be crying animated tears. I had no doubt that this was the picture Holmes had inquired about.

"I try not to judge the devout," said I, "but I find it disconcerting."

"Interesting, at the least. It's a photograph, whose model closely resembles the images in Renaissance paintings. The crying effect is quite clever. I think of—"

"Writing a monograph," I finished. "Your *oeuvre* threatens to rival Dickens's."

"Just so. But I was about to say, 'building a dark room.' Think of it, Watson! A library of photographic portraits of known felons in every police station. The late Allan Pinkerton—America again—initiated the concept, but it's been slow to catch on. That the victim of a crime might identify his assailant from an album might just render my profession obsolete; however, it's the aim of the true scientist to make himself redundant."

Curiosity got the better of me. "I would know more about this hiking trip across Europe. It's out of character for a man who scorns exercise for its own sake."

"But it was not. I accumulated a vast variety of data on the apaches of Paris, the pirates of Barcelona, and the Turkish janissaries. No student ever took out a more educational year from the university."

He paused then to draw in a lungful of air.

"Do you not smell it, Watson?"

"Cabbage. It seems to be the Yorkshire Pudding of America, if New York is any example."

"Philistine! I refer to the clear clean air of intrigue. The nation veritably reeks of it."

"It reeks, I'll give you that." Whereupon I strode to the window and wrenched it open. At that moment, a report sounded from outside. "It will take me some time to adjust to these devilish backfires."

"More than you may think, Watson. Step clear of the window!"

The admonition was twice effective for the pain in Holmes's voice. I whirled from the pane, and in so doing saw him leaning against the wall opposite, gripping his left upper arm. Blood seeped between his fingers.

CHAPTER XI.

LUNGO

"The curtain, Watson!"

I'd started towards Holmes; the look of alarm upon his face halted me. I flung the curtain crosswise of the window, obscuring any outside view of the room, and raced to him. In a trice I tore his sleeve from its seam and examined the wound. With a contrite glance towards weeping Jesus, I saw that it was but a graze. The bullet—for I was sure of the instrument—had slashed through flesh only; but the cut was deep. I leapt to my medical bag, which I'd had the ingrained good sense to keep separate from my trunks. It was the work of a few moments to disinfect the wound with alcohol and staunch the bleeding with gauze long enough to bind it.

I'd helped him to a chair, but it took all my strength to keep him from springing up from his seat. "I'm the master here," I told him sternly. "If you won't take rest, I'll have Mrs. L'Azour call for an ambulance, and you can impress the doctors with your deductions."

"You're a tyrant. I don't envy your patients. However, our man is long gone, if I give him the compliment due someone who can ambush me. Find the bullet, Watson."

If I may boast, I'd spent enough time in close proximity with death to have learnt the procedure. In short order, calculating Holmes's position at the time of the shooting, I found the rupture in the plaster of the wall a few centimetres from the spot where he'd been standing. It was the work of a minute to extract the lump of lead with my pocket-knife and place it in my patient's outstretched hand. He held it up.

"Thirty-eight caliber, I should judge. The copper jacket suggests it was fired by one of the new semi-automatics, such as the Spanish used in Cuba. Gas-fired, Watson; as if the agents of death weren't fast enough by way of the dependable old bolt-action rifle. A sniper's weapon. You'll remember Colonel Sebastian Moran, and his speciality in delivering death at long range."

"You can rule him out, at least," said I. "He's buried in Stranger's Field, with a broken neck his last trophy."

"I saw a telephone in the foyer. Be good enough to call Lieutenant Petrosino and inform him of this latest event."

"After I call the local hospital."

"Posh. I did worse to myself vaulting a barbed-wire fence in Wyoming Territory."

"When were you in Wyoming?"

He looked rueful. "I'm guilty of not giving you a complete account of my travels after the Reichenbach business. Tibet wears on one after a season. I found the range wars in the American West more interesting than the wisdom of Asia; for one thing, I learnt how to braid a lasso from horsehair, which may come in handy someday, although I know not how. Come, come! This bears no comparison to your wounding in Afghanistan."

"You'll promise me to remain quiet whilst I place the call? No working up a disguise from the bedspread and the coconut mat outside the door and gallivanting through Greenwich?"

He smiled abashedly. "I confess I took notice of that mat, with something of the order in mind, should the need arise. However, I'm allergic to coconut. Call our friend. I'll be here when you return, fortifying myself with the medicinal brandy in your medical bag."

"However did you know—?" I started. But I knew better than to press the point. I went downstairs, cranked the instrument in the foyer, and asked the operator to connect me with the Italian Squad.

Lieutenant Petrosino appeared within the hour, looking equal parts concerned and vindicated. "Did I not warn you, Mr. Holmes?"

"About the vicissitudes of the local geography," said my friend, stretched out in his dressing gown upon one of the brass beds; my trunks and his carpetbag had arrived in the interim. "You said nothing about opening a window; although I concur that was careless, given our situation. But let us not waste time assigning blame. You have the bullet; can you, with your ingenious American methods, trace it to its source?"

"Alas, I cannot, although my instincts tell me that a projectile should be traced as certainly to its source as a type-written letter to the typewriter." He smiled at Holmes's raised brows. "Yes, I have read your monograph upon that subject, along with many more. I have a standing order with all the publishers upon our two continents for anything new regarding criminal science. I have men searching the upper stories and rooftops of buildings opposite this one. Our bird will have flown, but someone may have seen something."

"Surely you can narrow down the list of assassins who elect to dispatch their victims at long range. I noted immediately upon taking possession of this room that the nearest point of vantage is two hundred metres."

"There are three." Petrosino seated himself in an armchair, placing his cap on the floor. He had a splendid head of black hair, streaked here and there with grey; as I judged him years shy of forty, I thought them earned through experience rather than time. "One, a veteran of the war in Cuba, is in a prison infirmary, dying of malaria contracted during his service in Santiago; he was an anarchist, who shot at an alderman and hit a dentist by mistake. The second, a lunatic with an inbred talent for marksmanship, died of a heart attack before he could carry out his threat to slay his estranged wife and her lover. His wild threats were discovered in a diary he kept. He shut down the shooting range in the carnival on Coney Island. The third—ah, *Dio!* He may be but a myth."

"Enlighten me," said Holmes. "There is no story more true than the apocryphal."

Petrosino shrugged; a purely southern Continental gesture, not to be duplicated by one of any other origin.

"I should not waste your time. *Lungo* is the name he's been given; it is the Italian for 'length.' It's said he shot to death the favourite candidate for the presidency of Macedonia whilst he was delivering a speech upon a platform, at a range of six hundred metres. Certainly the fellow died, and of gunshot; but the local authorities believe it was delivered at close range by a revolver in the hand of one of his own adherents, upon discovering he'd been denied a position that had been promised to him upon victory. The fellow was found guilty and hanged within a fortnight. The rest is rumor, undoubtedly encouraged by the defendant's attorney. Six hundred metres! *Impossibile!*"

"I find the impossible impossible. Watson and I were just discussing a man who shot a Bengal tiger square through the eyes at that very range, in front of a British general and his staff, who took the measurement afterwards."

"Then he is your man!"

"He's dead, unfortunately."

"If all who were thought dead were dead, the cemeteries would run out of space."

"Witnesses, again; among them the hangman, a Scotland Yard chief inspector, and the doctor who recorded the moment his heart stopped beating."

"He should have stuck to tigers." Petrosino scowled. "I consider this my fault. Directly Dr. Watson called, I placed Sergeant Fantonetti on suspension. He was the man who knocked at my door whilst we were conferring. Clearly he lingered outside, with an ear pressed to the panel. But for him, only we three knew you were stopping here instead of at the Brevoort. Unless you were followed?" His face showed a ray of hope.

"Those who have tried have found themselves followed, and by me. You will pardon me if I suggest your Italian Squad requires maintenance."

"I had hoped, by making it small, that I should be in a position to keep an eye upon its members; but as I said, this spawn's pockets are deep. Fantonetti has a wife and children. Perhaps he was not corrupted, but cooperated in return for his family's safety. My original intention was to ban married men from the squad, but it's the nature of my people to marry young and take comfort in old age from their grandchildren and great-grandchildren. Most of the single men I interviewed were either incompetent or easily compromised." He placed a finger alongside his Roman nose. "One develops a sense for these things."

"I can smell out a traitor myself or I wouldn't be here." Holmes groped inside the sling on his shoulder, which I had fashioned from a towel borrowed from Mrs. L'Azour, and withdrew his brier and travelling pouch. "Now that you're here, we may as well have our meeting. I gave you the particulars of the Venucci affair in my cable. What can you tell me about the Black Hand in England?"

"My acquaintances with the Italian language newspapers in London assure me that it hasn't the foothold there it has in America. Much as I would admire to credit the excellence of your law enforcement, *Il Mano Negro* scarcely bothered with England. Some one hundred sixty thousand Italians enter this country annually, bringing with them a healthy respect for *Il Mano Negro* from the old country: Little training is necessary, you see. A barbershop is fire-bombed, a tailor's is broken into and acid poured on the inventory, and the lesson is understood. Sometimes no demonstration is necessary, just that friendly little note with a childlike drawing of a hand and the directive, 'Pay or die.' You have received no such communication?"

"None."

"That is unusual. Can it be our Cousin Giovanni—for want of another name—jumped the gun, so to speak?"

"A contractor's eagerness speaks volumes. Either these fellows suspect I know more than I do, or wish to keep me in the dark. At all events, someone considered the problem important enough for our Uncle Umberto to send a cable."

"*Imbecille!*" Petrosino slapped his forehead. "All this talk of cables, and I forget. This awaited you at the hotel." He drew a yellow envelope from his sleeve and began to rise. Holmes, yawning, signaled him to be still.

"Read it, will you, Watson? I'm not the inexhaustible traveller you are."

"I begin to wonder." I took the envelope from our guest and opened it:

HAVE ARRESTED STRIPED SUIT PAOLO ROSSI STOP NOT
TALKING STOP CANNOT HOLD LONG LEST PAST REPEAT
ITSELF
   G LESTRADE

"Good old Lestrade," said Holmes. "He never passes up an opportunity to pour salt into an open wound. But with the billiards player
accounted for I can endeavor to place a face upon this new enemy."

"We have a name, at least," I said. "Lungo."

CHAPTER XII.

WE ARE GIVEN A HAND

Holmes drew upon his pipe. "Lieutenant, I should like your permission to investigate this incident."

"Were I you, I would consider an attempt upon my life more than just an incident."

"The late Macedonian presidential candidate might argue the point. I have narrowed the practical range in this neighbourhood to two hundred metres. Reason tells us the man capable of bringing down a national figure at three times that distance would have dealt a tourist more than a flesh wound, if murder were his intention. He seeks to frighten me back to my cosy digs. I must make his acquaintance, if only to inform him I'm not the quaking sparrow he thinks me."

I said, "I hardly think your vanity is worth the risk of death."

"My friend, if that's the construction you placed on what I said, I've misspoken myself. This was a feint, which has told me a little about him. In order to know more, I must observe him when he swings in earnest."

"I cannot offer protection," said Petrosino. "My responsibility is to my neighbors in Little Italy."

"It wouldn't be necessary." Holmes smiled at me. "This isn't the first time Dr. Watson has assisted in my preservation. Without a sharp-eyed fellow in the bush, a staked goat is nothing but a tit-bit for lions."

"Forgive me, but you don't know these lions. A tit-bit only whets their appetites."

"To know them is my intention."

"You have my permission to investigate independently. I suspect to withhold it would be to waste my breath."

"Thank you. One more question, and then you may regard your responsibility to our welfare as discharged. Who pulls the criminal strings in your jurisdiction?"

"That would be Gabriele Medusa, who holds court in his tonsorial parlour. Anyone in Little Italy can direct you there. But you will find him unhelpful, if not precisely discourteous. I have interviewed him many times, and all I can get from him is quotations from classical literature. He taught himself English in the New York Public Library."

The lieutenant rose. "I shall place an officer outside this room. I do not share your faith in these vermins' motives. Having failed to kill you at far range, their next attempt will be close up. They are artists with knives."

"You carry one yourself, I perceive." Holmes removed his pipe from his mouth and pointed the stem at an uncharacteristic snag in Petrosino's tidy uniform. "Are you a Rembrandt or just a Sunday painter?"

"Leonardo, if you please." Our guest twitched an arm; that was all it seemed. In the instant, a thin blade with a pearl handle appeared in his hand.

Holmes's reaction was no more tardy. In a trice, he snatched up his leaded stick from where it leaned against the night-table, and in the next moment the knife lay on the floor, its owner gripping the hand in which it had been held.

"Golze, the Austrian fencing master, taught me the trick," Holmes said. "I added a refinement of my own, pulling the punch to avoid shattering your hand. He wouldn't approve; Teutons do nothing by half-measures. We are not defenceless, Lieutenant. You cannot spare an extra man upon our account."

Petrosino shook the hand and worked his fingers. His smile was pained. "Very well. The proverbial house need not fall upon me." He stooped to reclaim his knife—and in the space of a half-second it was buried to its hilt in the wall a few centimetres to the right of Holmes's head.

"I would be honoured," said the lieutenant, "if you would include the item among your famous souvenirs. The squad confiscates them at the rate of a dozen per week."

Overcoming his surprise, Holmes chuckled and worked the blade loose from the plaster with the hand belonging to his good arm. He blew the powder off the blue steel and tested the edge with his thumb. "I shall use it to open all my correspondence henceforth, and think of you, *Tenente*, whenever I pay a bill."

"And I of you, when old age creeps up on me and settles in these bruised bones." He flexed his fingers, executed a smart little bow, and left.

From the landing, we heard a brief polite exchange between our departing visitor and the landlady. When presently I opened the door to her tapping, she looked sympathetically at Holmes. "Is the gentleman well?"

I had explained the situation to her when I'd asked to use the telephone. She had been stoicism personified, asking only after our welfare. "As his doctor, I can assure you he'll recover."

"This will help." She drew the cover off a china bowl on the tray she was holding. It smelled strongly of potato. "*Vichyssoise*," said she; "the French response to the chicken soup of the Hebrew. I am no cook, but the chef in the café on the corner is a friend. He delivered it himself, all dressed up as you see."

I thanked her and took the tray.

"If there is anything else, please call. That two gentlemen under my roof should be attacked: *Scandaleux!*"

"An estimable woman," said I, when we were alone. "The Gallic version of Mrs. Hudson." I stooped to place the tray across Holmes's lap, but he waved it away.

"Pray sustain yourself, Doctor. The digestive process murders sleep. Be alert, and wake me at midnight, when I shall take up the watch. To ignore Petrosino's warning would be inane." He knocked out his pipe in the tray on the night-table and drew the covers to his chin.

"I say, Holmes. There's more on this tray than cold potato soup."

"Oyster crackers?"

"No."

Sitting in the chair Petrosino had vacated, I had snapped open the folded napkin, whereupon a fold of stiff paper fluttered to the floor.

I put the tray aside and got up to retrieve and unfold it. The contents froze me to the marrow.

"You needn't read it aloud, Watson." Holmes was sitting up now, eyes bright, face flushed with excitement. "'Pay or die.' Is it in English or Italian?"

"Neither. I mean to say, that isn't the message." I turned the paper round and held it out so that he could see it for himself. It was blank but for the crude drawing of a human hand, dark with ink, and beneath it the legend:

BEQUEATH YOUR SOUL TO GOD

CHAPTER XIII.

ADVICE FROM A BARBER

"Better and better." Holmes moved to clap his hands, then forbore when his sling impeded the gesture. "They paraphrase Bacon. If I am to follow this advice, it would be worth it to be slain by a literary man."

"There are times when your sinister sense of humour wears upon one," I said, handing him the paper.

He turned up the lamp on the night-table and studied the item at close hand. He sniffed. "Hum. The singular smell of lampblack, the chief agent in the manufacture of India ink. If I thought Mrs. L'Azour untrustworthy, I'd suspect eavesdropping upon our conversation with the lieutenant. I refer to our friend the Bengalese hunter."

"A stretch, certainly. I assume the compound is hardly more in short supply here than back home. It need have nothing to do with the villain's old hunting grounds. I begin to think you've transferred your obsession to Sebastian Moran from—"

"Tut! If you expect me to honour my resolution, you must refrain from taunting me. However, the name is a misnomer. The ink is a product of China and Japan. The paper, interestingly, is a rice derivative. I spent some time in India after Reichenbach, directly I left Lhasa. It's as common there as foolscap, and nowhere else."

"Tiger Jack is dead, Holmes. We saw him cut down from the scaffold, and heard the physician's declaration."

"And yet these hands itch for a spade, to settle the thing *in toto*. But we needn't book passage yet, when Gabriele Medusa is so convenient."

"It's a worthy supposition," I said. "Petrosino said he knows his English-language classics."

"Well, we shall give him his orals tomorrow. Meanwhile, we must disturb our landlady once more. Fetch her, will you?"

I won't belabour the reader's patience with a detailed account of our interview with Mrs. L'Azour. She knew nothing of the note, swearing upon the crucifix she wore, and she was believable. The café proprietor who provided the *vichyssoise*, one *Monsieur* Blanc, was a compatriot, a "pious man" whose enterprise was extremely successful: Greenwich's bohemian population queued up into the street regularly to enjoy his simple but tasty country fare. He was assisted by his widowed daughter-in-law, who had lost her husband in the late war with Spain; she, too, was described as above reproach.

"I accept this *prima facie*, for the time being," said Holmes. "*Monsieur* Blanc seems impregnable. As to the daughter, our dangerous friends are patriarchal, disinclined to trust the fair sex in such matters. *Merci, ma bon femme.* We shan't disturb you again this night."

"*Ne pensez pas, monsieur.*" She curtsied and took herself out.

"You are wide awake?" Holmes asked me.

"I always am, after receiving a death threat."

"Indeed. I have the opposite reaction. This breed has a distorted concept of my life's value. Redundancy and warm bland milk are the same to me. Look sharp, Watson. Your fate is infinitely more important in my view."

Within five minutes, he was asleep, leaving me to sit up with my revolver at my elbow and every sound in that slumbering household increased tenfold.

We were undisturbed, however, during my vigil and then Holmes's, Eley in his lap. He insisted I douse the lamp, but I slept fitfully, and whenever I awoke I saw the strong planes of his face reflected in the minimal light leaking round the curtains, eyes aglow, like a cat's in the shaft from a lantern.

In the morning, he was as fresh as if he'd been the one resting, whilst I felt old and used. He made quite the dashing figure with his overcoat slung over his shoulders cloak-fashion, his arm in its sling, and the brim of his soft hat tugged rakishly down above one eye. Mrs. L'Azour could manage eggs and coffee; after breakfast we set out for Little Italy.

As Petrosino had promised, we found Medusa's lair without difficulty. The whole neighborhood knew of *La Perla*, a spacious shop with a spotless plate-glass window through which the winter sun shone strongly, with black-and-white tiles spotless and all the instruments of the barber's trade a-glitter: ranks of razors, clippers, brushes, personalized mugs in wooden racks, and three white porcelain chairs raised, lowered, and tilted by means of chrome handles. It was early. No customers occupied the corner where stacks of Italian periodicals stood within reach of the oaken bench and only one chair in use, by an absolutely stout man who set aside his newspaper and got up as we entered. He wore striped shirtsleeves, a boiled collar, braces supporting woolen trousers, and yellow gaiters on gleaming black shoes.

"*Buongiorno, signores!*" he greeted heartily, in a booming voice that seemed to be regulated by the counterweight of an enormous pair of black moustaches. His cheeks were red and round as apples and his hair slicked back and parted exactly in the centre. "My first customers of the day! Gabriele Medusa at your service. Who will be first?"

Holmes looked amused. "Are we so obviously not *paisan*, that you should speak to us so confidently in English?"

"No. There are Northern Italians here, some whiter than you; but they do not dress like Englishmen, and I know everyone in the neighborhood besides. By the process of elimination, I shall greet you as Sherlock Holmes and Dr. Watson, distinguished visitors to this shore."

"Good Lord!" said I. "I'm in the presence of two detectives."

"*Elementare!*" His eyes were as black and shiny as his shoes. "Ours is a small village surrounded by mountains of brick and steel. There are no secrets here, and when famous men from across the sea enter it—well, what use is there of newspapers? I myself read them only to improve my English."

"It bears little improvement," Holmes said. "I understand you learnt at the feet of its masters."

"I have been pleased to include Dr. Watson among them. His accounts of your exploits—"

Holmes produced the grim message we'd received during the night.

Medusa's jovial façade vanished, as if it had been painted on a canvas curtain jerked up into the flies by a zealous stagehand. He strode to the door, turned the key in the lock, drew the shade down over the glass, and beckoned us to follow him through a curtained doorway at the back of the shop.

This room was an office, banked with wooden file drawers, a solid desk with a green baize top, a tufted leather chair on a swivel, and lower chairs, leather also.

"*Sigaros?*" He twisted a fat palm toward a great humidor on the desk.

We declined. When we were seated, Medusa selected a pontoon-shaped cigar, bit off the end, spat it into a cuspidor, and set fire to it with a square wooden match. Wreaths of aromatic smoke filled the room. "'Bequeath your soul to God.' A travesty, to misquote a great writer deliberately."

"You deny any knowledge of it?" Holmes asked.

"Understand, I make no apologies for the life I live. In the village where I was born, a man without a title was a beast of burden, to be discarded the moment he was no longer useful. There were only two ways he could prosper, as a prizefighter or a criminal, and then only in America. I am no good with my fists, *signores*."

"Do you deny you sent someone to fire a bullet into our room in Greenwich Village?"

"I have heard of this intolerable thing. Yes, I deny it. There is no percentage in victimizing white men. Here, a peasant, a greasy wop, brings upon his death through arrogance or ignorance or stupidity; an investigation follows, another peasant is arrested, or perhaps the man to blame is never found: Either way, the police lose interest and apply themselves to the next case of arrogance or ignorance or stupidity. 'They come transfigured back, secure from change in their high-hearted ways.'"

"'Beautiful evermore, and with the rays of morn on their white shields of expectation.' Odd to cite Lowell on the subject of such creatures."

Medusa beamed, his garrulity restored. "You cannot know what it means to have this kind of conversation. I have pockets filled with pearls, and I live among swine; hence *La Perla*, the name of my establishment."

"Petrosino warned me you'd try to turn away my questions with cant. What do you know of a man called Lungo?"

"A fiction, invented by local housewives to frighten their children into bed. The *Tenente* is grasping at straws if he mentioned this chimera."

"As a matter of fact he adheres to your view on the subject. This is no fiction." Holmes put two fingers in a pocket of his waistcoat and dropped a small misshapen object onto the green baize.

The barber studied the spent bullet without touching it. "No evidence was necessary. If I doubted the rumor, your testimony confirmed it. I do not possess a firearm, *Signor* Holmes. If I found that any man I employ possesses one, he is fired. Some of these wretches have spent time in jail; petty offences all, caused by poverty and desperation, I make no judgment. To be searched by the police with such a weapon on one's person would mean further imprisonment, and a stain upon my reputation."

"'The stiletto, *la pistola*, the garrote.'" The detective quoted Luigi Pizarro. "The first and third are permitted?"

A pair of meaty shoulders rolled. "The streets are dangerous. Whilst a blameless tubercular is turned away at Ellis Island, a cutthroat may pass through the eye of the needle. One must protect oneself and one's family."

"I submit that strangling one's attacker with a length of wire requires something other than defence of self and home."

"You do not know our community. In London, the entire foreign quarter would fit inside Battery Park. There are some twenty millions of Italians here alone."

"That is one of the reasons Dr. Watson and I made this voyage: to see the enemy in its natural habitat."

"Sicily was much closer."

"Geographically correct. However, on that island, one Medusa is indistinguishable from all the others. When you truly wish to know how a man made his fortune, and upon how many backs, you must come to the place where the streets are paved with gold."

"I cannot help you, sir."

"Your grammar is faulty. The phrase you're looking for is '*will* not.'"

He smiled, this time without warmth. "I can see I must go to an Englishman when my English needs improving."

"Thank you for the refresher course in the classics, *Signor.*" Holmes reclaimed the bullet and stood. Medusa kept his seat.

"*Parla Italiano?*"

"*Un po,*" replied the detective.

The barber crooked his finger. Holmes hesitated, then leaned close to the desk. My hand tightened upon my pocketed revolver unbidden; all this talk of knives and strangling had set my nerves on end.

However, our host made no motion other than to place his thick lips close to Holmes's ear. His voice rustled in an unintelligible whisper.

The interview was ended. Medusa saw us to the door and unlocked it. When we were on the street, the shade he'd drawn flapped back up onto its roller.

"What did he say?" I asked when we were back on the street.

"*Il mondo e antiquato, y voi e anche immaturo per lo.*"

"What does it mean?"

"My usage is no doubt atrocious, and I can provide but a rough approximation: 'The world is old, and you are too young for it.'"

191

CHAPTER XIV.

PASTA AND THE PRESS

We walked the short distance to Petrosino's precinct, but a dusky-faced young officer told us he was still at home, having been up late the night before. Nothing in the polite young Italian's manner suggested he held us responsible for the inconvenience.

"A most dangerous man, Medusa," said Holmes, as we followed the policeman's directions. "No Napoleon of Crime, of course; but quite possibly a Richelieu. At the same time I'm reasonably certain he had nothing to do with what took place last night."

"What are your grounds?"

"He's afraid, Watson. His kingdom is built upon sand, held in place by the kerbs of Little Italy. This incident has international implications. He may be able to contain the local authorities through threats and bribery, but not the full weight of two vengeful governments. His parting words were as much a plea as a warning. He is not our man."

"Then we have come all this way for nothing."

"Emphatically not. We have flushed out Lungo. Plainly we pose a hazard to some nefarious plan. Lestrade was correct insofar as the Black Hand in London seeks to avoid publicity, hence its efforts to see that Pietro Venucci's final resting place remains final. But by taking the matter all the way to the United States, we have forced these fellows to take drastic measures to stop the investigation. Depend upon it, there is something more behind all this than just a dead gravedigger."

We entered a brownstone building whose interior smelled—refreshingly, not of the city's indigenous cabbage, but of cooked tomatoes and a delectable variety of herbs. On our way up the three flights to the lieutenant's flat, we heard arguments of differing decibels in Italian, a tenor singing an operatic aria on a gramophone (Caruso, perhaps), and an interesting debate between a woman speaking Italian and a boy speaking New York–accented English involving when he should be expected home for dinner.

The smell of Mediterranean cooking increased as we approached a door at the end of a narrow dim hallway, and positively gushed out at us as Petrosino opened the door. In place of his uniform he wore a stained apron over a brown woolen waistcoat and clutched a squat green wine-bottle in a woven basket under one arm and his short-barreled revolver in his free hand. Recognizing us, his wary expression broke into a genial smile. The weapon vanished beneath his apron.

"My friends, you are just in time for luncheon."

"We wouldn't impose," said Holmes.

"Absurd. I am a bachelor, who cooks enough in one day to feed myself all week. I have prepared pasta sufficient to satisfy the neighborhood. *Prego, entrare, e partire un po della felicita tu portare.*"

"*Grazie, mi amico*; although I fear we do not bring so much in the way of happiness. No," he said, when our friend registered alarm, "not another attack. Just lack of progress."

He took our hats and coats and hung them on a halltree and removed his apron. "We shall dine in five minutes."

The apartment was small but homey, a combination living and dining room and kitchen, with a worn but once costly rug on the floor, photos in oval frames of mustachioed men in stiff collars and solemn women in black bombazine, and a view through an open doorway of a single bed on an iron frame. A gramophone (possibly the one we'd heard on our way up the stairs) perched upon a shawl covering a spindle-legged table. Petrosino filled three glasses on an oilcloth-covered table from the squat bottle of wine, served us in threadbare overstuffed chairs pinned all over with antimacassars, and wound up the gramophone. The clear tenor voice issued from the great chrysanthemum horn.

"The doctor and I had the honour of meeting *Signor* Caruso in London shortly before we left," Holmes said. "In person his voice is magnificent."

"I was privileged to hear it as well, from backstage at the Metropolitan last year. I was in charge of ensuring *Il Mano Negro* held up its end of their bargain. The dinner the man had delivered to his dressing room would have foundered Diamond Jim Brady."

"Geniuses are often voracious. I seem to be an exception."

The lieutenant nearly choked on his wine. He mopped his lips with a great lawn handkerchief. "*Scusami.* I find your frankness refreshing after this morning's telephone conversation with the chief. He owes his position to the mayor, and the jargon required to maintain public office has rubbed off upon him."

"I trust he doesn't hold you responsible for what took place last night," Holmes said.

"I am sure it was no worse than what he heard from the mayor. You have spoken with Medusa?"

My friend provided him with a full account. Petrosino nodded. "I agree with your construction. He plays the buffoon to perfection, but he is too wise to stir up hornets larger than he." He sighed. "Someday, my chief will grant my request to revisit Sicily and rip up this noxious weed by the root. What is your next step?"

An alarm clock rang. Our host excused himself and rose. "The sauce, it burns. Shall we continue our conversation over our meal?"

Holmes agreed, and we sat down to a sumptuous repast. The pasta tasted of refined butter and the sauce was delicious. We complimented the chef.

"I thank you on behalf of my grandmother. She would curse me in her grave were I to share the secret outside the family. *Omerta*, it is not exclusive to *Il Mano Negro*."

"I wonder if I could prevail upon you for a favour," Holmes said.

"Anything."

"Would you notify the newspapers where we are staying? I wish to make a statement for publication."

Petrosino was as surprised as I was. "If that is what you wish; but will they not hamper your movements?"

"A little, but as those movements involve merely a ride to the docks, the inconvenience won't be great. We sail with the tide, assuming we can arrange accommodations."

"The department can help with that. You are abandoning your quest?"

"On the contrary," said Holmes. "I intend to lure our friend Lungo from his lair."

Whereupon he indulged himself with a second helping from the big bowl on the table.

Petrosino hung up the telephone in the foyer of his building. "*Di compiuto.* Your berth on the *Dolley Madison* awaits at six o'clock this evening, and the gentlemen of the Fourth Estate have been notified. If I know them, they will greet you at Mrs. L'Azour's front door. I would be honoured if you would allow me to deliver you to the dock in the chief's go-devil."

"Thank you, but so official a leave-taking may frighten our prey back into hiding."

We said farewell, and prepared to shake his hand, but Lieutenant Giusseppe Petrosino seized us each in an embrace that would bring a bear to shame. "*Addio, mi caro amicos!* I pray that our paths will cross again under better circumstances."

"And I, regardless of the circumstances."

I said as much, and the association was ended.

Our new friend had not exaggerated, for a gaggle of men in unwashed linen and battered bowlers boiled off the front steps of our boarding house the moment we appeared. Holmes quieted their simultaneous queries with hand upraised.

"No questions, please, gentlemen. We came to your splendid country on a matter of grave importance, but the trail leads back home, where we shall root out its source. I have nothing to add." He turned and sprinted up the steps with me in tow.

"Mr. Holmes!" This came in chorus. One voice, belonging to a tall man in tailoring somewhat superior to his colleagues, came to the fore.

"Pemberton of the *Sun*," he announced. "Is it true someone tried to shoot you in your room last night?"

Holmes paused in the open doorway. "That rumor is false. Mrs. L'Azour would tolerate no such inhospitality. I commend the comforts of her establishment to anyone who intends to visit your fine city. Thank you."

"But that sling—"

I followed Holmes inside quickly and pushed the door shut against the force from without. This was my first encounter with American journalism. At last I knew the full meaning of the word *press*.

CHAPTER XV.

I OWE MY LIFE TO A CIGAR

We hired a carriage, and within the hour we were aboard the *Dolley Madison*, which despite its gracious namesake was altogether a less lavish affair than the vessel that had brought us to the shores of liberty. It had begun life as a tramp steamer, and such improvements that had been made to upgrade its status were little more than cosmetic. A rat the size of a bull pup greeted us in the corridor outside our stateroom, a chamber scarcely more spacious than a monk's cell, with upper and lower berths bolted to the bulkhead and the pervasive odour of coal oil and fish. It lacked even a porthole.

"We should have sent ourselves with the luggage," I said. "The cargo hold can't be much worse."

Holmes was sanguine. He stretched out in the lower berth with his hands behind his head, the sling discarded as no longer necessary. "You'll forgive me if I don't join you in your plaint. I earned my first passage to this country stoking coal. Did you mark our fellow passengers?"

"I didn't see anyone carrying a rifle case, if that's what you mean."

"I should be disappointed if you had. Apply my methods."

"The mysterious party in the sun hat and smoked glasses caught my eye. I thought, 'There's a man with something to hide.'"

"I gave the purser a pound note in return for the information that the gentleman owns a tin mine in Bolivia that yields some one hundred thousand dollars monthly. He prefers to travel incognito, which explains the outlandish disguise. Evidently he's an admirer of Poe. Anyone else?"

"The East Indian princess or something, dusky-skinned, in expensive furs and pumps as fashionable as any I saw in New York."

"No one seems to know anything about her, but her bags are calf-skin, with gold fittings. Anyone can obtain fine clothing, but luggage is another matter. I wouldn't assign much to her nationality. The Mafia uses women only to procreate and keep house. Next."

The hoarse whistle blew. I clambered into the top berth before the movement of the ship could defeat me. "Your turn."

"The middle western farmer and his wife interest me, if only because I cannot conceive of anything less oceanic."

"I must have missed them."

"You were at my side when they passed us outside, looking for their cabin. Such types rarely wear overalls and flour sacking when they travel. His callosities were consistent with steering a plough, and a wheat stalk gifted with the power of speech could not sound more like Kansas.

"The invalided U.S. Marine has possibilities. I won't belabour your patience with how I arrived at the simple conclusion of his past occupation and injury. That branch of the service employs more sharp-shooters than any other. He's Nordic, but the Black Hand has been known to import its specialists, based upon merit and anonymity."

"He sounds like our man."

"There are three hundred forty-two passengers aboard this ship, excluding ourselves. Until I have eliminated three hundred forty-one from suspicion, he's only a wounded veteran with wanderlust." He took his hands from behind his head and tipped his hat forward over his eyes. "Wake me at eight bells, will you, Watson? When I said food is the enemy of sleep, I had yet to encounter *Nonna* Petrosino's pasta and sauce."

"And when is eight bells?" I asked; but his even breathing told me he was deep in the arms of Morpheus.

Although he had not mentioned it, I knew the importance of stay-ing alert whilst he slept. Ships and skullduggery went hand-in-hand. It was a simple thing to move about without attracting suspicion, catch one's victim alone in a dimly lit gangway or a tiny cabin such as ours, dispatch him, and dispose of the remains by way of the nearest porthole, or simply shove him over the railing on deck and let the sea do the rest. I sat on the edge of my berth with feet dangling, pistol within reach, endeavoring to subtract the churning of the engines and the wash of the waves from a stealthy tread, the doorknob turning by way of an unseen hand, and to stave off sleep; I, too, had eaten a heavy meal, and the sway of the lantern depending from a steel hook in the ceiling, slinging shadows up and down the bulkhead, was hypnotic.

I dozed more than once, but lightly. A squeak (rat? the door hinge?), a groan (the flexing of the hull? a breath held, then expelled?), and I woke with a start, the revolver already in my hand as by magic. When at last eight bells rang (eight o'clock, by my watch; nautical time is seldom so rational), warped by distance and the motion of the vessel, I was never so glad to hear such a sound.

As before, my companion took the second watch, which in the morning he pronounced uneventful. There were several seatings for each meal, the tiny dining room accommodating but ten tables. The food was edible, the coffee bitter. We observed our fellow passengers at table and on deck. To my overexcited imagination, at least one out of five qualified for inclusion in Holmes's planned photographic rogues' gallery. But by the second day out, my friend had eliminated the Bolivian millionaire, the Kansas farmer and his wife, and (to my disappointment) the invalided U.S. Marine. The first wagered sparingly in the little casino ("Only the rich are so close with a dollar," said Holmes. "Had he sprayed the bank notes about like water, I should have closed in"); the middle western couple were on their way to visit a nephew studying at Eton, and showed anyone who paused long enough a thick sheaf of Kodak portraits of a young man whose ears and nose were identical to the farmer's; and the detective's casual conversation with the retired soldier uncovered a plethora of information on how to prepare salmon steaks for a hundred men. He'd been a company cook, too busy frying potatoes to practise his marksmanship.

"Ruses are of course possible," was the learnt conclusion. "However, such evidence as we have seen requires many months to manufacture, and if Petrosino is right about the slayer of the Macedonian presidential candidate, our Lungo was in the Mediterranean at the time, in possession of bona fides more germane to that region."

We were in our stateroom, which we'd deemed the most secure place to share intelligence. The close quarters, and my mounting suspicion that either our enemy had chosen not to follow us home or had boarded a different boat, made me restless. I went out for fresh air.

The air on deck was bracing, stiffening my face and frosting my nose. I stood gripping the tarnished brass railing, gazing out at the choppy steel-coloured waves and remembered crossing a very different sea, weak from the lingering effects of enteric fever and promenading on the arm of an army nurse; thinking, then, that my adventurous days were over.

Smiling at my old naivety, I slid the silver case from my pocket and took out a cigar just as the wind changed, hurling spray over the railing and snatching the case from my hand. Instinctively I lunged to catch it before it fell into the ocean.

I heard a report, bent by the elements, but to an old campaigner a report just the same. There are no backfires at sea, and the noise that accompanied it, once heard, is never forgotten: the ear-splitting whistle of a bullet passing through the space where my head had been an instant before.

My soldier's reflexes, thank the Lord, remained intact. I threw myself to the deck and rolled, upsetting a wooden lounge chair and coming to rest with my back against the deck cabin, my hand groping for my revolver. My gaze swept the deck from stem to stern, the roof of the cabin, every porthole. The last were all shut, and I saw no one. The air was too icy for casual strollers. There had been just us two: myself and my would-be murderer.

CHAPTER XVI.

TRIUMPH

"Sharp, Watson! There isn't a moment to lose!"

No sooner had I blurted out my news than Holmes was on his feet, jerking open the stateroom door and shoving me out into the passage. He scrambled up the ladder to the upper decks with me close behind.

"I've been an egotistical fool, to think myself the only target," he said as we climbed. "A close call in the boarding house and a paper threat were intended as warnings, as I surmised. After they went unheeded—in a most public fashion, thanks be to the press—Lungo raised his sights, so to speak. Murdering you, the closest to me in all this world, would be an alarm not even I could ignore. I shall spend the rest of our lives, short or long, begging your forgiveness."

"There's nothing to forgive, Holmes." I was panting; years and an expanding waistline were taking their toll. Yet I remained close at his heels as we surmounted the last ladder and raced down the deck towards the scene of my near-assassination, revolvers in hand. "Obviously, he doesn't know you as well as I. You would never give up the search, with me or without me."

"I certainly should not, without you. I would hound this beast over both sides of earth and over all sides of land until he lay dead at my feet. There it is! Up we go!"

A steel ladder bolted to the deck cabin bore a tin sign reading CREW MEMBERS ONLY. The ship was pitching in the roughening sea. We put away our weapons to use both hands and clambered up onto the roof.

It was as high as I had ever been aboard ship, and I am no sailor. The surface underfoot was slick with wash and wind shoved at me, snapping my coattails. The sway of the craft forced me to my hands and knees lest I be swept overboard. Holmes, half-cat, half-housefly, dashed upright to and fro, eyes on the corroded steel at his feet. At length he cried out and pointed at a small oval depression in the generations of soot that had settled there from the smokestacks. There was but the one, and as we watched the wind freshened, blowing a fresh black layer onto the mark, obliterating it.

"Small," said he, and pounded his forehead with the heel of his hand. "Think! No, no foot so dainty among passengers and crew; at least, not the men."

"But you said—"

"You, there! You're not allowed up here! Go back!"

The harsh voice belonged to a man in a nor'wester yellow slicker and floppy hat secured with a band under his chin and large black boots on his feet. He was coming our way from the direction of the bridge, waving a heavy belaying-pin as if it were a bludgeon.

I started to explain ourselves, but before I could get a word out, Holmes flung himself down on one shoulder, skidding across the slippery cabin roof feet first, directly towards the advancing crewman. The soles of his boots collided with the man's ankles, knocking him down to his knees. But he kept his hold on his weapon and swung it at Holmes's head. Shouting, I launched myself to my feet and lunged for the belaying-pin. By sheer luck my fingers closed upon it—but it came away in my hand. He'd abandoned it to reach under his slicker. Out came his hand, holding something that resembled a long, narrow pipe; but Holmes had braced himself with his hands, and with a mighty kick knocked the object aside. Orange fire leapt from the end of the pipe, simultaneous with a report such as I'd heard before, and from that very spot.

But the shooter wasn't finished. The gun came back around; but by then Holmes had excavated his pistol. I drew mine, and fired it an instant behind his. The man in yellow dropped his long-barreled gun and fell on his knees.

"Catch her, Watson! We must take her alive!"

The ship was leaning hard to starboard. The crew member was sliding towards the edge of the roof. At that angle he would bypass the deck entirely and vanish into the ocean. I leapt, ignoring my terror of falling, and closed both fists on oilcloth, dragging the weight of the one who wore it away from the edge.

"Wait," said I then, panting from the excitement and exertion. "*Her?*"

The ship's doctor emerged from the tiny infirmary, looking grave. "She hasn't long. One bullet, and she might survive, with one lung. Two—" He shook his head.

"The lady offered no choice." Holmes spoke without regret. "Can she talk?"

"Yes; but don't be long. She's asked for a priest. We haven't one aboard, but there's an Anglican minister in Three-B. She must save some breath for prayer."

We found the patient lying on a cot under a thin blanket. Beneath her dusky colouring she was nearly as pale as the sheet. I judged her less than thirty, and reasonably attractive under normal circumstances. She had the long, almond-shaped eyes of Asia and her black hair was cut short. I barely recognized her without the wig; she was, of course, the "East Indian princess" I had seen our first day aboard. The foul-weather gear, including the clumsy black boots she'd pulled over her small feet, lay heaped in a corner. She had likely stolen the items from some sailor's slop chest to assist her in her final charge.

"You are not a priest." Her voice, although weak, had the musical accents I associated with her country. Earlier, she had roughened it in order to sound masculine.

"You know who we are," said Holmes coldly. "Why did you not ask for a Hindu holy man?"

"I was baptized in my father's church. Colonel Sebastian Moran was an Irish-Catholic."

"It can do you no good now to keep your story secret."

She closed her eyes, shuddered with a sudden spasm, then opened them wide and bright. "If I miss the priest, will you tell him my confession, that I may be saved?"

"I shall."

She spoke, interrupting herself only when pain racked her. Her name was Lakshmi Moran, the only child of Colonel Sebastian Moran and an Indian mistress. Moran had never publicly acknowledged her, but when she was of age, he took her along on his tiger hunts and amused himself by teaching her to shoot. To his amazement, she had inherited his natural talents. Thinking her useful to his civilian employer, the late Professor James Moriarty, he'd promised to send for her after he'd resettled himself in England.

"You inherited more than his marksmanship," ventured Holmes. "Morality is a trait inbred or not at all."

"Hear me out. My mother died of typhus whilst we were waiting. I was sixteen, a half-caste, scorned by whites and natives alike. I cut my hair, disguised myself as a boy, and joined a Sepoy regiment, where after proving myself on the firing range I was transferred to a company of sharpshooters. I was the best they had, and until I began to develop physically, I managed to dissemble my sex.

"Eventually, I was discovered, and dismissed without ceremony. But I had managed to save enough of my soldier's pay to buy a steerage ticket to England, to be reunited with my father. It was not until I made inquiries in London that I learnt he'd been hanged for the murder of a man named Ronald Adair and the attempted murder of a man named Sherlock Holmes."

Lakshmi then made her way as a woman of the streets, but only as a means to an end. She learnt to disguise her mature womanhood, and through her contacts in the London *demimonde* applied for a position as an assassin for the Black Hand. Her first assignment, once she had proven her skill, was to slay a candidate for office in Macedonia who had pledged to rid his country of organized crime.

"Conscience, what is that?" said she. "I had learnt at first-hand that human life was disposable."

The Mafia never suspected her gender, and named her *Lungo* in honour of her gift.

"Length; a generous compliment." She laughed weakly, coughed, waited for breath. Her mouth foamed pink at the corners. "Upon reflection, I'm sure some of my colleagues guessed my secret, but by then I was so successful they kept silent rather than face their superiors' wrath. *Omerta* has been my *padrone* all these years."

When it was learnt that Sherlock Holmes had gone to America to meet with an expert on the Mafia, Lakshmi bought a ticket—this time at first-cabin rates—on the next ship.

"I toyed with you in New York; it pleased me to make you quake, by deliberately missing a clear shot and sending you that crude note. I should have been more professional, and less artistic. When the newspapers announced you were returning to England to continue the investigation, I bought a berth under an assumed name, donned an expensive disguise—for murder pays well—and made my attempt at sea: I would kill Watson first, and when you came running to investigate, ambush you when you were in shock at the loss of your friend and most vulnerable."

"For what reason?" Holmes pressed. "The Mafia in England wanted to prevent the disinterment of Pietro Venucci to avoid publicity, but surely it would stop short of following us to America and escalating the operation."

There wasn't much time. Her eyes were glassy and her voice had fallen to a whisper. Then she stared at him with complete lucidity. A smile tugged at her lips.

"You mean you don't know? The great detective failed to deduce? I was not sent. I came on my own; to kill the man responsible for my father's death."

CHAPTER XVII.

TRAGEDY

My tale is nearly told, but there is a coda.

With Holmes's help, the pin-setter's murder fell to his partner, Rossi, the billiards sharp. "A man who can manipulate balls upon a table can surely find his way round so quaint a system as an English gaol," said Holmes, whose testimony at the Assizes convicted Rossi and the guard he'd bribed to let him into the victim's cell. Just who set the mechanism in motion is unknown to this day.

In the flurry of all this attention, the Mafia kept silent whilst Magdalena Venucci escorted her father's remains back to Sicily.

Some six years after the events I have related, Holmes shared with me a cable he'd just received:

AT LAST CHIEF AGREES SEND ME SICILY BEARD THE DEVIL IN HIS DEN STOP UNABLE VISIT WAY OUT BUT LOOK FORWARD TO IT WAY BACK STOP BUONA FORTUNA MI AMICO
J PETROSINO

"I look forward to it also," said Holmes. "I receive a letter from him occasionally, keeping me abreast of his inexhaustible activities on behalf of his honest brethren. He fails more often than he succeeds; but in this he isn't alone. You have much to answer for, Watson, touting my triumphs whilst dissembling my tragedies. Your intuition regarding the Indian woman was just, unscientific as it was, whilst my dismissal was based upon blind dogma."

He was a master at chiding one whilst paying him a compliment, and so I ignored his remarks. "It will be good to see him. I hope our pasta and tomatoes rise to his standards. I dream about that meal often."

It remained a dream.

The reports in the London newspapers were brief: On 13 March, 1909, after sending home encouraging reports of his progress, Detective Giusseppe "Joe" Petrosino was shot twice in the back by two men with revolvers on his way to police headquarters in Palermo. His murderers were never arrested.

Holmes laid aside the *Times*, drew Petrosino's pearl-handled knife from the drawer of his desk, and tested the blade once again with his thumb. "This isn't the end, Watson. I'd hoped to retire to an apiary in Sussex next year, or the year after, if there is no war. But the bees must wait. This spawn—forgive me if I break my oath—"

"They are Moriarty's sons," said I grimly. "May their tribe decrease."

"So it will—with you at my back. Would that Petrosino had had a Watson of his own."

THE END